THE MISSOURI RIVER MURDERS

Other books by David E. Unruh:

Train to Cheyenne

THE MISSOURI RIVER MURDERS

•

David E. Unruh

AVALON BOOKS
NEW YORK

Published by Avalon Books,
an imprint of Thomas Bouregy & Co., Inc.
160 Madison Avenue, New York, NY 10016

Library of Congress Cataloging-in-Publication Data

Unruh, David.
    The Missouri River murders / David E. Unruh.
        p. cm.
    ISBN 978-0-8034-7666-0
    1. Tennessee—Fiction.   2. Missouri River—Fiction.
3. Murder—Fiction.   I. Title.
    PS3621.N67M57 2011
    813'.6—dc22
                                            2010046217

PRINTED IN THE UNITED STATES OF AMERICA
ON ACID-FREE PAPER
BY RR DONNELLEY, BLOOMSBURG, PENNSYLVANIA

To Curt Southall, Dick Woodin,
and my daughter, Kristine,
all of whom reviewed my manuscript
and gave me helpful suggestions. And to my
biggest fan, my wife, Carol.

Prologue

Tennessee, 1864

A man and a woman conversed in hushed voices as they saddled two horses.

"I wish this were over," she said.

"It will be soon, and with it all our troubles."

"Do you love me?"

He dropped the reins of his horse and pulled her to him with both arms. They kissed, and then she laid her face on the lapel of his wool coat. He held her there until her horse sidled against the two of them, as if to remind them what they were about to do. He released her, and they finished their task and led the horses out of the barn and along a trail into the woods. They stopped, and he handed his reins to her to hold. He walked farther on the trail to a point where it led onto a road, then quietly walked back to her.

"This is far enough. We should be able to hear the cart go by. We'll let it go for about an hour, and then the moon will be up. We'll pick up the track and let them lead us across the line."

A half hour later they heard a single horse. They didn't speak. He thought it could be a scout or even a spy. Or it could have been two tree trunks swaying in the breeze. Several minutes later they heard the cart, and they began following, after he judged the passing of an hour.

Every few minutes they would stop and listen for a moment. One of them would dismount and look for the wheel tracks of the cart and then remount and continue following. At about five in the morning, they could see the cart ahead as the sky just started to gain light. They spurred their horses and galloped up to the cart. There were people riding in it and at least one person on foot. There was also a horseback rider with the cart. All of these people ran or galloped away and melted into the forest. The man yelled out to one of the riders, "Jonathan!" The rider reined his horse around in answer to his name.

"Who is it? Identify yourself." But the man who had shouted said nothing, rode up, and shot Jonathan in the chest. The woman rode up and joined him. She was shocked when she saw the lifeless form on the ground.

"You killed him!"

"Did you think you could outrun him carrying seventy-five pounds of gold?"

"You didn't say you would kill him."

The man didn't want to argue. "Watch for those other people in case they come back." Hurrying, he dismounted and went to the cart, where he found a few bundles of clothes. He threw these to one side and found what he was looking for—two heavy satchels. He lifted one up to the woman, who draped it over the saddle in front of her. The other he slung over his shoulder. He could hear hoofbeats from up ahead on the trail.

"Let's go! Quickly!"

They rode down the trail a ways and into the forest, where they stopped and listened for anyone following. They heard no one, but his plan was in disarray. They couldn't go back the way they had come, in the event the gold was missed and they were followed, and ahead of them there was someone on the trail who might be waiting to ambush them.

"Russellville is just north of here," he said. "We'll go deeper into the woods and then keep the sun on our right. We should start seeing farms before too long, and as soon as we get our bearings, we'll find our carriage and clothes. The rest will be easy."

But it wasn't easy. The woman, being unused to hours in the saddle, fell behind just as a Union patrol approached. She slipped into a creek bottom as her companion spurred his horse for a nearby forest. They both escaped, but it would be two years before they would find each other again, and it wouldn't be a happy reunion.

Chapter One

February, 1866

Colonel Barnard Clinton Culpepper paused on the steps of the courthouse and took a deep breath. The sky looked like snow, but there was no wind. The day was still trying to establish itself, to go down as a snowy day, or a windy day, or maybe even a clear day. It was past noon, but it was not possible to characterize the weather as yet.

Still, Culpepper's day had established itself. His long-awaited court-martial for desertion in the face of the enemy during the final months of the Civil War was over. He had been cleared of the charge and that was all he needed from this day. It might have been better if some of his former command and some of his friends were standing beside him, congratulating him, sharing his victory and sense of relief. But in the months since the charges had been brought against him, he had lost most of his friends in the Army. His career was irreparably damaged and, with the end of the Civil War, his contemporaries were scrambling to preserve their own careers as a war-weary Congress scaled back the armed forces. Culpepper had decided before the court-martial that he would resign his commission, no matter the outcome. As soon as that formality was accomplished, he would be a civilian for the first time in twenty years.

At the bottom of the steps was the young man who had testified on his behalf, Daniel Barton. Barton's testimony was in conflict with the majority of witnesses who testified, but he was

4

unshakable in his version of events. His frank manner in answering questions had given him a greater credibility. And all the other witnesses had testified more to save their own reputations than to damage Culpepper's. Barton had been only an observer; he had nothing to lose, no matter what the final verdict might be.

Danny Barton was trying to decide what to do with himself, now that the court-martial was over, when he saw Colonel Culpepper descending the steps toward him. He hadn't worked for the colonel long enough to know any details of his personal life, but he had been alongside him in battle and respected him as a commander. He could tell that the colonel wanted to speak to him, and he waited for the stern officer to join him.

"Lieutenant Barton," the colonel said, and extended his hand without waiting for a salute.

"*Mister* Barton, now, sir," said the former officer, taking the colonel's extended hand with a smile.

"How long were you a prisoner?"

"Thankfully not long, sir. It was a bad time."

"Yes, I understand. I want you to know that I managed to rally most of one platoon, and we came looking for you, but you and all the rebels were gone by that time. We inventoried the bodies and did not find yours, and that gave me hope that you were merely a prisoner."

"Yes," Barton said.

"I'd like to thank you for coming to this hearing and testifying. I understand you came all the way from Missouri."

"Yes, sir."

"And you'll be headed back there now?"

"I don't know. My family has only a small farm, and I'm not needed. Since the war began, I promised myself that if I survived, I'd see more of this country."

"That's admirable, young man. How far is your home from St. Louis?"

"A long day's ride on a good horse or a two-hour train ride."

"I'd be pleased to have your address. If things go well for me, I'll soon be needing a reliable man."

Barton removed the court-martial summons from his pocket and wrote his address on it. He handed it to Culpepper.

"I'm glad the court-martial turned out the way it did, sir," he said.

"Yes."

"Will there be charges brought against the officers who pulled their troops away from the battle?"

"No."

"As I said inside, I couldn't believe it when I heard them sound the retreat. I think that was the only time those officers were in front of their men." Barton grinned wryly.

"War finds a man's weakness like nothing else can." Culpepper was humorless.

"I reckon that's a fact," Barton agreed. "If you don't mind my asking, sir, what are you going to do now?"

"Mr. Barton, I have bought a Mississippi River steamboat, and it's being refurbished in St. Louis to make it more suitable for the Missouri River."

"I woulda thought one river would be like the other."

"Not at all, young man," Culpepper said. "To travel the length of the Missouri, a boat should be lighter, more powerful, and have less superstructure to catch the prairie winds."

"I reckon I need to do some learnin'," Barton said. "Is there a chance I'd be working on your boat?"

"That is precisely what I need you for. You'll be my aide . . . and more."

"More?" Barton questioned.

"A boat is like a small town. You'll be the peace officer."

"I've never done anything like that."

"You know how to handle weapons, and by your testimony today, I think you can tell a good man from a bad one."

"I still reckon I need to do some learnin'," Barton said.

"I believe you're the man for the job. Do you have any doubts?"

"No, sir."

"Very well."

"I'd better get on down to the train station, sir. It's been a pleasure to know you, and I'll be ready when I hear from you."

"Thank you again, Mr. Barton. You'll hear from me within the month."

Culpepper headed for division headquarters, and Barton began his walk to the train station.

Chapter Two

Early April, 1866

Melinda LaFramboise watched the sunset from her second-story hotel window. She had already booked passage on the *Str. Missouri Princess* and was scheduled to leave in the morning. She had one more evening in St. Louis. There was enough time to meet someone interesting and wealthy, or at least entertaining. She would soon need money; the small fortune in gold that she had stolen two years ago was gone like goose down in a whirlwind. Her circumstances had forced a change in her role. She had been a charming and lovely lady of Indianapolis society, eating and drinking with the better people, enjoying the good life. But in the past months, she had been forced to face the reality of her situation. No husband, no wealthy suitor, no man—of all the men she knew—who might be willing to support her as she desired. These thoughts left her restless. She checked herself in the mirror and left her room to go to the bar in the hotel.

Because women usually don't go into a bar unaccompanied, Melinda found a seat next door in the dining room where she could see the entire room. She stealthily watched the men coming into the room, sizing them up in seconds and then averting her eyes when what she saw held no promise, or waiting and making eye contact with them when they appeared to have that certain combination of wealth and foolish adventure that would enable her to manipulate them. To Melinda's advantage, the dining room was nearly full.

"Would you mind if I joined you?" He was medium height, slightly paunchy, and very well dressed. Melinda had made eye contact with him as he entered the room and smiled her most enticing smile. Her prospects for the evening now looked good; his, after this moment, did not.

Four hours later, the man was unconscious in a chair in his room, very drunk, and the woman he knew as Emily was returning to her room with most of his cash. She locked her hotel room door and then went to her window to look out. Everything was dark, and there was no sound from the apparently empty street. She had never been forced to leave a room by the window, but she always appraised her chances, just in case. Her companion of the evening would not awaken for many hours, she was sure, and by that time she should be well up the Missouri River.

The next morning Melinda hired a carriage to take her to the waterfront. The scheduled departure time for the *Missouri Princess* was nine A.M., and it was already after eight. When the carriage brought the steamboat landing into view, she could see that the steamer was no longer taking on freight. She settled back into the carriage seat, confident that she was safe. The carriage drove down to the landing, and as it was reined to a stop, Melinda leaned forward to talk to the driver. She spoke with a pleading note in her voice, her face close to his.

"I'm traveling to join my husband in Omaha. He is in the Army and is due to leave for the frontier in a few weeks." She pressed the coin into the man's hand, making sure her ungloved hand caressed his slightly. "My father wants to stop me; he doesn't care for my dear William. If he asks about me at the hotel, would you avoid answering, if you can? I must see my husband before he leaves to fight Indians." It was a lie, of course, but it had the desired effect on the driver.

"You can count on me, Miss." The man was captivated by the beautiful woman. Melinda thought it was too bad she didn't need someone to lay down his life for her at that moment, because this driver surely would have. He took her hand to help her step down from the carriage, putting his other hand on her waist to steady her. Far from acting offended, she smiled gratefully for the assistance she didn't really need. He followed her with her luggage as she walked up the landing stage to the bow. She thanked him again, and he reluctantly returned to his carriage.

It was traditional to have the women's accommodations toward the rear of a steamboat, where a boiler explosion would be less lethal. The boilers were usually as far forward as possible to balance the weight of the engines and paddlewheel. The purser welcomed her aboard and then pointed out the stairway to the main cabin, informing her that he would see that her luggage was sent to her. Five minutes later, Melinda made herself comfortable in the ladies' area of the main cabin.

It was a comfortable cabin, made to accommodate eight refined women. She could spend the entire trip without once leaving this part of the *Missouri Princess*. Meals were served four times a day in the area adjacent to the ladies' cabin. When the evening meal was over, a heavy curtain was drawn across the room to separate the dining area from the ladies' sleeping quarters. The dining room then became the men's cabin, but the more affluent male passengers booked small sleeping compartments, separated from the big room by individual curtains. Additional men could sleep on the carpeted floor, if they didn't mind the card games being played around them.

Most steamboats on the Mississippi and the Missouri rivers could offer this type of accommodations at a lower price than a hotel. Private staterooms on the upper, or Texas, deck were about the same price as a hotel room and included meals.

So Melinda had the opportunity to either keep to herself or mix with gentlemen of some potential. Melinda would have liked access to the Texas deck, but there were no staterooms available; even if there had been, she was conserving her remaining funds. The pretenders on the cabin deck would suffice for her entertainment and enrichment until she got to Omaha.

Shortly after Melinda boarded the *Missouri Princess* three men boarded the boat. They were dressed in work clothes. Two of the men wore sidearms, and all of them carried long guns and bedrolls. After some discussion with the purser, they arranged for deck passage. This meant that they would share in the work of loading and unloading and in the gathering and cutting of wood once the *Princess* was beyond the last wood hawk on the river.

Chapter Three

Josephine watched the platform as the Chicago and Alton train slowed to a stop in Springfield, Illinois. Most passengers would stay onboard and continue to Alton and East St. Louis, where they would cross the Mississippi on a ferry to St. Louis. She was getting off here, and, as always, she told herself that this might be the town where she would at last pick up the trail of the woman she was trying to find. She took her train case and walked to the door of the car, catching herself as the train came to a final stop. The conductor took her arm as she stepped out onto the platform.

"I'll see that your trunk is put inside the station, Miss Wainwright."

"Thank you, Mr. Kennedy. I appreciate all the help you've given me."

"Not at all, Miss. I hope you find the woman you're looking for."

For just a second Josephine's face was taut, and then she smiled a thin smile.

"Thank you again." She turned to walk into the little station.

Inside the station she confronted a wall with notices and advertisements pinned to it. She found one ad for a hotel and one ad for a rooming house. There was a telegrapher on duty in the station, and she walked to his window.

"Ma'am?" he asked.

"Could you tell me where a lady should stay for one night in Springfield?"

The telegrapher looked at the nice clothes that Josephine was wearing, a full dress of a subdued print with lace at the collar and sleeves. At that moment her trunk was brought into the station and stood up on one end near the door to the street. He decided she was a woman of good breeding.

"We have two places for women," he said. "Moore's Boarding House is two blocks east, one north, and has rooms for women traveling alone. And there's the Springfield Hotel, which is across the street."

"Which would you recommend for a woman such as myself?" she asked.

"You would be safe in either place," he said politely, "but perhaps more comfortable in the boardinghouse."

Josephine said nothing, but waited for an explanation.

"There's a bar in the hotel, and a piano, and there's sometimes a lot of noise. Most women prefer the boardinghouse."

"That's very helpful. Thank you," Josephine said and then continued, "Perhaps you can help me further. I'm from Kentucky, and my husband's brother there is very ill. His sister was traveling this way, and I'm trying to locate her so that I can let her know how serious the situation has become since she left."

The telegrapher was now thoroughly charmed by the young, nicely dressed woman.

"I see a lot of passengers from my window here. Could you describe her?"

"She's about my age, a little shorter than I am, and has curly red hair. She's, well, striking."

The telegrapher raised his eyebrows, but shook his head. "I can't say I've seen her."

"Well, thank you anyway. One more thing, if you don't mind. How can I arrange to have my trunk taken to the boardinghouse?"

"I'll see to it, Miss . . . ?"

"Wainwright. Josephine Wainwright."

"Nice to meet you, Miss Wainwright. I'm Fred McNeill. Your trunk will be there within the hour."

"Thank you, Mr. McNeill. Good day to you."

"Good day to you, Miss Wainwright."

The mud in the street was nearly dry. Josephine lifted her skirts just enough to keep them out of what mud there was. A man driving a carriage slowed to let her cross and then tipped his head as he passed. Josephine stepped up onto the boardwalk in front of the hotel.

Josephine entered the hotel lobby and approached the desk. The desk clerk looked up from his books and smiled a welcome for her.

"Good afternoon, miss. May I help you?"

"Oh, I hope so. My name is Josephine Wainwright, from Kentucky. My husband's brother there is very ill, and I'm trying to locate his sister. She was traveling in eastern Illinois. Her name is Melinda LaFramboise. She is about my age, a little shorter perhaps, and has curly red hair."

"Let me review our register. How long has she been away from home?"

Josephine didn't know how to answer. Melinda LaFramboise had been gone for over two years. Six months ago she had been arrested in Chicago, but had forfeited her bail, and it was only conjecture that she had headed west. Josephine had been in many hotels and towns like this one and had not found one trace of Melinda. She doubted that she would be able to persuade the clerk to check the register for the full six months.

"Our last letter from her was written two months ago," she said, and watched his face to see if he accepted this.

"Very well," he said without betraying any doubt of her sincerity. "Let's start with yesterday and go back through the ledger. I must say, I can't recall any person of that description staying with us."

He began turning pages, and on the page from two days previous he found the name M. LaFramboise.

"Oh," he said in surprise, "sure enough. Only day before yesterday." He turned to glance at a calendar. "I was in St. Louis that day."

"How long did she stay?"

"She left us the next day. Just a moment." He turned and went into a little office, returning in less than a minute. "We had her trunk taken to the C&A train station. Before sunrise."

"That's very helpful. Thank you." Josephine smiled her warmest smile. She left the hotel and returned to the train station.

"Mr. McNeill, I have found that my sister-in-law was here two days ago. She probably caught an early train the next day, yesterday. Where might she have been going?"

McNeill looked at a train schedule.

"The early train goes to East St. Louis. She probably took the ferry across the river to St. Louis."

"What time does the next train leave for East St. Louis?"

"Five tomorrow morning. It leaves the same time on Mondays, Wednesdays, and Fridays. There'll be a ticket agent here in the morning, if you would like to ride that train."

"Thank you very much, Mr. McNeill. I see my trunk is still here. It might as well stay here until tomorrow morning."

Josephine left the train station and walked to the boardinghouse, where she got a room for the night. She was closer to Melinda, her brother's killer, than she had ever been, and she was almost too excited to sleep. She and Melinda had not known each other well, living more than thirty miles apart in Kentucky, but she knew she would easily recognize Melinda and thought perhaps Melinda would recognize her also.

If Melinda were in St. Louis, Josephine would have to find her and alert the authorities before Melinda saw her and tried to get away. If Melinda had left St. Louis for the frontier, well, that presented a number of problems. St. Louis was a hub, with steamboats going south toward New Orleans or the Ohio River, north toward St. Paul, or west up the Missouri River. And there were several railheads along the Mississippi and Missouri, the most important of which was Omaha, where the transcontinental railroad was being built across Nebraska. If Melinda escaped to the western frontier, it would be much more difficult to find her.

All these ideas and concerns kept Josephine awake for several hours, but she managed to get a few hours of sleep before waking just before four A.M. She quickly dressed and let herself out into the early morning. There were few lights along this back street, but a boardwalk led all the way to Main Street, which was lit by several lamps fastened to the buildings there. She walked toward the train station along the dark boardwalk, carrying her train case.

As Josephine passed the alley that ran parallel to Main Street, a man stepped out in front of her and grabbed her throat with one hand and her free hand with the other. She slammed the train case into his head, and he released her collar and hit her in the side of her face with a fist. She went down, stunned, and he leaned over her with a knife in his hand.

"Let's see what's in that case now, missy," he growled.

Josephine could see the knife and thought she was about to die. She kicked as hard as she could with both feet and screamed. The man staggered back. She scrambled to her feet and swung the train case with all her might, connecting solidly with his head again. He crumpled to the ground and was silent.

Josephine gasped for breath. She could feel blood running down the side of her face, and when she touched it, she cringed from the pain. Her neck was bruised from his grip, and her right side was tender from her fall. But she was alive and otherwise unharmed.

Two men came running up the side street.

"What's going on here?"

"Who screamed?"

Josephine still couldn't get enough breath to speak. She held her train case in one hand and braced herself in case these men were in league with the man who had attacked her.

"What happened?" One of the men stopped in front of Josephine. There was not enough light to see the laceration on the side of her head.

Josephine spoke in a raspy voice. "He attacked . . ." Her voice failed, but she pointed at the motionless form on the ground.

One man walked to the building nearby and lit a lamp that was on a shelf on the outside wall. He carried it back to where Josephine stood. Her bleeding face and bruised neck told most of the story, and her attacker lying on the ground told the rest. One of the men knelt beside him and turned him over. His folding knife was impaled in his chest. Josephine gasped.

"This bum is dead," the man said.

A third man, wearing a badge, turned the corner from Main Street and walked toward them.

"What happened here?" he asked.

"We heard this here woman scream and ran up here and found her and then saw this guy on the ground and Phil says he's dead." The man was obviously becoming excited.

"All right, all right," the police officer said to try to calm the man. "Is she all right?"

"She ain't said much."

"Are you hurt, miss?" the officer asked.

"I'll be all right," Josephine rasped, and then added, soundlessly, "I think."

"Put that lamp down here." The officer knelt beside the dead man and looked at his face and then at the knife still standing in his chest. "Did you do this?" he asked Josephine.

Josephine shook her head and mouthed the word *no*. She tried to say more in explanation but couldn't produce sounds yet. The officer looked at her and then directed his questions to the men.

"Phil, have you or your brother seen this man before?"

Both men shook their heads.

Another police officer came into the alley. The first officer began going through the dead man's pockets. He found some tobacco, an empty whiskey bottle, a few dollars, and some dried beef, but nothing to indicate the man's identity. He stood up and addressed the second officer.

"Brian, stay with the body. I'll send someone over to take care of it as soon as I can." Brian nodded. "The rest of you, come with me. We're going to the office so we can talk about what happened here."

Josephine's heart sank. She would miss the train to East St. Louis, and Melinda would gain a day on her. She tried to protest, but no words would come out, and she realized there was no help for it. She picked up her train case and followed the officer.

In the police headquarters, Josephine and the two men who found her were questioned at length. The police sent for a doctor, who attended to Josephine's cuts and bruises as effectively as he could in the dim police office and in front of other men. While he was doing this, Josephine was thinking about her next course of action.

Josephine had found that there were two riverboats leaving St. Louis for St. Paul, and one, the *Missouri Princess,* leaving for Sioux City, all within the next twenty-four hours. She would doubtless be too late to get passage on these. Surely there would be others, but if Melinda were on any of the three leaving soon, how could Josephine catch up? The only thing to do was to get on the river as soon as possible and hope for the best.

There were also stagecoaches and wagon trains leaving from St. Louis. Would Melinda ride a stagecoach or join a wagon train? From what Josephine knew of Melinda, she thought this was not likely. A riverboat, even a Missouri River boat, had amenities and refinements that made it many times more comfortable than a stagecoach. Yes, a riverboat was the most likely method of escape for Melinda, and most likely up the Missouri River toward the frontier. Josephine told herself that she had to be thorough in her search at every stop, even if it meant disembarking and boarding a later boat.

"I don't think I can do any more for you, Miss Wainwright. You're going to be sore for a few weeks."

"Thank you, Doctor. I'll be fine, I'm sure."

"Well, take it as easy as possible. It would be better for you if you would let me put you in the hospital."

"I have to get to St. Louis, Doctor," she said. "Someone is waiting for me there." Not quite true, she thought to herself.

"Well, then, I'll leave you with the police."

Josephine looked at the policeman who had been questioning her with a question of her own in her eyes. He looked over his notes and then pushed himself back from his desk.

"I have all I need, Miss Wainwright. I'm sorry for what happened to you, and I'm sorry I had to detain you," he told her.

"I understand. I'll be going then." She got up from her chair and couldn't hide the involuntary wince of pain.

"I'll get a carriage for you, Miss Wainwright."

"Thank you. Perhaps that would be best."

Twenty minutes later, Josephine was back in her room at the

boardinghouse. She had taken advantage of the carriage ride to retrieve her trunk from the train station. There wouldn't be a train until the day after tomorrow, and she would need more personal things. She had also formed a new plan.

It was too dangerous for a woman to travel alone. She could write to her father and await his arrival before continuing her pursuit of Melinda La Framboise, but that would take weeks and Melinda's trail would be cold by that time. She had another, more dangerous tactic: she could become a man, or more convincingly, a boy. She had passed for a boy before, when it was convenient and safer than moving around as a girl, and, although she was an adult now, she felt her slight build would still allow her to do so convincingly. She would need to do some shopping tomorrow. In the meantime, she began a letter to her father informing him that she was very close to Melinda and was planning to ride a riverboat up the Missouri. Then she laid down on her bed fully clothed and, in seconds, was asleep. She awoke in time for supper downstairs, which she ate hurriedly, and then returned to her room where she slept through the night.

The next morning she was more stiff and sore than she had expected she would be, but she managed to dress with only a little pain and took breakfast in the boardinghouse dining room. Then she walked down the same street where she was attacked and onto Main Street.

Josephine's shopping list was unusual. She came upon a store that sold used clothes, most of them children's and adolescents' castoffs. She found two pairs of pants, a shirt, and a wool sweater that had obviously belonged to a teenage boy. None of these garments was in good shape, and that was her preference. She also found a pair of boots and a stocking cap. A sturdy bag with a drawstring completed her purchases at the store.

There were two gunsmiths along the main street of Springfield. One was large, with a barred window in front and many shiny rifles and revolvers on display. The other was small and dark inside. Peering in, she saw an old man leaning over his workbench. He didn't look up when she entered, so she walked over to him. He still didn't look, but he spoke. "What?"

He continued assembling some small, intricate mechanism, peering at his work through half-spectacles. Josephine realized that he could probably smell her cologne and had already dismissed her as frivolous.

"I want a gun," Josephine stated.

"Everybody wants a gun." He continued working, having yet to look at her.

"I want a small gun," she said.

"Figures," he said low. He still didn't look up.

"Do you sell guns here or just growl at people who happen to walk in?"

Now he looked at her with just a trace of smile. "I do both. Hard to say which I'm better at. What kind of gun do you want?"

"Small. Powerful. Easy to load, easy to shoot."

"Not interested in hunting," he mumbled. He put his work down on the bench and got up stiffly from his stool. Josephine didn't reply. "Follow me," he said.

He went to a cabinet, opened it, and removed a small revolver.

"This is a Colt Baby Dragoon. It holds five .31 caliber balls." He handed it to Josephine and watched how she handled it.

The little pistol was well used. The grips had lost their varnish; most of the blue was off the barrel, and when Josephine turned it over, the wedge that held the barrel to the frame fell out onto the counter. She scowled. The gunsmith sensed her displeasure.

"I can let you have that one for fourteen dollars."

"No, thank you," Josephine said and handed the pistol back to him.

He looked at her closely for the first time. Her collar didn't quite cover the bruises on her neck. He didn't waste words.

"You're the woman who was attacked just around the corner yesterday."

"Yes."

The gunsmith picked the wedge up and inserted it back into the frame. He put the pistol back in the cabinet and removed a small derringer-like pistol, which he displayed in his open hand for Josephine to see.

"I make these myself."

Josephine was interested. "How does it work?"

"It holds two shots. To shoot, you pull the hammer back and pull the trigger. One barrel fires. When you pull the hammer back the second time, it automatically drops or raises the firing pin to the other chamber. Do you understand that?"

"Yes," Josephine said. "How do you load it?"

"It uses a .44 short Henry rimfire cartridge. Open the breech, drop in two cartridges, and it's ready." He opened the breech in demonstration and then closed it. "Let me see your hands."

Josephine didn't understand. She tentatively extended her right hand. It was not a lady's hand; until she embarked on her quest to find Melinda LaFramboise, she had worked for her father as a stable hand and horse trainer, from the time she could first walk.

The gunsmith briefly examined her hand. "This gun kicks like a mule bein' branded. You might be able to hang on to it. For one shot anyway."

"How much will you sell it for?"

"I make one of these a month and usually sell them before they're finished. I finished this one yesterday and three different customers are coming in today to look at it. I sold the last one for twenty-five dollars. I'm going to get twenty-eight for this one."

Josephine didn't hesitate. "I'll take it. I want ten cartridges and a bottle of gun oil."

The gunsmith nodded. He wrapped the gun in heavy brown paper, then the ten cartridges, and finally the bottle of oil. Josephine took the packages and handed him the money.

Josephine returned to the boardinghouse with all her purchases. She made arrangements with Mrs. Moore, the lady who owned the house, to store her trunk and train case. She packed the duffel bag with her sweater, extra pants, and some personal things. She already had a canvas coat that was well worn and matched her newly purchased clothes. She loaded the pistol and put it in an inside pocket of the jacket. She soaked the brown paper in oil and wrapped it around the eight remaining cartridges.

At four A.M. the next morning, Josephine wrote a thank-you note for Mrs. Moore and left it on her dresser. Then she let herself out and walked to the train station, dressed as a boy, where she bought a ticket to East St. Louis. Within an hour, she was on her way across the Illinois countryside.

Melinda LaFramboise was now four days ahead of her, but Josephine consoled herself that she was closer to finding her than she had ever been.

Chapter Four

St. Louis, Missouri, April 15, 1866

Charles Felden, pilot on the *Str. Barnard Clinton,* watched from the deck of the pilothouse as his first mate, Steve Allenby, directed some men on the shore who had pulled two carts of barrels as far as the starboard gangplank. There was a brief discussion that he couldn't hear, but he could tell from the gestures that the men wanted to leave the barrels on the shore. The first mate looked up at Felden, and Felden shook his head. The men pulling the cart refused to budge. Felden held up one finger and then descended the ladder to the first deck. He walked directly to the men.

"Get these barrels up on the deck."

"We got 'em to the boat. They're yours now," the bigger man said, and started to remove them from the carts.

"I'll tell you one more time: get them up the ramp and onto the deck."

The four delivery men were typical waterfront toughs, not accustomed to backing down. The biggest man smiled. He was sizing up the sixty-year-old pilot and looking forward to using his strength against the older man. But Felden wasn't backing down either. A small group of the *Clinton*'s roustabouts were gathering behind Felden.

"Throw 'em in the river!" Felden ordered.

The mate stifled a smile as he asked, "The barrels or the men?"

The *Clinton*'s roustabout crewmen were all smiling now and

looking forward to a little entertainment. Felden took a step forward and the crew followed.

"All of it," he answered.

The four delivery men realized they were outnumbered and held up their hands.

"All right, all right, we'll take 'em up," said the smaller one, hastily.

"When you get 'em up there, get off my boat. Don't ever come back, understand?" Felden didn't wait for a reply, but turned and walked through his amused crewmen, who parted like plowed soil. He ascended the ladder and resumed watching the process of loading. Captain Culpepper joined him on the pilothouse deck.

"Trouble?"

"Not much, Captain. It's over," Felden replied without elaboration or emotion.

"Very well."

The captain stood with his arms folded, watching the activity on the deck and at the steamboat landing. He was still standing there when the first mate ascended to the pilothouse deck with a handful of papers two hours later.

"All cargo is aboard, Mr. Felden."

"How does she sit, Mr. Allenby?"

"She's drawing four, three and a half, at the first frame, and four, one, at the stern."

"That sounds good. How are the bilges?"

"She's making a little water. Nothing serious."

"She'll tighten up in a day or two."

"I'd expect so."

Both men knew that the *Clinton* had been sitting high in the water since the last trip in the fall of last year. But Felden left nothing to chance.

"I want her pumped dry when we come on watch and when we go off. Log the time in minutes and seconds until the pump loses prime."

"I'll see to it," the first mate replied.

"Are all the passengers onboard?"

"Not the women. They're waiting at the hotel."

The *Clinton* was not scheduled to leave until the next day. The fires were lit but not stoked; there was no steam as yet. Felden knew that they could be underway in two hours, and although it was already after noon, on this part of the river they could travel at night. He also knew that the captain wanted to make two trips this season, so every day was precious. He looked at the captain, who replied to the unspoken question as if he were reading Felden's thoughts.

"We'll not cast off on the first anniversary of Abraham Lincoln's death, Mr. Felden."

The pilot nodded and then turned to the first mate.

"Send the purser to the hotel to inform the women passengers that we will be escorting them to the *Barnard Clinton* at eleven in the evening. Tell the mate to have all roustabouts on deck at fifteen 'til midnight."

The first mate left the papers with Felden and descended the ladder to find the purser. Captain Culpepper had not moved since first coming out on deck. Without turning to face Felden, he spoke. "When Mr. Singletary takes over the watch, I want to meet with all the officers in the pilothouse."

"Yes, sir," Felden replied.

"There will be a young man, Daniel Barton, coming onboard soon. He will be my aide. Inform him of the meeting."

"Yes, sir," Felden repeated.

Felden was puzzled. He hadn't heard about Barton before, and he couldn't fathom why the captain needed an aide. There was a purser to handle the finances, a steward to oversee the passengers and their care, the mates handled the deck operations, and the pilots were responsible for the navigation and welfare of the hull.

Captains on the U.S. waterways were not licensed, but pilots were. Any man with sufficient money or influence with the owners could be appointed a captain. In Culpepper's case, he owned a controlling interest in the *Clinton,* and thus assumed the role of captain, but he didn't seem like the type to want or need an aide. Felden made a mental note to question Barton alone before the meeting, if there was any opportunity.

Two hours later Barton and seven officers were gathered

outside the pilothouse. Culpepper opened the door and beckoned
them in. The pilothouse was scarcely large enough to hold nine
men, but his habitual brevity spared them a long period of discomfort.

"Gentlemen, we'll be making two trips up the Missouri this
year. The first trip starts at midnight tonight, and, God willing,
we'll reach Fort Benton in June. The second trip will start in July,
early I hope. We'll go as far upriver as possible, given the prob-
ability of lower water. There will be a layover to take on additional
freight at Council Bluffs, and from there we'll tie up after dark
most nights at the pilot's discretion."

The captain paused. No one commented, and he continued.
"We'll stand regular Navy watches beginning now. I want the
oncoming watch on duty fifteen minutes before the hour. Watches
will continue even when we begin tying up at night, and we'll
keep steam in the boilers." He was watching the men's faces in-
tently to see if any of them had a problem with this order.
"Watches will continue without interruption until we tie up here
in St. Louis in July."

The captain didn't think it was necessary to explain to these
experienced officers that the boat and cargo were too valuable to
let everyone sleep, even when not underway.

"I'd like to introduce you to my aide, Daniel Barton."

It was obvious which man was Barton. In addition to being at
least ten years younger than the youngest officer, he was the only
one not in uniform. He was wearing wool pants and jacket over
a wool vest and white shirt with a ribbon tie. Not obvious to the
officers was the Colt Army .44 with a short barrel strapped to his
chest, high inside his jacket under his left arm. He nodded his
head slightly and met each man's gaze in turn.

"Mr. Barton is our law enforcement officer. He is to be obeyed
in all matters except navigation, on which subject he will be silent." The captain looked at each man to make sure he understood, including Barton. Captain Culpepper was not accustomed
to having his directions questioned, and no one did.

"Mr. Singletary, give us a report on cargo."

"We have mostly building supplies. There is also flour, sugar, salt, and coffee in the aft part of the lower cabin. Iron tools, hardware, and thirty-two barrels of whiskey are in the hold. There are eleven barrels of gunpowder stored in each powder magazine. Twenty-nine horses."

"Very well. How about passengers?"

The purser stepped forward.

"We have twenty-six men onboard now. There will be two more at midnight, along with seven women and fourteen children. There are sixteen roustabouts on each watch. We will have ninety souls onboard at castoff."

The purser shuffled his papers and continued. "The captain has the Texas cabin, the pilots share the Iowa cabin, the mates share the Ohio cabin, the engineers share the Illinois cabin." He had to pause before continuing; he raised his eyebrows and then went on. "Mr. Barton has the Minnesota cabin, Mr. and Mrs. White have the Vermont cabin, Mrs. Lee and her two daughters have the New York cabin, Mr. and Mrs. Williams have the Pennsylvania cabin. The rest of the men will sleep in the men's cabin forward, and the four remaining women will sleep in the ladies' cabin aft. The ordinary roustabouts will sleep on deck. I'll sleep in my office off the main salon."

"Does anyone have any questions or comments?" the captain asked.

Allenby, the first mate, was forthright. "It's unusual to assign a cabin to a single man," he stated, looking at Barton.

The peace officer was a question mark to most of the officers. Greg Singletary had learned the story, however, and he also knew the captain was happy to let him speak.

Singletary nodded in Barton's direction. "There have been incidents of Indians attacking boats on the Upper Missouri. In Mr. Barton's cabin is a large chest containing sufficient arms and ammunition for us to repel such attacks. They will remain under lock and key until needed."

"Who decides that?" Felden asked.

"The captain, the pilot on watch, and Mr. Barton."

Felden nodded, satisfied.

There was also a safe bolted to the floor in Barton's cabin, in which would be stored gold from the Montana gold mines on the return trip. Singletary didn't think it necessary to mention this, but he was sure most of the officers would learn about it one way or another in the course of the voyage.

The meeting broke up, and the officers on watch began the task of making the boat ready for the river. The steward went immediately to the galley to organize the cook and his helpers. Felden, off watch now, walked the boat from bow to stern, looking in every compartment and cabinet. He opened every hatch over the bilge and, lying on his stomach with a lamp in one hand, looked at everything he could see from that position. He chatted with the engineer and several of the crew. He was followed every step of the way by Barton.

"This vessel is not in bad shape," Felden remarked, as he was reaching the end of his inspection.

"That's good to know," Barton replied. "From what I've heard, she doesn't have a good reputation."

"What have you heard?"

"One pilot died at the wheel of unknown causes. She spent one summer on a sandbar. Four passengers came up missing on one trip. Another pilot told me she's cursed. Fires, cholera. Don't know how much of it is true."

"That much and more, but there's no such thing as a curse. She's had bad officers, that's all."

Barton made no comment. He felt that the officers currently onboard were competent, but he knew he wasn't qualified to properly judge them and didn't want to talk without knowledge. Felden appreciated this.

"How long have you known Captain Culpepper?" Felden asked.

"I served in his regiment during the war and was assigned as his aide for a month," Barton replied.

"What kind of commander was he?"

"Fearless" was the first thing that came to Barton's mind, but he added, "He was hard but fair, I guess. I never talked to him outside of the line of duty until after his court-martial."

"Court-martial?"

The law officer didn't want to answer, and Felden sensed this and was ready to let the matter drop. Barton was quiet for a long time while the senior pilot carefully examined the pitman rod, the long hardwood timber that linked the piston of the steam engine to the crank on the stern wheel. It was reinforced at both ends by metal plates, which held the bearings. He wiped a fine coat of oil and dust away to expose the metal.

"I'm looking for stress cracks," Felden said. "Any sign of weakness." It was the first words he had spoken in explanation of his inspection tour. Something in his tone prompted Barton to speak.

"Culpepper was accused of abandoning his command. Almost all of his officers were from one wealthy family, and they were"—he paused to find the right words—"they were there for the glory, but they didn't inspire their troops. Culpepper put up with them and tried to teach them how to fight, right to the end.

"In the fall of 1864 he was leading a charge against what looked to me to be a smaller number of the enemy. His horse was shot out from under him, and his company officers turned and ran, taking the troops with them. They ran into another company of rebels, and this threw them into total confusion. They had never been without their leader. The pursuing Confederates had a turkey shoot."

"Where were you?" asked Felden.

"At Culpepper's side. I was his aide. I gave him my horse, but by that time the enemy was all around us. They shot the horse, and it went down with Culpepper. Then they shot me and must have thought we were both dead because they took up pursuit of Culpepper's regiment and left us."

This was a lot of information for the pilot to digest. He had not thought much of Barton when Culpepper initially told him about the young aide, but it was obvious now that he had more to learn about Mr. Barton.

"You weren't captured?"

"No luck. I was," Barton replied. "Culpepper found yet another horse and rode off to join his regiment, but he was too late. They were almost all dead, were wounded, or had deserted. The Southerners, probably realizing they had been lucky, retreated and found me."

"Where were you shot?"

"I took a minié ball off my ribs. It hurt, but wasn't very serious."

"Were you a prisoner of war?"

"Yeah, for only a month, and then I was exchanged. It was a hard month, but I was exchanged along with some prisoners who had been there for over a year. They were like ghosts. Skeletons of ghosts."

"Yeah, I saw some of those guys." Felden shook his head. "Worst thing I ever saw."

"The only good thing is that it's over."

Both men were silent with their respective memories of the war. Then Felden got back to the subject they had been discussing.

"So, let me guess. The family didn't want the truth about the behavior of the officers to come out, so they decided to make Culpepper the scapegoat. Right?"

"That's the way I put it together." Barton grinned an ornery smile. "But I spoiled their party. I told my story; it helped and they dismissed the charge, but Culpepper resigned his commission anyway."

Felden's opinion of Culpepper had already been high, even though they had spoken very little. Felden knew human nature and was able to make accurate judgments about a man's character in a short amount of time. This information from Culpepper's aide led him to believe he would find it satisfying to work for the captain. And, also, he began to like the young warrior Barton.

"Let's go see if the purser has the galley in order, Mr. Barton."

Barton didn't misunderstand this pointed suggestion. "Good idea." The two men walked eagerly to the galley to get a meal in the early evening.

At 7:45 P.M. Felden, still accompanied by Barton, arrived at the pilothouse to relieve Greg Singletary. Captain Culpepper was there but said nothing, observing the communication between the two pilots without comment. It was still a few minutes before eight P.M. when they had finished covering everything.

"Mr. Felden, if it's all right with you, I think I'll leave the pilothouse and see if I can find some food in the cook shack," Singletary said.

"Go right ahead. Greg, I'll see you at midnight," Felden said.

Barton followed the pilot just as he had followed Felden.

"You eaten yet, Mr. Barton?" Singletary asked.

"I'm always able to eat, sir. Would you like some company?" Barton asked. He was naturally gregarious.

"That'd be all right."

Singletary was not gregarious, but he wanted to know more about Danny Barton. He didn't have the conversational skill that Barton had, however, and the aide got much more information from Singletary than he got from him.

"How is the senior pilot selected?" Barton asked.

Singletary scowled briefly, but Barton's direct way of talking was disarming. The pilot was thoughtful as he spoke. "I've been boating on the Missouri for fourteen years, mostly on steamers between Council Bluffs and St. Louis, but I've brought twelve keelboats all the way down from Fort Buford and seven from the falls. I don't know anyone else except Joseph LaBarge who has more time on the Missouri. Captain Culpepper hired me, and I recommended Charles Felden to him. Felden has twenty-eight years on the Mississippi, but only one trip on the Missouri. That was as my junior pilot on the steamer *Iriquois*."

"Why did you leave the *Iriquois*?" Barton asked.

"Ice took her out at St. Louis last winter."

"Is it hard to get hired as a pilot?"

"No, not if you're licensed, but it's hard to find a captain and vessel as fit for service as Culpepper and the *Clinton*."

"Does he pay well?"

"They all pay well."

"Are you going to do a walk-around before you find your bed?"

"Don't have to. Felden did it, and if he didn't find anything, I won't."

Singletary and Barton finished their meals and made their way to their respective cabins.

Chapter Five

Greg Singletary came to the pilothouse at exactly 11:45 P.M. Captain Culpepper was in the pilothouse, as he had been all evening. Ten minutes later the mate came to the pilothouse to report on the bilges as ordered. Then Singletary sent him to the engine room for a report on the steam. The purser confirmed that all passengers and stores were onboard. He brought a mug of steaming coffee for Singletary.

In the meantime Danny Barton, after a short nap in his cabin, had been prowling the main deck. He made a note of the location of every deckhand's "nest." He would come back later to see which one was sleeping in which nest. He had a general list of the cargo, and he accounted for all of it. He looked at the horses briefly. He was something of a horseman himself, although he had never owned one. He noted that there were no saddles with the horses, and he stopped by a lamp and checked his manifest, finding that there were no saddles listed.

The boiler room was full of activity. Deckhands were stoking the firebox, stripped to their waists, even though the spring St. Louis evening was cool. The fireman opened the try cocks on the boilers, each in turn, every ten minutes. Using a long oak stick, he adjusted the "pea" on each safety valve arm and then lifted the valves on each boiler, careful to be out of the way of the release of steam, and let them reset.

Barton watched all of this with fascinated curiosity until finally the fireman, flattered by the attention of the young man, spoke.

"You ever seen a boiler explode, son?"

"I saw a locomotive get hit by a cannonball."

"Well, multiply that by ten and that's what these boilers could do."

"Why would they explode?"

"Pressure against hot steel. With all the safety features of a modern boiler, you'd think it couldn't happen, but it still does."

"Human error?" Barton guessed.

"That's part of it. First, something fails. Then the human doesn't catch it when he should. It's almost never the case that just one thing goes wrong."

Barton knew there would be more, that the fireman was delighting in telling this as much as he enjoyed hearing it. The fireman continued.

"These are new boilers; they're rolled from five-sixteenth-inch steel. That's a sixteenth thicker than some of the older boilers. And the rivet holes are drilled, not punched."

"What's the advantage of drilled rivet holes?" The young officer wanted to know everything.

"Less stress on the steel. Less chance of failure. These boilers have been tested to 250 psi, and the safety valves are set at 125 psi."

"I appreciate you answering my questions," Barton said, shaking hands with the fireman. Then he walked aft, following the steam pipes until he arrived at the engine room. The engineer was oiling linkages and looked up with a scowl as Barton walked in.

"What do you want?" the engineer growled.

"I'm Danny Barton," he said, as he extended his hand. The engineer ignored it. "I know who you are," he said in the same tone of voice.

Just then the steam whistle blew a blast, and the engine room bell rang for slow reverse. The engineer glanced at the steam pressure gauge and then opened a valve that applied steam to both engines. The port engine moaned a long *whuuufff,* and then the starboard engine did likewise. There were windows on the outside wall, and Barton went to one and quickly glanced out. The boat backed so smoothly that there was little sensation of motion; the illusion was that the boat tied alongside had started forward as it moved slowly past the window.

Now the bell rang for slow ahead, and the engineer and striker became very busy—the engineer working on the starboard engine, the striker working on the larboard one. The engineer bypassed the steam to the exhaust stack, stopped the wheel, and then lifted the fifty-pound connecting rod that worked the valve linkage from its hook, as the striker did the same on his engine. Two levers were thrown, and the connecting rods on each side were dropped into their lower hooks. This effectively changed the valve timing of the engines by one-hundred-eighty degrees. The engineer applied steam to the engines as he released the wheel.

The engines *whuuuffed* and the larboard engine's pitman rod moved to the end of its seven-foot stroke and began returning. Then the starboard engine's pitman rod, out of phase by ninety degrees, went through its own cycle. Barton stayed well out of the way, pressed against a wall, as he watched the activity.

As much as Barton wanted to stay and watch the engineer, he wanted more to be in the pilothouse during the maneuvering into the river. He said aloud, "Thanks," to the engineer, who didn't acknowledge it, and left the engine room for the pilothouse.

Outside, he saw that a crowd had gathered at the landing to cheer the departure. There was a small band playing, and people were waving and shouting. People on the boats on either side of the *Barnard Clinton* waved and shouted good wishes for a safe journey. Barton quickly climbed up to the pilothouse.

Singletary was the pilot, although Felden was still in the pilothouse. Neither the senior pilot nor the captain did anything or said anything as Singletary watched all sides of the steamer, looked out into the river, swung the wheel, and rang the engine room bell. In reverse, the paddlewheel forced water against the rudders, causing the stern to swing. Then, in forward, the wheel would be swung to the other extreme, and the boat's rearward travel would continue, only slowing slightly, and the stern would continue its swing.

The current in the river affected the stern first, and that was to the advantage of the pilot, as the boat ponderously aligned itself bow first into the current.

"Got 'er now," Singletary stated, as the boat found the channel, almost perfectly aligned with the current. He rang for half ahead, and the *Clinton* stopped its rearward motion and began fighting the sluggish current. After a minute, the lights of St. Louis started falling behind, and Singletary rang for full speed. Full revolutions on the paddle wheel amounted to approximately twenty, with four exhaust valves operating at ninety-degree intervals. Eighty times a minute there was a mighty *hommmp* that reverberated up and down the river. The first voyage of the *Str. Barnard Clinton*, under the command of Captain Barnard Clinton Culpepper, had begun.

Chapter Six

Most of those horses will be dead before you get into the Dakota Territory," Little Joe remarked.

Steve Allenby, the first mate, looked at the boy. His clothes were obviously hand-me-downs; his coat was worn nearly through on the sleeves and was stained. He could have been eighteen and small for his age, or perhaps only fourteen. He didn't have the appearance of someone who had knowledge of horses, much less actual experience. But, Allenby had to admit, he was a good worker. He was stowing wood for the boilers, and although he couldn't keep up with most of the other roustabouts because of his slight build, he was giving the task all the effort that he could muster.

"When you get the wood moved, come and see me," Allenby told the boy.

"Yes, sir."

The *Clinton* was making good time upriver. It was her first voyage since being rebuilt following an encounter with a snag on the Upper Mississippi.

Allenby looked around the deck once before ascending the ladder to the pilothouse. On the way, he passed Danny Barton.

"Mr. Barton," he said. "Could you give me your opinion on a matter?"

"Sure," Barton said.

"Do you know anything about horses?"

"Some."

"What's your opinion of the horses we're carrying?"

"I reckon I'd have to look 'em over."

"What I mean is, are they being taken care of properly?"

"That's not my business, but since you asked, I'd say no."

Allenby thought for a minute and then told Barton, "There'll be a boy coming up soon. I'd like you to be here when I talk to him."

Allenby, Barton, and Felden entered the pilothouse. Captain Culpepper had his usual position, behind the pilot against the back wall, watching everything. Greg Singletary was at the wheel, cursing under his breath as he fought a twenty-mile-an-hour crosswind. He worked the *Barnard Clinton* around a horseshoe bend; it went head to wind for five hundred yards, during which time the bow kept trying to chase its tail. After that was handled, he had to deal with a crosswind from the other side.

"I hate these afternoon watches!" He swore again.

Charles Felden just smiled. Singletary grumbled constantly about one thing or another, but he was a skillful, if uninspiring, pilot.

"Let's ask the engineer to take the slack out of the cables. I was having a little trouble myself this morning."

"Yeah?" Singletary didn't think Felden ever had trouble doing anything.

Allenby addressed his senior pilot. "Mr. Felden, I'm going to report early for my watch right now so that I can take care of a small matter," he said. "Is there anything I should know?"

"I'll talk with Erickson before he goes off watch and pass his information on to you when you're ready," Felden said.

"Thanks," Allenby said. "I'll be back as soon as I can." Allenby left the pilothouse, and Barton followed him. They waited on the hurricane deck, leaning on the rail.

"There's a young decker who thinks he can do a better job of caring for the livestock," Allenby told Barton.

"Who takes care of them now?"

"Whatever roustabout is in the area when they need food or water. We haven't been doing much for them other than that."

Allenby and Barton saw Little Joe coming up the main staircase and waited on the cabin deck to meet him.

"Let's go down to the main deck, kid," Allenby said. He

motioned to Barton as he and the boy took the passenger stairs to the main deck. Once there, they walked into the freight area where the horses were kept.

"What needs to be done here?" the first mate asked.

"They have too much room. They need to be packed in tighter so they can't hurt each other."

Allenby nodded. "All right. What else?"

Little Joe pushed at a large horse dropping with his toe. "This place is filthy. No one cleans it right. If one of them gets the slightest cut, it'll get infected, and you'll have to put the horse down."

"All right. What else?"

"Once we get past Omaha, there won't be many woodhawks, will there?"

Allenby raised his eyebrows. This boy seemed to know a lot about the river.

"No, most mornings we'll get our own wood."

"Take the horses out and work them. Do you have saddles?"

"No."

"I can ride bareback. The other horses can be used for dragging wood. I'll be ready to chase one down if he gets away. Do you have any harnesses?"

"We've got plenty of leather. Make one up for me, and I'll have more made. How many do we need?"

"One more."

"All right. Anything else?"

"There will be," Little Joe promised.

Allenby looked over Little Joe's shoulder at Barton. The officer nodded his head. He, too, was impressed by the young man.

"All right," Allenby said. "You're the official hostler. Your only job is the horses. Report to me or this man behind you. I'll tell the mate and the engineers so they'll let you do your job."

Little Joe stuck his hand out, and Allenby took it and shook it.

"Where are you bunking, Little Joe?" Barton had the feeling that because of the boy's small size and confident attitude, he might be victimized by some of the rougher crew. He had taken an instant liking to Little Joe and felt protective.

Little Joe narrowed his eyes and replied, "I've got a spot next to the starboard powder magazine."

"I've got a cabin to myself. You want to move in with me?"

"No," the boy answered without explanation.

Barton was taken aback. "Well, I just thought . . . never mind." He shrugged.

"Thanks for the offer," Little Joe said hastily.

"Come get me if you need any help with the horses," he said, and then he and Allenby returned to the pilothouse to observe the change of watch.

Barton let himself into the pilothouse, but he stayed silent until Felden had the watch running to his satisfaction. Felden got a report from Singletary on the miles traveled, the pumping of the hold, the amount of wood consumed during the previous watch, the amount of wood available, maintenance being performed, and many other less important matters, and then Singletary left to get some sleep. Allenby made a similar exchange with David Erickson, the second mate going off watch.

"Where did that kid come from?" Barton asked Allenby.

"He booked deck passage at St. Louis," Allenby responded.

"There's something about him that seems . . . I don't know what, I reckon."

"He's an unusual boy, all right."

"How old do you reckon he is?" Barton asked.

"Sixteen."

"His voice hasn't changed."

"Yeah. Maybe it was a lot higher when he was ten." Allenby shrugged.

Barton had talked enough about Little Joe. He changed the subject and directed his questions to Felden, who was spinning the wheel and leaning into the windows of the pilothouse to better see the river.

"How do you tell where you are in the river at night?" he asked.

Felden smiled as he thought about it. How do you tell someone about the many signs that a pilot looks for in the dark of night on the Missouri River? The head pilot replied slowly as he swung the wheel. "My compass and my watch tell me approximately where I am on the river. I can see the outlines of the trees and hills against the stars on both sides. The bow lights let me look at the surface of the water a few hundred feet ahead. On certain bends I can feel the current pulling the boat. There are some lights along the river that I have learned to rely on."

"And you're thinking about all those things at the same time?"

"You don't really think about it. The easy nights are when the moon is up half full or better. The impossible nights are when the wind blows."

"Because it blows the boat around?"

"Yeah, but more than that, it masks the water so that you can't read it."

"Have you ever run aground?"

"Yes."

Chapter Seven

As the *Str. Barnard Clinton* rounded a left-hand bend four hours out of St. Joseph, the *Str. Missouri Princess* came into view. Her bow was high, and her wheel was in reverse, throwing cascades of water against her stern. Charles Felden was on watch and he rang the engine room to slow. The *Princess* was right in the middle of where the channel had been last year, but she was obviously aground. Steve Allenby immediately sent two leadsmen to the bow, one with a lead line, one with a marked pole.

Felden had several problems to deal with. The first priority was to not run the *Clinton* aground. Then there was the danger that the *Princess* might come off the bar, but not have steerage, and drift down onto the *Clinton*. He wanted to get into a position to help the grounded steamer, but he couldn't, and wouldn't, jeopardize the *Clinton* to do it.

The engineer, also reading the situation, had the engines throttled at a setting that let the *Clinton* hold station downstream from the *Princess*. Felden called all hands on deck with a whistle. The first mate came to the pilothouse.

"Mr. Allenby, take the yawl over to the *Missouri Princess* and see if she wants our help." Felden had his eyes continuously on the river ahead or on the grounded steamer and nowhere else.

"Yes, sir."

The captain had been taking it all in and spoke. "If they want help, our terms are two hundred dollars per hour to put a line on them, in advance."

"Yes, sir." Allenby went to the rail and yelled to the roustabouts who had come on deck. "Skip, Two-ton, Little Bit, Gary,

41

Humpback, Weedeater! Prepare the yawl; we're going for a ride."
Then he descended to the main deck to direct the launch.

While Felden worked the wheel to keep the *Clinton* in deep
water, Captain Culpepper watched the *Princess* through binoculars. He could see only the larboard side. On that side there were
five men in the water with shovels scooping sand from under the
larboard bow. There were probably five more on the starboard
side. The idea was not to shovel away the sandbar, but to channel
the current in such a way as to wash sand from under the hull.
They had started in waist-deep water, but they were having some
success, and shortly they were in past their elbows. One of the
men stepped into a deeper spot and was suddenly swept off his
feet. He tried to get his feet under himself, but each time the current would take him again. As the water took him down current
alongside the steamer, passengers watched, but none made an
effort to help him. The drifting man was now in serious trouble,
as he was in water too deep to feel the bottom.

Captain Culpepper stepped to the rail of the hurricane deck
and shouted to the launch crew. "Man overboard off the *Missouri Princess*. Look lively with the launch!"

The *Princess* had managed to get a skiff in the water, but there
were only two men onboard, and they had no experience with a
rowboat. The skiff turned and wheeled in the eddies, with little
productive effort by the inept crew. In the meantime the yawl from
the *Clinton*, manned by six oarsmen and directed by the first mate,
made steady progress against the lazy current.

The hapless man in the river was no longer able to keep his
head above water. While Allenby had his oarsmen maneuver so
that they would intercept the estimated drift of the man, the crew
in the skiff from the grounded steamer abandoned their mission
and awkwardly made their way back to their mother vessel. They
knew there was nothing to be gained by recovering a body; there
would be an inquest that would delay the voyage, and the man's
back pay would have to be sent to his family. With no body, there
would be none of this. The crew from the *Clinton*, however, was
not ready to give up.

Allenby's front oarsmen leaned far over the gunwales of the

skiff, each putting one arm into the water up to the shoulder, while the remaining four men continued pulling into the current. Allenby encouraged them, never silent.

"That's it! That's it! Harder on them oars, now. Gary! Weedeater! Get deeper, try to touch the bottom! That's it, that's it. Pull a little deeper on the port side! Two-ton, that means you. You're lettin' 'er get off line. Harder on them oars!"

Suddenly they heard, "I got 'im! I got 'im! Somebody get another handful here!"

Weedeater had his right hand on the drowning man's coat collar. He grabbed the man opposite him for an anchor and pulled hard. The oarsman behind him pulled his oar onboard and turned around to help Weedeater. They both heaved, and over the gunwale came the man who had been swept away. He was a black man, young, poorly dressed, unconscious, and not breathing.

"That's it," Allenby said. "Just heave 'im over the gunwale, maybe he'll drain out." The man's legs were still dangling in the water. "You hang on to him, Weedeater. Let's go, men. Pull for the *Missouri Princess.*"

The man didn't exactly drain out, so Weedeater lifted him by his pants and then let him back down on the gunwale. He repeated this about five times until the man vomited riverwater and half-digested food into the skiff. Then his eyes opened, and he gasped for breath. A cheer of encouragement went up from the oarsmen.

The captain had watched all this through his binoculars. "Mr. Felden," he announced. "I'd say your first mate has just saved a human life."

"Looks like a black man from here," Felden replied, not taking his eyes off the river ahead for more than a second at a time. He had to keep the *Barnard Clinton* in good water and also watch the *Missouri Princess* in case she suddenly came off the bar and drifted down on him.

"Yes," the captain said.

Allenby directed his oarsmen up the river until they pulled alongside the *Princess*. The deck crew threw him some lines, and his men tied the yawl up as he jumped onto the main deck of the *Princess*.

The rescued man was lying in the bottom of the skiff. Although his eyes were open and moving, he was not able to raise himself up. Allenby's oarsmen lifted him by his arms until he was in a sitting position, and then they left him to gather his strength in his own time.

The captain of the *Princess* met Allenby on the main deck. He extended his hand.

"Captain Edward Smith."

"First Mate Steve Allenby."

"Let's go to my cabin, Mr. Allenby."

"Very well." Allenby glanced around at his men to see that they were staying with the skiff and followed Captain Smith to his office.

The captain's office was also his cabin, directly behind the pilot-house. He entered the pilothouse briefly to tell the pilot where he would be if there were any changes. Then he showed Allenby into his cabin and motioned him to a seat.

"As you can see, we're aground. We've been here since yesterday. We thought we could grasshopper forward, but had difficulty and didn't realize the cause. We've sprung a few boards and have taken on water. The mate didn't notice it until today." The captain was obviously not happy with his mate. He continued, after scowling momentarily. "We're currently pumping the bilge, and I believe that by evening we'll have dry bilges and soon thereafter be free."

"So how can we help you, sir?" Allenby asked.

"In several ways, if it pleases you to do so," the captain replied. "We have nearly exhausted our wood. We would like to buy fifteen cords from you and are willing to pay double for it."

"I'm sure the captain will agree to that."

"Then we have several passengers we would like to transfer to the *Barnard Clinton*. We intend to return to St. Joseph for repairs. A single woman and three men are all adamant about not being delayed on their journey."

"We'll find room for them. Will that be all you require from us?"

"I believe so. I can't ask your captain to delay his journey unduly, but if he is still within sight when we escape the sandbar, I will greatly appreciate his watching us long enough to make sure we don't sink. I have less confidence in this crew than I had two days ago," he said with more than a little sarcasm.

"I'll relay that to him, sir. How do you propose to transfer the wood?"

"When you get ahead of us, maneuver into our current stream, throw it over, and we'll pick it up with pikes and in our skiffs. We'll prefer the biggest pieces you have, of course."

"Very good. Oh, by the way, we fished out one of your crew, a young black man. It looks like he is recovering."

"Yes. Lucky for him you came along."

The captain went to the safe in his cabin, opened it, and removed cash with which to pay for the wood.

"This amounts to what we would have paid for thirty cords of wood in Kansas City. We'll be happy to receive fifteen cords from you." He handed some of the cash to Allenby. "I'll have the transferring passengers on the bow shortly." He handed Allenby the additional money. "And please tell your captain that should we meet again, I'll not settle for less than buying him dinner and drinks for an evening."

"Yes, sir. Thank you, sir. I'll pass that message to him."

Allenby and Captain Smith shook hands, and the first mate returned to the main deck. He was puzzled to see the young black man still sitting in the yawl, apparently recovered from his near-drowning ordeal. Standing on deck adjacent to the tied-off yawl was a young black woman in a large draping shawl, surprising in the heat of the day, a white woman in elegant attire, and three white men. The black woman was anxious about the rescued man, who refused to reboard the *Princess*. The four white people were the passengers who had not wanted their trip delayed.

The mate on the *Princess* addressed Allenby. "The worthless black don't want to work for us no more. You're welcome to take him and his woman. You can leave 'em on a sandbar or take 'em on up the river. They been more trouble than they're worth."

Allenby looked down at the black man sitting in the skiff. "What's your name, fella?"

"Abraham," he answered.

"Are you all right now?"

"Yes, sir."

"Well, Abraham, we'll take you onboard the *Barnard Clinton*, but you'll have to work or we'll kick you off at a wood station. Same goes for your woman."

"I works good," he said. "Liz'beth works good like me."

"Very well. Everyone be seated." He looked at the other four passengers. They each stepped gingerly into the yawl. Then the black woman stepped in, but even though she was young, she was awkward on her feet and was forced to put one hand on the shoulder of the man called Humpback. He scowled, but said nothing. As soon as everyone was seated, Allenby stepped in at the stern. The yawl was overloaded, and the oarsmen were handicapped in rowing because of the extra people crowded in, but they drifted and rowed back down to the *Clinton*. In no time they reached her and were shortly tied off to her starboard side. The four white passengers stepped over to the *Clinton* first, and then the black couple, Abraham and his wife, and last, the oarsmen and Allenby. The oarsmen lifted the trunks of the passengers onto the steamer deck.

As soon as the yawl was hoisted aboard, Felden rang the engine room for full speed. His leadsmen were still on the bow, awaiting the forward progress of the steamer so they could take soundings. He had had ample opportunity to read the river and found the new channel with no difficulty. The *Barnard Clinton*'s engines huffed their deep, raspy moan, great black clouds issued from the stacks, and the paddles churned into the muddy waters, sending the boat surging ahead.

Felden thought he knew Captain Culpepper's mind well enough that he rarely asked for guidance . . . and never for advice. But as the last of the cordwood was thrown over to drift down to the *Missouri Princess,* Felden, without turning, addressed Culpepper. "We'll be around the bend in half an hour. Should we ease back a little in case they need more assistance?"

"No," Culpepper answered. "That captain has already cost his boat more than I would have asked to pull him free. A day's delay is equally costly for us."

"Yes, sir." The head pilot and the captain agreed on most things. Now they were both silent as the *Clinton* made for the bend. Just before they entered the bend, Culpepper used his binoculars to look the *Missouri Princess* over one last time, and then, satisfied that her predicament was unchanged, set the glasses down on the counter and fixed his gaze ahead.

On the *Princess* things were starting to happen. With her wheel in reverse, and the men in the river channeling water under her bow, she was making sternway, inch by inch, then feet by feet. Then, an hour after the *Clinton* had disappeared around the bend, the bow slipped into deeper water and suddenly she was free. The pilot left the wheel in reverse for a minute while she floated into deep water once again. His intention was to turn her back downriver.

But something wasn't right. When the wheel started turning forward again, the helm was sluggish. She seemed to be sitting bow low in the river. The pilot shouted to the mate to check the bilges. In minutes the mate was in the pilot house, and there was a flurry of activity on the forward main deck.

"She's stove in at the water line portside, and there's more water in the bilge than we thought. Water is pouring over the starboard guard, and the pumps aren't keeping up."

The pilot thought for a minute and then turned to the captain. "I recommend we run her right back up on the bar, sir. We can pump her dry and try to make repairs on the bow."

It was the captain's turn to think to himself. Putting her back on the sandbar would mean they would be where they were yesterday with no gain. There were other sandbars between here and St. Joseph. They could shift weight aft or even throw some over to raise the bow as high as possible. St. Joseph was four hours away at normal speeds, and they could get more pumps and professional repairs there. He had lost too much confidence in his crew to think they could improvise repairs adequate enough to get them all the way to Omaha.

"Water is coming in starboard?"

"Yes." It was the mate who answered, but the captain had addressed the pilot.

"First, dam the guard with anything we have. Shift the passengers and excess crew to the aft larboard decks. Move freight to the stern. Build up the fires. Use pitch and the driest wood we have. Set the peas all the way out on the safety valves. Lash the safety valve down on the port boiler. When a safety valve lifts on the second boiler, lash it down. If number three lifts, put all the passengers off. Make for St. Joseph as if your life depended on it."

An hour later they were gaining on the water in the hold. A crew was working on the damaged port bow, shoving various materials into the hole and then nailing boards over it. The speed of the *Missouri Princess* tended to lift the bow and that was an advantage. Both starboard and larboard guards were above water. The second safety valve had not lifted. The crew was stoking the fire as aggressively as they could, and the wood was laid out next to the boilers in readiness.

Then disaster struck. An eager roustabout tried to throw a bucket of coal oil into the firebox and spilled some on the deck. Fire spread forward and got into the wood that had been stacked in readiness and some of the lighter cargo that had been transferred forward to make room for heavier items at the stern. As the engineer was putting the fire pump into gear, the second safety valve lifted, then the third, and one minute later the port boiler blew up, leaving a gaping hole in the side of the steamer.

Boiler explosions on riverboats were usually catastrophes, killing most of the people onboard and disassembling the boat into a pile of scrap and splinters, but, occasionally, they were less lethal. Owing to the fact that the port boiler was the one that burst, and the passengers and extra crew were on the starboard side, lives were spared.

The pilothouse collapsed into the hole left in the cabin deck. The pilot and the captain climbed out and gained what was left of the hurricane deck. The engineer had been tending the fire pump instead of the boilers and was struck by debris, but escaped serious injury. Excess steam vented out the portside, and the engines lost power. The stern wheel swished to a stop. The force of the explosion spread fire all over the main deck, and there were no longer fire pumps to attack it.

The *Princess* was as good as lost. She was drifting with complete loss of power, burning and sinking at the same time. Passengers were jumping overboard, fighting for floats and trying to get the skiffs off the deck.

The mate was running back and forth, trying to direct firefighting efforts and bilge-pumping efforts, and seeing how many people had been hurt in the boiler explosion. He was effective at none of these.

The pilot stayed on the hurricane deck, trying to find a way to work the rudders in an attempt to find shallow water near the shore. Having no speed through the water, the rudders were mostly ineffective, but he would take anything he could get. He rigged clamps and a block and tackle on the steering cables and found he could move the rudders, but he had to re-rig after every movement.

The captain descended to the main deck and managed to find some crew with level heads. They launched a skiff to pick up the desperate passengers who had jumped or been thrown into the river, and then they hauled a line to the near shore and tied it around the stump of a large cottonwood. Without steam, the capstans wouldn't turn, so they couldn't pull forward, but the anchor line was cleated to the bow, and the boat began to swing toward the shore.

The captain took control of the firefighting efforts, and when it looked as though they would have success, he began directing the care of the injured. There were eleven men injured by flying debris and seven suffering from steam burns; nine would die that day, and seven others were never found. The *Str. Missouri Princess* sank in seven feet of water at the bow and nine feet at the stern. Some of her passengers were picked up by a downriver steamer, while others managed to make it to shore. The captain stayed onboard to protect what was left of the once-magnificent steamer. Much of her regular cargo was lost or scavenged by flat boaters downstream. Months later she would be dismantled for salvage, and her patched hull used as a wharf boat. The *Princess* was one of hundreds of victims of the unforgiving Missouri River.

Chapter Eight

Little Joe divided the horse corral into two corrals with a sturdy railing and put all the horses into one. Then he began shoveling the empty one. There was a large door that opened onto the main deck guards, and there was no step between the deck and the walkway. A removable railing allowed him to push the manure right into the river. When that was done, he used a washdown hose and a stiff broom to clean the deck down to bare wood.

Next, Joe carefully examined each horse and brushed it. Each horse got a few minutes of his attention, so he was at this task for over an hour. The horses had already gotten to know him and responded in kind to his affection. He fed them and ducked out of the corral, took his coat from the railing, and put it on.

Danny Barton had been watching, and when Little Joe saw him he turned away while he buttoned his coat, then turned back and smiled at the officer.

"Hello, Mr. Barton. Do you like horses?"

"Some. Not all."

"These are good horses. They're starting to like river life."

"Well, I guess they should. They don't work, they just eat, and they've got the best friend they'll probably ever have." Barton said it to be funny, but he was sure he could see Little Joe blush a little. *A shy kid, in some ways,* he thought. "How about raiding the kitchen?"

Little Joe grinned widely. "That sounds good. I worked right through dinner."

"Stand out next to the rail, and I'll hose your boots off."

"Good idea."

When that was accomplished, they climbed the stairs to the

cabin deck. It being the late afternoon, there was no meal being served, but it was too long for either of them to wait for supper. Barton took Little Joe into the cook shack, and the cook, who had taken a liking to Barton, readily supplied them with food that they took up to the hurricane deck. Once there, they sat on a bench, eating and watching the sun get low over the river.

Little Joe opened the conversation. "I heard you served under the captain during the war."

"Yeah, I was a clerk for just a few months. Then I was his aide for a few weeks until I was captured."

"Did the Confederates treat you well?"

"No," he said, "but they treated me as good as they could. They were all starving. Even after a month, I was in better shape than my guards."

"How'd you get away?"

"I didn't. I was exchanged for some of their men who had been captured."

"Did you go back into battle?"

"No. By the time my wound healed, the war was nearly over."

Little Joe had apparently satisfied his curiosity and was silent as he ate.

"Did you have relatives in the Army?" Barton asked.

"My brother was killed."

"Sorry to hear that, Joe."

Little Joe had no reply. His attention was taken by something on the main deck. He set his food down, stood up, and leaned over the rail, looking forward. Then he sat back down and resumed eating. It wasn't until they had both finished that Barton learned what had gotten Little Joe's attention.

"Mr. Barton, I think I should show you something," Little Joe said.

"All right." There was a question in Barton's voice.

"Follow me to the bow." They got up, and Barton followed the boy down to the main deck and to the bow. There they found Abraham and his wife working on making the harness that Joe had requested.

"This is Abraham and his wife, Elizabeth," Little Joe said.

Barton was uncomfortable. He hadn't been around many blacks and all his opinions of them were based on hearsay, much of it conflicting.

"Hello, sir." Abraham stood up and bowed. Elizabeth sat cross-legged on the deck with her flowing skirts spread around her. Barton decided to hide his discomfort and extended his hand. Abraham's eyes widened. He smiled and then took Danny's hand.

"They've got a little nest next to the horse corral," Little Joe informed Barton. No surprise, considering they were black. Most of the white men onboard would not have tolerated sleeping in close proximity to former slaves. He felt a little sorry for the couple who had proven to be good workers, but knew he could only cause trouble if he moved them closer to the other deckers.

Joe made a startling announcement. "Elizabeth is pregnant." This surprised everyone. Abraham and Elizabeth had been hiding her condition, afraid they would be put off the boat if discovered. Barton was speechless, but Little Joe wasn't.

"When is the baby coming, Elizabeth?" Joe asked.

Elizabeth didn't answer. She put her hand on her abdomen and looked at Abraham. He didn't say anything; they were both flustered and scared.

Little Joe put his hands on his hips. "The baby is coming any day, Mr. Barton, and it's going to be born in horse manure!" Barton could only stand there, looking from Elizabeth to Little Joe. The boy continued, "If one of these mares was about to foal, I wouldn't let her do it here!"

Barton was thinking rapidly. This situation couldn't be allowed, but short of putting them ashore at the next town, what could be done? It would cause a rebellion on the main deck if he moved them away from the corral to sleep where the other deckers slept. And it was unthinkable that they would be allowed onto the cabin deck.

How did Little Joe know anything about pregnancy? If Barton had had time, he might have surmised that Little Joe had grown up in a large family. He might have helped his mother in childbirth, particularly if there were no women around. Before he could form these thoughts, Little Joe demanded his attention.

"You offered to share your cabin with me, Mr. Barton." Joe paused as he watched his face to see the realization of what he was about to ask hit before he could ask it. "You could let Elizabeth use it for a few weeks."

It was less of a request than a command. Little Joe, in spite of his youth, was taking charge of a very unusual situation. Abraham was panicked and shaking his head. He was almost ready to grab Little Joe and pull him away from Barton to erase what had just been said. Black people had been made to suffer greatly for affronts like this just a few years ago. At the least, he was afraid that his wife could be put off, and he be forced to stay on the boat and work.

Barton couldn't believe his ears. This request from a mere boy was as brash as if Little Joe were a general. He turned it over in his mind. They were two days out of Omaha, where they could put the couple ashore and assure the baby and mother of better care than could be had on the *Barnard Clinton*. But even two days could be too long if the baby was coming any day, as Little Joe had claimed. If the crew would not tolerate close company with the black couple, the ladies on the cabin deck were even less likely to. But if he could find space for them on the Texas deck, that might work, particularly if they were installed there under the pretense of being personal servants to the officers. He couldn't decide this on his own; he needed to involve the captain. He looked at Elizabeth.

"How do you feel, Elizabeth?"

She looked at Abraham and then down at her abdomen. "I feel heavy," she replied and looked up at Barton as she gently rubbed her unborn baby.

"Stay right here. I'll be back in a few minutes." Barton left the couple and climbed to the pilothouse. Little Joe stayed behind, his hand on Elizabeth's shoulder.

Barton found Captain Culpepper in the pilothouse, where he spent most of his waking hours. Greg Singletary was on watch, maneuvering the *Clinton* through a crossing. The channel traversing the crossing was shallow, and the risk of grounding great.

There were two leadsmen on the bow, taking turns casting their weights out ahead of the steamer. It required good timing to throw the lead out and then let it feel the bottom just as the boat caught up to it so that the line was straight down. The line was knotted, and knowing the distance between the knots gave the leadsman the exact depth at that instant. He would call the depth to the pilot, and in the meantime the other leadsman was repeating those actions. If a leadsman was getting comfortable soundings and the surface looked good, one leadsman was adequate, but on this crossing Singletary needed two. He was busy with the wheel, holding the *Clinton* to the desired course, and listening for the soundings.

Barton entered the pilothouse but kept quiet until the crossing was safely accomplished. Looking ahead he could see that there would not be another crossing for at least ten minutes, so he chose this time to speak. "Captain, I have a problem I need to discuss with you."

"Go ahead."

"You remember the black couple who we took onboard from the *Missouri Princess*?"

"Yes."

"They're sleeping next to the horses; it's the only place available to them."

The captain took his eyes off the river and looked at Barton. Singletary turned slightly to hear better.

"The woman is about to have a baby."

"Oh, for mercy sakes!" Singletary blurted out. He turned around and looked at both the captain and the security officer, shaking his head in disbelief.

"Take me down there, Mr. Barton," the captain said.

Barton led the way down to the main deck and to the corral. When they got to the corral, the couple's sleeping area on top of a box holding the corral tools was made obvious by a bedroll and a small canvas bag holding their few possessions. Horses stood right next to the box, which was just outside the corral.

"This will never do," the captain said.

This comment made it easier for Barton to put forth Little Joe's audacious solution. "I'd be willing to give up my cabin until the baby is born, or until we get to Omaha where we can put them off," he said. Without realizing he was doing it, he held his breath.

"No," the captain said. Barton let out his breath and the captain continued. "We can't have them in the same cabin as our arsenal and the ship's safe. We'll put them in my cabin. What's their destination?"

"Montana," Barton answered.

"They can have my cabin until they decide to leave the boat, whether that's Omaha or Montana. I'll move in with you."

Without thinking, Barton said, "There's only one bunk in my cabin." Then he regretted saying it.

"You'll sleep on the floor."

"Yes, sir."

"Who's taking care of the horses?"

"The young decker, Little Joe."

"I expected less. Tell him I'm pleased with the condition of the horses and their quarters."

"Yes, sir, he does a good—"

"Take care of moving the couple. I'll clear my cabin out right away."

"Yes, sir."

The captain turned and climbed back up to the pilothouse. Barton went out to the bow to tell Little Joe and the black couple what the captain had said.

By the time the sun had set, Elizabeth was in the captain's cabin, resting in an overstuffed chair. Abraham was still obligated to work, so he was finishing the harness down on the main deck. Little Joe was tending to his horses, and Barton was walking the boat, stem to stern, deck by deck.

On the main deck, the crew was putting tools away and quitting work for the night. As soon as the cabin passengers had been fed, the roustabouts and deck passengers were allowed to climb the stairs to the cabin deck and get their last meal for the day.

One of the traits that Captain Culpepper valued highly was honesty. On many riverboats the steward was given money for provisions and anything he saved went into his pocket. Such a person might ring the dinner bell at short intervals so that no one had a chance to eat too much. Or allow only small portions, or, if given the opportunity, purchase small plates and bowls for the dining room. They might also accept huge tips to provide special meals to affluent passengers. Culpepper would tolerate none of this.

The meals served on the *Clinton* were not as fancy as those served on the Mississippi River steamers, but no one left the table hungry. Culpepper was particularly interested in seeing that the laborers were well fed. Everything Culpepper did with the *Clinton* was done with the thought that the renovated vessel would be traveling the western rivers for twenty or more years. This would be about fifteen years better than the average. He wanted and expected absolute loyalty from the senior pilot to the lowliest deckhand.

Barton walked into the dining room on the cabin deck just as the cook rang the bell for the last call. There were still a few cabin deck passengers at the long table, but they had finished eating and were merely socializing. When the first of the roustabouts appeared in the dining room, these passengers arose and went to watch the card games or get a drink at the bar.

The roustabouts and deckers ate buffet style. The cook's helpers laid food out on a table and were first in line, and then the others crowded in and helped themselves.

Barton walked through the room, briefly checking each card game and noting which men had guns on their belts. He saw the three men who had left the *Missouri Princess* sitting by themselves at a table, drinking and talking. Their demeanor did not suggest trouble, but two of them had gunbelts and the other had a Springfield carbine at his knee. If they decided to cause trouble, it would be big indeed. The young officer went to the table, dished a meal for himself, and sat to eat with the crew. The voyage had not been long enough for Barton to make friends in the roustabout crew, so the ones sitting next to him were silent.

When he had finished eating, Barton again wandered through the game tables. He had seen plenty of card games while in the Army, and he knew that poker players in a typical card game had varying levels of skill, all kinds of luck, and a wide range of honesty. After watching at least one hand at each of the five tables, he went to the bar.

"Lucky, give me five new decks," he said.

"Sure, Mr. Barton." He smiled. "Have you seen a few . . . uh . . . discrepancies?"

"Yeah. One deck has five aces. One deck has tapered cards. Might as well change 'em all."

"These are new and straight," Lucky said as he placed five new decks on the bar. Barton took them and one by one replaced all the decks.

His efforts had an unforeseen effect. One player was too hasty in modifying the new deck and was observed by a man who had just lost a big pot.

"You cheatin' cow chip!" the drunken loser exclaimed and pushed back from the table, pulling a revolver from inside his vest.

The accused man sat quietly and began sweating. He was armed, but he knew he didn't stand a chance of getting to his own weapon while the angry loser had his own revolver aimed right at him. No one else at the table dared move. The other card games stopped, and all eyes were on the man with the gun.

Officer Barton stepped quickly up behind the drunken man and put the barrel of his .44 against the man's head just behind his ear. With his other hand he pressed the drunkard's gun down until it was pointed at the floor. Then he pulled it from the man's hand and stood back.

"Do you have proof that man was cheating?" he asked the drunkard.

"Spread his cards out," the man answered.

Barton leaned over the table and fanned the cheater's cards out on the table with his left hand. There were six cards and the back of one was not quite the right color. It was from the old deck. The gambler could lay his cards down, and the back would be hidden. Then he could palm the card out when he tossed the cards to the next dealer.

The cheater reached inside his vest, but before he could withdraw the gun, Officer Barton had his own gun leveled at the man's chest.

"Put your hands on the table, mister," Barton ordered, and the man complied. The officer reached into the man's vest and pulled out a derringer, which he pocketed. As he was taking a pair of handcuffs from his jacket pocket, the cheated gambler grabbed someone else's gun, cocked it, aimed it at the gambler, and pulled the trigger. It didn't go off, but he was cocking it again when a third man pulled his own gun with the intent of joining the fray.

Barton aimed his own pistol at the cheated gambler, who turned toward him and had thoughts of aiming the misfired gun at him. Barton cocked his own gun and extended it to within six inches of the bridge of the man's nose. The man decided to drop the gun he had snatched from a man at his side. The officer turned to glare at the third man who, without expression, lowered his gun and pushed it back into his belt.

Barton locked one side of his handcuffs around the cheater's right wrist and then yanked the man to the floor and dragged him to the bar, where he locked the other cuff to the foot rail. "When we stop for wood in the morning, you're getting off. Any more trouble, and I'll throw you over in the middle of the river."

He returned to the table where the other players were watching his actions. "Does anybody know how much money he sat down with?" he asked.

"Looked like about fifteen dollars," one man said. No one disagreed.

Barton counted out fifteen dollars from the cheater's winnings. "Divide up the rest among yourselves." He stuffed the fifteen dollars into his pocket. No one objected, but a man who had watched the incident spoke, barely suppressing his anger.

"You just about got yourself killed, kid. You better figure out what you're doin'."

Barton had no reply.

During this episode the three men from the *Missouri Princess* had their hands on their guns but made no move to take sides in the event. For the next hour the games were peaceful and the room was relatively quiet until the door from the walkway opened and Abraham came in. He went directly to Barton.

"Mr. Barton, Eliz'beth is havin' her baby. She needs help."

Chapter Nine

Harold Robertson watched as the last customers left the bank, and his clerk, Henry Miller, locked the door behind them. It had been a busy week, and much to his satisfaction, deposits had exceeded withdrawals.

Omaha was booming. What had been a campsite across the river from Council Bluffs a decade ago was now a town of thousands, with new people coming in daily. This growth had been made possible by three events: the selection of a northern route for the transcontinental railroad, the successful navigation of the Missouri River by a number of steamboats, and the cunning vision of a group of real estate speculators who had laid out the town site prior to the Civil War.

Robertson had been too late to take part in the original commissioning of the town, but he did come in time to establish a bank with his savings. His bank wasn't the only bank in Omaha and it wasn't the biggest, but it was the most profitable. He avoided long-term loans and high-risk loans. He was shrewd enough to recognize the ventures that would yield early profits, and he plunged readily into these with what he had on hand. He disliked idle money and kept the bank's cash hovering near zero. Not true of his own reserves, however. He kept a substantial sum aside that he called "road money," in case his world started caving in.

The banker sat down at his desk and finished his correspondence for the day: letters to investors, letters offering capital and the terms, and letters asking for information.

He lived alone in a moderate-sized frame house. His maid cooked and kept house and lived in an adjacent cottage. In the year he had lived there and engaged the housekeeper, they had not grown fond of each other or become friends; it was just business.

Neither had Robertson made close friends with other residents in Omaha, but he knew all the important people. He drank with them, played cards with them, and listened closely to all their conversations for opportunities that might benefit him. The background that he shared with these men was a tossed salad of fact, half-truths, and outright lies.

He had been, as he claimed, an officer for the Union. But not a company commander; he had been a spy and never wore a uniform. Worse, he had also traded secrets to the Confederate forces when it benefited him. He hadn't been discharged to take care of his dying wife, as he occasionally related; he had simply abandoned her when he was presented with an opportunity to enrich himself at the expense of the doomed Confederacy. In one daring, dangerous night, he intercepted the fortune that enabled him to elevate his life. The ragged, unshaven, unclean man who had skulked around the battle lines for four years, selling information to both sides, was now a well-groomed, clean-shaven banker, whose tongue was as slick as his face.

The businessmen of Omaha could not quite see through the respectable veneer that Robertson wore. He had years of experience at deception, and although some of his acquaintances had reservations, what was obvious to them was that almost everything he touched turned to gold. It hypnotized them.

Omaha was a wide-open boomtown. There were fortunes to be made, if you weren't afraid to move quickly and decisively. And knowing Harold Robertson seemed to be of value if making a fortune was your intent. That didn't mean you had to invite him into your home, but if you could bring yourself to trust him with your money, as many did, it paid off handsomely. So far, at least.

Robertson held the massive ledger book close, and Miller's chair scraped on the floor. It was after five o'clock. He put his correspondence into a desk drawer, locked it, and looked up as Miller came into his office.

"All done then, Henry?" he asked.

"Yes, sir." Miller handed Robertson the summary of the day's business and placed the safe drawer on his desk. The banker studied the summary as his assistant stood patiently in front of his desk. He made several pencil notations on the meticulously handwritten document with his pencil.

"I see two of our loans were paid off today, one in advance?" he asked.

"Yes, sir. McGuire made his last payment and Jensen paid his off, although it wasn't due until fall."

"In cash, of course?"

"Yes, sir," Miller answered. "I was glad to see the cash come in. I cashed several railroad checks this afternoon."

Miller didn't know the overall financial picture of the bank or how much reserve there was in the safe. He would have been alarmed to know that there was almost none.

"Very well, Henry. That will be all for today. I'll see you Monday morning."

"Yes, sir. Here is my pay voucher for you to sign, please."

"Of course." Robertson took the check from Miller, signed it, and handed it back.

"Thank you, sir," Miller said. He counted out his week's pay from the drawer and filed the voucher after making another entry in the ledger. Then he left Robertson's office and took his coat and hat from the coatrack.

A knock on the outer door distracted both men. Miller walked to the door and peered around the drawn window shade. He said over his shoulder, "It's John Swanson."

Swanson was the telegrapher from the Western Union office. Miller opened the door as Robertson got up from his desk and walked briskly to meet the man. "Come in, John," he said. Miller, anxious to get home and afraid that the telegram might mean additional work, wasted no time in leaving the bank. Swanson came in as Miller left. He handed the telegram to Robertson, and his somber expression told the banker it was not good news. Robertson unfolded the paper and read in disbelief.

MISSOURI PRINCESS AND CARGO LOST LITTLE PINE BEND STOP
NINE DEATHS STOP SENDING FULL REPORT BY STEAMER STOP
AWAIT INSTRUCTIONS STOP CAPTAIN E. SMITH ST. JOSEPH

The bank's major investment was scattered along the banks and the bottom of the Missouri River. He had talked the shareholders into this, his largest venture being the purchase of a Missouri River steamboat, and although they had been hesitant, his salesmanship had carried the day. It was well known that Mississippi River steamers were moneymakers, even if short-lived. The average steamer on the Upper Mississippi lasted only five years, most being taken by snags that pierced the hull, some suffering boiler explosions (these were the most deadly), and a few from fire or collision with a bridge or another steamer. In spite of these frequent mishaps, or perhaps because of the great risk, it was a hugely profitable business.

On the Missouri the business was in its infancy, other than those steamers run by the American Fur Company. But the Army was now shipping large amounts of supplies to the Indian country, businessmen were shipping goods, and emigrants were using the riverboats to get across the prairie and pick up the Oregon Trail. The demand for transportation exceeded the supply. A riverboat seemed like a wonderful investment, and it would have been, if handled by an honest and competent bank.

The problem was that Robertson had inflated the estimated cost by enough that he didn't need to use any of his own money; furthermore, he had not purchased insurance, pocketing that money. If he used his own money to cover the loss, he would be short by some twenty-two thousand dollars, his bank would fail, and he would face prison. His choices were few.

The telegraph office was two doors down from the bank. Swanson, the telegrapher, had hand-carried the telegram to the bank. Robertson silently read the telegram again and then looked at Swanson. He had to keep this news quiet as long as possible.

"Thank you, John. This is distressing news. I'll want to meet with my principal depositors as soon as possible. Can I ask you to please not let anyone know of this? I feel it is my duty to be the first to give them this news."

"Certainly, Harold. I always keep telegrams confidential." Robertson was not sure of this.

"It's not the disaster it might appear to be at first glance," Robertson explained. "I am so relieved to see that there was so little loss of life, and the vessel and its cargo were well insured." Two lies. Robertson cared little for human life, and there was no insurance.

The telegrapher excused himself and scurried back to the telegraph office. Robertson watched him walk back toward the telegraph office and then sat down and began making plans.

It was Friday, so the bank and the telegraph office would be closed for the weekend. There was a risk that Swanson would not keep his secret until Monday. Robertson had to make some decisions quickly.

He would have to leave Omaha. He was already known and being sought in New Orleans; St. Louis was a little too close to New Orleans for safety, so the western frontier looked good to him. The railroad tracks were almost to Fort Kearney. He could take the train that far and then transfer to a stagecoach. The stage line would eventually take him to California via either Salt Lake City or Santa Fe. Or he could travel by riverboat up the Missouri to the gold fields in Montana. But first, he must eliminate John Swanson.

Robertson took a small pistol from his desk and put it in his pocket. As an afterthought he took his letter opener, a long thin blade, and let himself out of the bank, locking the door behind himself, and walked toward the telegraph office. As he approached, he saw Swanson likewise letting himself out of his office and locking the door.

"Harold, the river is high today, and water has flooded the lagoon again," Swanson said. "I'm betting I can grab a catfish by the tail and have him for dinner tonight."

Perfect, Robertson thought. He replied, "Do you mind if I walk with you?"

"Not at all. If there's one catfish, there's probably twenty."

An hour later, Swanson was facedown in the Missouri River, and the banker was back in his office, putting all the cash from the bank into a satchel.

Chapter Ten

Let's go, Abraham!" Danny spun Abraham around, and they headed for the door. Danny paused at the door and surveyed the room. The cheating gambler was still chained to the foot rail at the bar. The games in progress were quiet and appeared under control. The heavy curtain that separated the ladies' quarters from the main salon had been drawn for the evening, giving the few ladies onboard their necessary privacy. Danny had the brief thought that he might need one or more of these ladies, but he decided to talk to Elizabeth first. He followed Abraham to the stairs leading to the first-class cabins.

In the captain's former cabin Danny and Abraham found Elizabeth on her back in bed, using her elbows to keep her head and shoulders off the pillow. Her face was shiny from perspiration, but she seemed not to be in any pain.

"Elizabeth, how are you doing?" the officer asked.

"I hurts pow'ful bad, Mr. Barton, but it goes away for a time." She lowered her head to her pillow.

Abraham went to his wife's side and knelt down, taking one of her hands in his. "We'll help you, 'Liz'beth. Me and Mr. Barton."

Elizabeth gave Abraham a look that was overlaid with patience, but that said that she had real doubts about any help the two men might be able to supply. She squeezed his hand and then looked at Danny.

"Get Little Joe," she said.

"That boy can't be much help, Elizabeth. I'll have one of the ladies come . . ."

"Shoot, Mr. Barton," she interrupted. "Joe ain't no boy. She be

64

a woman." She smiled weakly at him with an expression on her face as if he was just a little boy needing help tying his shoes. "And them fancy ladies ain't gonna wanna help a black baby come into this worl'."

"No, Little Joe is a boy. You're going to need a woman," he insisted.

Elizabeth chuckled softly. Just as she had always thought. White men weren't any smarter than black men. "Fetch Little Joe, please, Mr. Barton."

Danny straightened up and started to go, but he turned back. He started to say something but shook his head and left the stateroom.

On the hurricane deck, he nearly ran into Captain Culpepper. "Sorry, sir."

"Not a bit of it, Mr. Barton. Are we about to have a new passenger?"

The captain's aide was uncharacteristically flustered, and the captain had noticed. It was only a short journey from that observation to assume that the pregnant woman was about to give birth.

The last few hours had been very eventful for Danny. A cheating gambler, a near gunfight, a pregnant former slave, and then a woman dressed as a boy, if Elizabeth was to be believed.

"Well, yes, I think perhaps so, sir. I . . . I'm going to get help. I don't think I . . ." He stopped in midsentence. He tried to see the captain's face in the darkness. "Elizabeth . . . that's the black man's wife . . . Elizabeth . . . uh . . . just told me that Little Joe is a . . . woman!"

"*Hmph!* Then that's the person you need to help you," the captain declared.

"Yes. Yes, I'm going to find him, uh, her. I'm going to find Little Joe." Barton looked at the captain's face in the shadows.

"I'd suggest you not waste time, Mr. Barton." The aide couldn't see, but he could hear the amusement in the captain's voice.

"Yes, sir!" He took the stairs two at a time down to the main deck to locate the young boy, young girl, woman, Little Joe.

* * *

It was almost midnight and both pilots were in the pilothouse, as well as the mates and Captain Culpepper. Danny was standing on the cabin deck between the door to Elizabeth's cabin and the stairs to the pilothouse. She had been in labor for almost three hours, but nothing had happened yet. Josephine was in attendance, and Abraham was helping. All Danny could do was wait in the dark and listen to the moans of the steam engines and the sound of water under the hull and the stern wheel.

In the pilothouse there was some discussion regarding the position of the *Barnard Clinton* on the Missouri River. "If we haven't passed the big barn with the light on the peak," Greg Singletary said, "we're below Cooper Creek."

"We haven't passed it," Charles Felden replied. "I put it a half hour ahead."

Felden had been navigating in the dark for four hours, but Singletary was confident that, in spite of his limited experience on the Missouri, he knew the river. Furthermore, he knew Felden wouldn't make a statement concerning the progress of the steamer unless he knew it to be absolute fact.

Felden rang the bell eight times as the second hand on the pilothouse clock lined up with the other two hands at exactly midnight.

"Here you are, Greg," Felden said, as he stepped back from the wheel.

Singletary stepped up in the darkness of the pilothouse and put his hands on the wheel. He turned the wheel slowly and slightly in each direction and felt the two hundred thirty feet of steamboat respond. This reassured him a little. The wheel felt good, the engines sounded good, everything was in order, but he decided to play it safe.

"David, put a leadsman on the bow and send me a scribe. I'm going to chart the bottom for an hour or so."

"I'll be right back, Greg," David Erickson said and left the pilothouse quickly. Felden, far from being insulted by Singletary's action, completely approved but said nothing and followed the second mate out of the pilothouse. As he passed Barton he paused and spoke. "Any news?"

"Not yet, Mr. Felden."

"Have you had a chance to talk to the woman?"

"You mean Joe, or whoever she is?"

"Yes."

"No, she's been busy in there with Elizabeth." Barton nodded toward the cabin door. "I'm kinda anxious to see what she's up to, though."

"Yeah, me too. Keep me informed."

"Yes, sir."

"You'd better get some sleep, son. We'll be in Omaha tomorrow, and it'll be a busy day."

The young officer wanted to protest, but he realized that the pilot was right. He turned to Elizabeth's cabin and opened the door slightly.

"Joe, I'll be in my cabin if you need me." He didn't wait for a response, but walked around the hurricane deck to his own cabin. The captain was just retiring for the night in what had been Barton's bunk.

"Mr. Barton."

"Captain."

"The lamp is yours. Good night."

"Good night, sir."

Barton rolled out his bedroll on the floor, turned the lamp low, and lay down with his clothes on.

In the pilothouse Erickson had taken on the role of scribe. He had entered all the soundings in a well-worn notebook that Singletary used for keeping track of the shifting river channel. At one A.M., Singletary had dismissed the leadsman. He had confirmed Felden's assessment of their position and was satisfied. A three-quarter moon had passed its zenith but was still above the trees, and Singletary was having no difficulty reading the surface of the river. Not that he could relax. It was night, there were no navigation aids, there were known and unknown snags every mile of river, and all he had to do was not hit any of them, not run aground, and not hit either bank or another steamboat that happened to be going downriver. But he was up to all those challenges.

"So did you hear about that hostler, Little Joe?" Erickson asked.

"I heard he's pretty picky about the way those horses are kept. Sounds like he's big for his britches."

"Big for his dresses is the way it turns out. Big for *her* dresses, that is." He chuckled.

"What!" Singletary was incredulous.

"Yeah, Joe is a girl, or maybe a woman."

"That's ridiculous."

"Maybe so, but that's the way it is."

"That skinny boy is actually a woman?" Singletary asked.

"Yep."

"How'd they find out? Who found out?"

"That Negro woman is having a baby, and I guess she had it figgered out. She asked for Little Joe's help. Then it kind of unraveled."

"Yeah, I heard about the black woman. She's in the captain's cabin." Singletary shook his head.

"Yeah, practically next door. For a hard man, the captain sure has some soft spots."

"I wish they were still on the *Missouri Princess,*" Singletary grumbled.

Singletary had had very little exposure to other races. He was uncomfortable around Africans and Asians, and, because of various stories he had heard, he didn't trust them. But he didn't trust a lot of whites either. Erickson, on the other hand, had supervised black slaves on the levees for years and regarded them with more respect than most Southern white men.

"Did you know there are black pilots on the Mississippi?" Erickson asked. This was in fact true, but he said it more for Singletary's reaction than for information.

Singletary was pressing against the window glass of the pilot-house, watching a ripple glide by on the larboard side that was a telltale sign of a snag. He didn't acknowledge the statement for a moment, but then he straightened up and spoke through clenched teeth. "I don't think we'll be taking any more soundings, Mr. Erickson," he said. The implication was clear; he wanted to be alone. Erickson slapped Singletary on the back, let out an audible chuckle, and walked out into the night.

At three A.M. the *Barnard Clinton* was quiet. Elizabeth was catching short naps between labor pains; Abraham was asleep sitting on the floor and leaning against her bed. Barton and the captain were asleep in their cabin, and the officers who were off the clock were all also sleeping.

The moon was now behind the trees, and the river was more difficult for Singletary to read. It had also widened out. The *Clinton* was negotiating a long left-hand bend that was followed by a long right-hand bend. The crossing was almost certainly going to be shallower than the channel. Singletary rang the engine room for half-speed to give himself some time to set up the crossing. He also signaled for a leadsman again. In less than a minute, a roustabout appeared on the bow with a lead line and began throwing it.

Pilot Singletary maneuvered the *Clinton* away from the right bank and into the crossing. The water began to shoal out, and the leadsman kept throwing the lead and calling the numbers up to the pilot. The water was suddenly only four and a half feet deep, and the pilot rang the engine room for dead slow. Soon the *Clinton* was drifting back into deeper water. Singletary again rang for half-speed, and the *Clinton* began making forward progress again, but slightly more southerly than before.

Erickson put a second man on the bow with a marked stick, a technique more useful than a lead line in very shallow water. Then he climbed up into the pilothouse. He was no longer in a joking mood; he was strictly professional and well aware of the difficulties that the pilot was dealing with.

The moon was so low that it was no direct help at all, but as often happens on the Missouri River, low clouds were gathering right over the river. They reflected the smallest fraction of the moonlight down to the water.

The soundings were consistently around five feet, and Singletary was confident that he was in the deepest part of the crossing. He had a foot of water between the bottom of the *Clinton* and the sandy bottom of the river. He could see the outlines of the trees on the shore against the stars. The left bank, which he was approaching, faced north, and Singletary guessed that the trees were not as tall on that side. If that was the case, he could be close enough to start the *Clinton* turning. A two-hundred-thirty-foot-long sternwheeler took a lot of river to turn. He looked at the approaching bank and listened as the leadsman called out the soundings. He waited, holding the wheel steady.

Singletary might not have seen the snag if he hadn't been watching for the approaching bank so closely. "Snag!" he shouted and spun the wheel to starboard. The leadsman braced himself and continued throwing his line. A third roustabout, who knew his job well, ran to the edge of the larboard bow and pointed both arms at the snag. The *Clinton* slowly turned to the right and the roustabout's arms swung left as he kept them pointed right at the snag. When his arms were at right angles to the steamer, the pilot spun the wheel to larboard, and the boat began turning back to its original heading. In minutes the snag, visible only as a V pattern in the surface of the water, had slipped by and was behind them.

Just as Singletary began a right turn to line up along the bank that he still couldn't see, the leadsman found six feet of water, then seven, then eight, and Singletary could see the trees of the left bank lining up parallel to his course.

Captain Culpepper had awakened when the engines changed speed and had been standing behind his pilot in the dark pilothouse. He had said nothing until now. "Nice work."

Singletary nodded without looking around. The captain left the pilothouse to return to his cabin. Erickson patted the pilot on the shoulder and also left to tend to matters on the main deck. It was now three thirty A.M.

The river was straight for a mile or more. Felden would be in the pilothouse to take over the watch in fifteen minutes. Singletary was looking forward to a few hours' sleep as soon as he could hand the wheel to Felden. He wondered how the black woman was doing. He admitted to himself that he hoped she was doing well, and that the baby would be born without complications. The two had caused no trouble since coming onboard and seemed to be good workers.

There was even less light now than there had been, but Singletary knew that the channel went to midriver here before crossing to the north shore. He eased the *Barnard Clinton* to the middle of the river, listening for the soundings through the still open pilothouse window.

Suddenly a light appeared in the middle of the river. Then another, and another. It was a flat boat, a large one, Singletary could tell by the number of lanterns that were suddenly being lit. He spun the wheel hard to starboard as he blew a long blast on the steam whistle.

The term *flatboat* encompassed a wide variety of rivercraft, the main feature in common being that they had no power. They were built upstream, loaded with cargo for some port downstream, and pushed out into the current with long poles. Their crew was small because there was little to do. Being unpowered, they had right-of-way over powered vessels on the river. Further, the crew often extinguished their lanterns at night, lighting them only when they were in danger of being run down.

This flatboat was dead ahead of the *Barnard Clinton*. Singletary had instinctively spun the wheel to the right, but now the flatboat drifted in the same direction.

The *Clinton* was now lying crosscurrent in front of the approaching flatboat. Her paddle wheel was under full power and was throwing cascades of water as she skidded sideways and tried to make headway on her new heading. Singletary had hoped to avoid the flatboat completely, but at the very least he wanted the impact to be on an angle if possible. Accordingly, he spun the wheel left to swing the stern.

The flatboat was barely a boat length away, as the *Clinton* was at a forty-five-degree angle in the current, not far from the right bank of the river. With just a few more yards of headway by the steamer, and a lot of luck, a collision would be avoided.

Alerted by the steam whistle, Culpepper, Felden, and Erickson entered the cabin. The first mate, Steve Allenby, was not far behind. They all kept silent as Singletary struggled to avoid a collision. Barton had also awakened to the sound of the whistle, but he stayed outside on the hurricane deck. He walked to Elizabeth's cabin and put his ear to the door. He could hear voices, but he couldn't make out any words. He remained outside the door and watched what he could see of the approaching flatboat.

Singletary rang for full astern and waited for the paddles to change rotation before he spun the wheel to the right. This action would continue the swing of the stern without making too much headway. The flatboat had passed the bow of the *Clinton*, and as the steamer slowed and the stern continued to swing, it looked as if the collision might be avoided. But the paddles did not reverse in time to stop the forward progress of the steamer and she ran out of water, stopping on a sandbar.

The wheel churning in reverse might have saved her, but the flatboat struck the wheel, knocking several buckets loose. There was a horrible crunching sound as the damaged buckets spun under the stern and ground against the hull. The engineer stopped the engines and blew off the excess steam. The *Str. Barnard Clinton* was aground and without power. The flatboat, scarcely damaged, drifted away with the sound of raucous laughter from the crew.

Singletary allowed himself the luxury of a strong curse, and then he started issuing orders. The mate and the off-watch officers were at his command, and he took full advantage of it.

"Erickson, get a crew into the yawl with a hundred-fifty pounder and take it out one hundred feet off the larboard bow." With no power, the steamer could be lost if she came off the sandbar on her own.

Erickson nodded and left the pilothouse on the run.

"Allenby, get the starboard yawl and start sounding the river down current behind us. We'll need four hundred yards to give the wheel a chance to bite. Let me know if we have it."

Allenby followed Erickson.

"Mr. Felden, have one of the engineers get a crew on the buckets and give me a report as soon as you can on the damage. Make sure they pin the wheel."

Felden nodded and left.

The pilothouse was now silent; only the captain and Singletary remained. The air was thick between them. The rule for pilots was that the pilot was responsible for whatever happened to his vessel, no matter what the cause, and Singletary had grounded the captain's fine steamboat on the easy part of the river. He wasn't sure what he could have done that would have avoided the accident, and he tried to put that into words.

"Captain, I . . ."

"Mr. Singletary, I'm going to wake up the cook and get the kitchen going," the captain interrupted. "We're in for a long night."

"Yes, sir." Singletary slumped dejectedly as the captain left him alone in the pilothouse.

Groundings in the Mississippi and Missouri rivers were usually not considered emergencies. In forty years of steamboating, a variety of techniques had been developed to cope with the shifting sands of the river bottoms. As in the case of the grounding of the *Str. Missouri Princess,* the initial incident might not spell trouble. It's how the officers and crew cope with it that makes it either a routine delay or a disaster.

As soon as Felden took over the watch at four A.M., Barton entered the pilothouse. He wanted to talk about the incident, and since Elizabeth was still in labor and most of the passengers were still asleep, he had little to do. The captain was still in the kitchen; the two men had the pilothouse to themselves.

"How bad is it?" Barton asked.

"She'll survive," Felden replied.

"So, it's not bad?"

"Every delay is bad." Felden launched into a two-minute lesson in economics. "The boat has the potential to make a fixed amount of money per trip. If she makes all her ports on schedule, you could even calculate what she makes per hour. The longer we stay here, the less money she makes."

"What does she make per hour?" Barton asked.

"I don't know, but you can bet Captain Culpepper does," Felden replied. "And there's more."

"Yeah?"

"This isn't the Mississippi. There are two periods of high water;

right now we're riding on spring rains. In May the water gets low, and we'll have a tough time coming back down. Then in June the river will be high again with Rocky Mountain snowmelt. Those are the only two periods of high water; the water will get shallower as the summer wears on. Culpepper wants to get to Fort Benton soon enough to make a second trip."

"Do you think we'll make it?"

"Most people don't think we'll make it even once."

"But what do you think?" the officer insisted.

"This boat is powerful and doesn't take much water. It's built low so that the prairie winds have less effect. Singletary is one of the best pilots on the Missouri. If there's water, we'll get there."

Barton was to the point. "What could Singletary have done differently to avoid grounding?" he asked.

"Made his initial turn to larboard. Left."

"Is that what you would have done?"

"That's what I'd be wishing I had done." Felden grinned sardonically.

"The kitchen is operating, Mr. Felden. Can I bring you some coffee and something to eat?"

"Call me Charles, Danny. Coffee will be fine."

Elizabeth delivered a healthy baby boy at sunrise with the able assistance of Josephine Wainwright. Two hours after the event, Danny found Josephine on the main deck, taking care of the horses. She looked exhausted, but pleased.

"I guess it's not just the horses that are lucky to have you aboard," he said.

"Give me a hand here," she said as she urged the horses into the alternate corral.

Danny swatted the horses on their rumps with his hat as Josephine pulled them by their manes to guide them through the gateway.

When all the horses were relocated, Josephine wearily began cleaning the floor. Danny dragged a hose over to help. Ordinarily, Josephine would have scolded anyone who might have tried to help her, but she was nearing her limit. It had been both a physically and emotionally exhausting twenty-four hours.

Forty-five minutes later, as they were finishing, she paused, leaned on her shovel, and looked purposefully at Barton. He returned the look.

"I see two questions on your face, Mr. Barton," she said. He said nothing. "You want to know why I'm dressed like a boy, and why I'm traveling alone on the frontier."

Danny shrugged as he motioned her to stand next to the railing so he could clean her boots.

She continued. "The first question is answered by the second. I'm dressed like a boy because I'm traveling alone on the frontier." But she didn't say why she was traveling on the frontier.

When her boots were clean she performed the same service for him, and then she spoke more about her intentions. "I'm going to continue to travel as a boy for that reason, and I ask you not to betray me," she said, looking directly into his eyes. This time she wasn't commanding, she was pleading, and the look in her eyes did all the betraying. Danny saw her as a woman for the first time. He wondered how he had not seen through her masquerade; it seemed so obvious now.

"Let's get something to eat, Jo," he said.

"You're not curious about my purpose in traveling alone on the river?" she asked.

"I reckon it's your business," he answered. "You need to know, though, that all the officers now know you're a woman."

"Just tell them not to treat me any differently," she said.

"I'm going to try to get a stateroom for you," he said. "We're leaving some first-class passengers in Omaha, and there might be a stateroom available."

"I'm getting off in Omaha," she said, believing that Melinda LaFramboise would be getting off there also.

"Oh." He couldn't hide his disappointment.

"I'm still ready to eat," she said. They walked together to the kitchen.

It was early afternoon, nearly ten hours after the grounding of the *Clinton*. Felden was on watch in the pilothouse. There was nothing for him to do, but he could be found quickly if there was a question or a progress report.

While the repair crew labored on the buckets, lines had been run out fore and aft. It was thought by all the officers that the *Clinton* was not grounded badly. Her hull was still tight and taking on no more water than usual. The plan was to winch her astern with steam up and slack on the bowline. Then, when she was afloat again, pay out the bowline and let her drift over the stern anchors. With the bowline made fast, the stern anchors could be retrieved. All that was needed at this moment was for the repair crew to report their task finished, unpin the wheel, and allow the engineer to turn the paddle wheel slowly to make certain that everything was running true.

"Felden, we're ready," Singletary said.

"Very well, Mr. Singletary. I'll give you time to get to the engine room. When I ring for slow ahead, the engineer will turn the paddles as slowly as possible and as many revolutions as it takes to assure the wheel is true. When I see the wheel stop again, I'll ring for half-speed astern, and Allenby will have the stern lines winched in on both sides. We'll see if we can put this boat back in the channel."

"All right, Mr. Felden." Singletary left the pilothouse to fulfill his role according to the senior pilot's instructions. If the steamer came off the sandbar with no further problems, the visual evidence of his piloting error would be only a memory that would slowly, but surely, fade as they continued their adventure up the Missouri River.

When it wasn't a regular mealtime, Danny would usually go to the side door of the kitchen off the cabin deck rather than walk through the main salon, which was the dining room at mealtimes. Josephine had adopted this habit also and was welcome in the kitchen because she often brought catfish for the kitchen staff. Today they were both tired and entered the main salon on their way to the kitchen, talking as they walked.

"We'll get off this sandbar soon?" Josephine asked.

"Yeah, I think so. Let's grab some biscuits and get up on the hurricane deck."

"All right." Then she stopped and turned toward him. "I wish I didn't have to get off at Omaha." She watched his face to see his reaction to her statement. He smiled, but seemed puzzled. She wanted to say more, but she didn't know how to express her feelings to this young man, and she wasn't sure she wanted him to know more than what she had already said.

"I reckon we all travel roads we'd rather not," he said. He started to put his arm around her to guide her into the dining room and then pulled it back. She was no longer the young boy that he had thought he knew.

Suddenly Josephine grabbed his arm and pulled him to one side, using him as a shield. From what, he didn't know.

"Let's get out of here," she said, low and urgently.

Danny didn't wait for an explanation. He put his hand between her shoulder blades and guided her back out the door. Once outside, he stopped and turned her around to face him. "What's going on, Jo?"

Josephine took a deep breath and then said, "Get me something to eat. I'll wait for you on the hurricane deck." Before he could protest, she hurried away to the stairway leading to the top deck.

Felden rang for slow ahead and then waited for the wheel to turn. He could feel the *Clinton* shudder slightly, as first the starboard engine pushed on its pitman arm and then the larboard pushed likewise. Although the steamer was still aground, he thought he could feel a slight forward motion, like an eager dog on a tight leash. It could be that during the hours they had been anchored and without power, some of the sandbar had washed out from under the hull. The danger was that sometimes it made a new sandbar in the eddies behind a grounded hull. But in this instance, a crew in a yawl had sounded for a hundred yards behind the steamer, and there was adequate water to float her.

A roustabout came into the pilothouse. "The paddles stopped, sir," he reported, and then bolted out of the pilothouse.

Felden rang for half-speed astern and again the steamer trembled, only this time the trembling became a slow vibration as the wheel spun up to half-speed. But the steamer stayed on the sandbar. Allenby was on the aft-hurricane deck, walking quickly from side to side, watching the stern anchor lines take up slack and begin pulling in concert with the paddles. His counterpart, Erickson, was on the bow, watching the deckhands preparing to pay out the bowline. Allenby had served on coastal schooners with less line and anchors than the *Clinton*. Culpepper had equipped his steamer well. Because of Allenby's saltwater experience, he would describe the steamer as well-found, but riverboats were separate from many of the traditions of the sea. She was, in river terms, merely well equipped. In fact, many officers did not assign gender to a river vessel, referring to a steamer as *it*, rather than the centuries-old tradition of *she*.

Josephine was sitting on the hurricane deck, dangling her legs over the side and leaning on her folded arms on the middle rail. She had a bird's-eye view of the churning paddle wheel and the efforts to winch the steamer astern, but her eyes were closed. Danny walked up behind her and rather than shouting over the sound of the splashing water touched her on the shoulder and offered her a large biscuit. She turned and smiled drowsily at him and accepted the biscuit.

"I've got a jar of coffee and some cups. Want some?" he asked.

"Thanks."

Danny eased himself onto the deck beside Josephine. He put the jar and cups between them. She poured coffee for both of them, and they ate and drank in silence for several minutes.

"There's a woman onboard who murdered someone. My brother. She murdered my brother," she said, breaking the silence. Danny watched emotions march across the young woman's face.

"And you just saw her," he said slowly.

"Yes, and I didn't want her to see me."

"Who is she?"

"Her name is Melinda LaFramboise."

"What now?"

"She wasn't alone when my brother was killed. I want to watch her and see if she leads me to the man who actually pulled the trigger. I want both of them to stand trial."

"Will you recognize him if you see him?"

"No."

"Will he recognize you?"

"Not likely, but she might, even the way I'm dressed."

"Tell me about this woman, Jo," Danny said.

Josephine waited a long time to reply. He watched her face patiently. Finally she said, "I'll have to go back a few years." She shifted her weight on the edge of the hurricane deck to a more comfortable position. "My real name is Josephine Wainwright. I'm twenty years old. I grew up in Kentucky on my father's ranch. He farmed, raised cattle and sheep, but what he was most well known for was breeding horses.

"I had three older brothers. My oldest brother, Jonathan, was fifteen years older than me and was born with a deformed foot. He could ride, with a special saddle, but he couldn't march a step, so he never entered the war. He left home in 1854 and started farming in Tennessee, about forty miles south of my father's ranch. Like my father, he was successful.

"Beginning in 1855, and about once a year until the war started, my father, who objected to slavery, would gather a string of ponies and ride down to my brother's farm. Once there, he would trade the ponies to the locals for as many slaves as possible and take the people back to Kentucky, where he would sign papers freeing them. As you know, Kentucky was a slave state, even though they did not secede, so he kept knowledge of this activity from our neighbors and moved the freed slaves north as quietly as possible. He was doing nothing illegal, just not always acceptable in Kentucky.

"I accompanied him on many of these trips, disguised as a boy to avoid trouble. Sometimes, my father would be contacted by mysterious people who would ask him to assist escaped slaves. At first he refused, but he later agreed and found, to his surprise, that my brother had been a part of the underground railway for many years. It was a natural operation for them, but it caused my brother much torment; he tried to be loyal to Tennessee, and after the war started, to the newly formed Confederacy. He worked hard to supply the Confederate Army with food and supplies, but he couldn't abide slavery."

Danny suddenly looked at the shore. "We're moving!" he said, as he realized that the stern lines were winching in and the *Clinton* was sliding backward.

In the pilothouse Felden rang the engine room to stop, even though he could still hear and feel the hull sliding on the bottom. He wanted to assure that the paddle wheel was turning forward as soon as possible. His anticipation was spot on; the paddle wheel rolled to a stop as the stern lines pulled the steamer free. Felden could feel that the hull was afloat, like a slumbering beast, awakening slowly. He blew the whistle four short blasts. The *Clinton* continued making sternway, and when she was about to drift over the stern anchors, Allenby shouted to lift the anchors aboard and then ran the length of the hurricane deck to let Felden know.

Felden had been watching and signaled Erickson on the bow to snub the line to the bow anchor, which had been set off the larboard bow, in the channel. The steamer crabbed sideways into the main channel, and Felden rang for half ahead and gave one long blast on the whistle. The action on the stern anchors was repeated on the bow anchor, and the *Str. Barnard Clinton* was under way. A cheer went up from the crew.

"Nice work," the captain said, as Felden rang for full ahead.

Danny had stood to watch as the steamer backed off the sandbar, but he knew Josephine had more to say. He sat down.

"I think we're free, Jo. Finish your story."

She spoke wearily. "My father became ill in 1862, and I began to make the midnight trips into Tennessee, still disguised as a boy, to assist escaping slaves. I knew the way through the forest blindfolded. I guided many former slaves into Kentucky to a farm north of my father's ranch, where they received food, clothing, forged documents, and directions to the next refuge on the railway."

"How many slaves did you help?" he asked.

"Over thirty that we were aware of. We knew that there were others tagging along in the dark, and that increased the risk of being caught, but we couldn't chase them away," she replied. "And my father bought and freed about half that number also."

Danny whistled low.

Josephine continued. "Then, in 1864, a shipment of gold was stolen from the Union Army by a group of men posing as Confederate soldiers. One of the men may have been a double spy. He approached my brother about returning the gold to the North with some refugee slaves. My brother, genuinely patriotic, was in an impossible position, and regardless of which way he really felt, he agreed to do so."

"Your brother would have been shot by either side if he had been discovered."

"Yes, but he was shot by the man who arranged the shipment. It was a contemptible scheme to get the gold through Confederate territory and Union lines so that he could have it for his own," she said bitterly. "Our method of escorting slaves was for me to ride some distance ahead to ensure the route was clear. If I came across someone on the trail or saw something that made me suspicious, I would circle through the forest and warn my brother. It didn't work this time.

"About half past five in the morning, when the sky was just beginning to show light blue in the east and we were well inside Kentucky, I heard several shots behind me. I turned my horse back to see what had happened. My brother was lying on the road; the slaves were gone, and so was the gold. It had been in two satchels, which would have been possible for two people to carry on horseback for at least a short distance. My brother was still alive, barely, and he whispered to me, 'Tell Rachel I love her,' and then he died. I cried for a long time. Finally, when the sun came up, the slaves came out of hiding and helped me load his body into the wagon. This was a brave thing for them to do. We finished our journey to the ranch, where I hid them, as I always did, in a false wall in the main house. They left the next evening, but one of them told me he clearly saw the man who shot Jonathan and that there was a woman with him."

"But you never saw that slave again?" he asked.

"Not until we found the *Missouri Princess* aground. The man we pulled from the river, Abraham, was that slave . . . former slave."

"How do you know that Melinda LaFramboise was involved?"

"She lived about thirty miles south of us, on the same road that led to Jonathan's house. We often stopped there on our way south, to get water for our horses. She was devious and spoiled, and she left home with no explanation on the evening that Jonathan was killed and was never heard from again. Abraham described her well. She was the woman."

Chapter Eleven

Melinda LaFramboise did not feel the *Barnard Clinton* move to the rear on the sandbar, but when the engines went into forward, she and everyone else in the main salon felt it. Then they heard the cheers from the crew. Several people arose and went to a window or a door to observe the progress of the steamer. One man turned around and announced that they were going forward. At that news, several others got up and went to a window or a door to observe. Melinda was disdainful and somewhat depressed. She remained seated, sipping a drink of whiskey and water that she was sure had some Missouri River in it. It was cloudy and seemed almost gritty.

The journey so far had been unproductive for her. Without a cabin of her own, there was no way she could offer hospitality to a man, and there were no men who had a cabin to themselves other than the young officer Danny Barton, who seemed not to have a job. There were many single, well-dressed men onboard, but they were all sleeping in the main salon after hours.

During the day, the entire cabin deck with the exception of the kitchen and the purser's office was open. The kitchen was all the way forward, and the bar was on one side next to it. There was a small area for gaming tables and then a long table ran half the length of the cabin deck. There were berths inset into the forward sides of the main cabin, covered with curtains, for the men. Beyond that was the ladies' area that was furnished with soft chairs and settees that converted to beds. When the aft portion of the salon was cordoned off by a heavy curtain in the evening, female stewards would make up the number of beds required to accommodate the ladies.

Melinda's days were spent chatting with passengers, most of whom she considered boring. She was certainly the center of attention, with her sparkling good looks and soft Southern voice, and she was much in demand as a good luck charm by the men who spent their days and nights gambling. This was all very entertaining, but, even though many of her drinks were paid for by whichever gambler she happened to be favoring that particular evening, there was still an inevitable drain on her small purse.

Melinda had learned that the *Clinton* would be visiting Omaha, and then Council Bluffs. Omaha was the gateway to the West, but Council Bluffs would afford her the opportunity to get back to civilization. This excruciatingly slow trip up the Missouri River had given her a taste of the frontier that convinced her she would be happier on the eastern side of the Mississippi.

There was risk for Melinda in returning to familiar surroundings, but she was becoming ready to accept that risk rather than go through the slow torture of trying to thrive, or even just survive, on the western frontier.

"Miss LaFramboise, I'd like to buy you a drink so that we can make a toast to our extricating ourselves from the sandbar."

The man was about forty, dressed in an expensive wool suit, and attractive enough that a flirtation with a younger, beautiful woman would not seem inappropriate.

"That's very kind of you, sir, but how in the world did you know my name?"

"Everyone on the boat knows your name, ma'am," the man replied. "You are truly a flower on the prairie."

For various reasons, some people learn to yawn on cue, and some learn to cough or sneeze when desired. Melinda had a most unusual skill; she could flush with apparent embarrassment at will, and she did so now.

"You are too kind, sir, and I accept your offer."

"Not at all. What would you like to drink?"

Melinda leaned forward to whisper as loudly as possible, "Do you suppose you could explain to the bartender how to make a mint julep? I have not had a proper mint julep since I left Kentucky."

"It would be my pleasure," he said. He walked to the bar under Melinda's watchful eye and had a brief conversation with the bartender. Then he came back to the table where Melinda sat.

"Allow me to introduce myself, Miss LaFramboise. I am Delbert Winston Gray, from Baltimore, but currently from Seattle."

"Oh, my goodness, Mr. Gray, you are a long way from home, aren't you?" Melinda's eyes opened wide, giving her an innocent, vulnerable look.

"Call me Del, Miss LaFramboise. And may I call you Melinda?"

"Oh, please do, Del." She clasped his hand, but only briefly.

"To answer your question, I have been building my business in Seattle for several years, and now I have liquidated my assets in Baltimore and will cast my fate into the Northwest."

"How fascinating, Mr. Gray . . . Del. How on earth will you get to Seattle from the Missouri River?"

"I'll take the steamer as far as possible up the river. The captain has confidence that we'll not turn back until we're well past the mouth of the Yellowstone. Then I have a wagon with my worldly possessions and four horses in the cargo bay. I'll follow the federal wagon road from Fort Benton to Seattle."

Melinda put her hand on her chest as if she were out of breath. "Oh, my goodness, Del, it sounds so dangerous!"

"The trip is not without risk," he admitted, "but it is much preferable to a stagecoach ride across the Rocky Mountains of the Wyoming Territory. And once I decided not to pursue that route, I realized I could bring much of my personal property with me."

The bartender brought Melinda's mint julep and set it in front of her. The fact was that Melinda had found his mint juleps more than satisfactory, but she wanted to demonstrate her taste for her companion's benefit, and also let him do something for her. The bartender brought a whiskey for Gray, which he raised in a toast.

"Here's to our successful extrication and the continuance of our mutual journey."

Melinda raised her glass. "Yes. And here's to your journey to Seattle and your reunion with your family."

Gray raised his glass in response. "I regret to say I have no family, my dear. I've been married to my business for many years."

Gray had excelled in manufacturing during the Civil War. He had turned a small foundry into a major supplier of weapons for the Union. When victory for the Union seemed sure, he sold the foundry and traveled to the far Northwest to begin again. He had always been too busy for a social life, but now the combination of endless days on the steamer and the appearance of a beautiful Southern woman had distracted him slightly. It would seem that he was too naive to see through Melinda or recognize her for the opportunist she was.

Melinda, for her part, was having second thoughts about leaving the steamer. This traveling businessman was charming, attractive, and, if not wealthy, at least comfortably well off. She liked him, which was unusual, for she genuinely liked few men. It was suddenly a less appealing option to leave the boat at Council Bluffs. In addition, it might be possible to secure a stateroom after the steamer called at Omaha if she spoke up quickly. This would allow her to entertain Gray away from the curious eyes of other passengers. Usually, the men she let into her life fell into one of two categories: unattractive to the degree of being repulsive, or attractive physically but without means or ambition to take care of her. An attractive, ambitious, successful man was a tantalizing and rare oddity. The afternoon passed quickly for the two of them.

Another conversation between man and woman was taking place on the hurricane deck. Danny and Josephine were again sharing some food as they watched the scenery slowly unfold at either side of the steamer.

"How is Elizabeth doing?" he asked.

"She's doing fine. And the baby also."

"Are they getting off at Omaha?"

"There's no reason to. The captain isn't going to ask them to, and they have always said their goal is Montana Territory."

"But you're still getting off there?"

"It depends on Melinda LaFramboise. I'm going to do whatever she does. And if she doesn't lead me to her partner, I'll have her arrested without him."

"In Omaha or Council Bluffs?"

"The steamer is going to both towns?"

"Yes," he answered. "The captain told me we'll tie up in Omaha first, to unload some freight for the Union Pacific, and then we'll cross the river to pick up additional freight for various ports upstream."

"When will we get there?"

"We should have been there yesterday, but running aground set us back."

They were silent for a moment as they remembered all the events during the time the steamer was aground. Danny spoke first. "What would Melinda do if she knew you were onboard?"

"She'd run, if she could."

"And if she couldn't, your life would be in danger." His voice echoed the concern expressed in his words, and he impulsively took Josephine's hand in his.

Josephine looked grim as she said slowly, "So would hers." Her hand tightened on Danny's.

Chapter Twelve

Charles Felden was navigating through a submarine forest of snags. The *Clinton*'s engines were down to half-speed, which meant that she was making almost no headway against the Missouri River. Miles upstream, spring runoff the last few years had forced the swollen river against a forested bank and tumbled many cottonwood trees into the river. Some of these trees were mere stumps, having been cut down for fuel in previous years; some were massive, living trees that had the dirt around their roots washed away. Floating for a while, eventually the roots hooked up on the bottom, and the current and debris sheared the branches off, leaving a blunt "spear" facing any boat working its way up the river.

The senior pilot was cannily working the edges of the channel, with two leadsmen on the bow. Snags in the deeper water of the middle of the channel were much more difficult—sometimes impossible—to spot, and the angle of the spear was more deadly. In shallower water along the edges, the snags were usually visible and lay flat in the river, making them less lethal but still dangerous.

Captain Culpepper was also in the pilot house, watching his skillful pilot take the two hundred and thirty by thirty-six by five and a half steamer through the snags. Just as when he was a regimental commander, he habitually carried a pair of field glasses around his neck on a strap. Occasionally he would use them to scan the river ahead, but even when he spotted a snag on the *Clinton*'s course, he remained silent. It would have been a breach of pilothouse etiquette to offer any suggestions without being asked, and Felden didn't need to ask. His eyesight was perfect, and his knowledge of the riverbed, supplemented by Singletary's notes, was without equal.

But then Captain Culpepper saw something through his field glasses that moved him to speak. "Mr. Felden, there appears to be the body of a man hung up on a snag five hundred yards upstream."

Felden glanced quickly around to see the angle of the captain's field glasses so he could determine where on the broad river the captain was looking. Then he scanned the river.

"Yes, sir, I see it. It's well out of the channel."

"Signal the mate to the pilothouse. We'll take the yawl out and see what must be done."

The pilot complied. When Captain Culpepper saw Steve Allenby climb the stairs, he said, "Carry on, Mr. Felden," and stepped out of the pilothouse to meet the first mate.

Danny Barton's natural and professional curiosity prompted him to also answer the call to the pilothouse. He was standing beside Allenby as the captain explained, "Mr. Allenby, I want to take the yawl out."

"Yes, sir." Allenby mistakenly assumed that the captain wanted to check the river channel ahead of the steamer and was surprised at this. He was reasonably certain that Felden would not have asked for this kind of assistance or interference, but it was not his place to question the order. He walked to the edge of the cabin deck and leaned over to shout, "Skip, Two-ton, Little Bit, Gary, Humpback, Weedeater! Launch the yawl. The captain and I are going for a ride."

Barton wanted to go also, but he was not a skilled oarsman and didn't want to be dead weight, so he only helped launch the yawl. He had his own field glasses, and once the yawl was in the water and the oarsmen were pulling, he climbed to the pilothouse. He also was perplexed at what appeared to be an unnecessary action by the captain.

Barton stayed outside the pilothouse, thinking that Felden was too busy to talk, but Felden saw him waiting outside and beckoned him in with a tap on the window and a gesture. The pilot was to the point. "There's a dead man up ahead," he said.

Barton raised his field glasses and scanned the river in the direction that the yawl was headed. Now he understood. "I see him," he said.

The yawl had no trouble outdistancing the laboring steamer. Shortly it pulled up alongside the snag that had captured the dead man. The oarsmen held station while the captain and the first mate inspected the body.

"What's to be done, captain?" Allenby asked.

"Secure a line around his feet and then cut the snag and bring him onboard."

Little Bit spoke up. "I can slit his gut and cut him loose, and he'll sink like a rock."

Allenby gave Little Bit a quick, dark look and answered the captain. "Yes, sir." He made a slipknot loop in a short line. "Drop back and come up on his feet, you men, so I can put a line on him."

The six oarsmen worked as one, complying with Allenby's order. Allenby leaned over the bow as the yawl came up directly down current from the dead man and once again held station. He slipped the loop underwater and around the man's feet, tightening it, and then he let out some line.

"All right, men, move up to his head so I can cut his jacket loose."

The oarsmen did this, and when the body came loose from the snag, they maneuvered away as the two oarsmen in the stern pulled the body into the yawl. Then they stroked for the *Clinton*.

Alongside the steamer, the men lifted the body onto the deck and then went about reloading the yawl onto the hurricane deck. Barton was there to meet the yawl, and he, the captain, and the first mate gathered around the body. Barton went through the man's pockets and found a pencil, three keys, and a few coins. There was nothing to let them know who the man was, but Barton made some assumptions.

"This man ordinarily wears eyeglasses; see the indentations on his nose. He wears them all day long, so either his eyesight is terrible or he spends his days where he needs to read. Also, he's not dressed for rough outdoor work. This isn't the kind of man who would be working on the river, so I'm guessing he didn't meet an accidental death."

"Very well," the captain said. "We'll take him to Omaha and turn him over to the authorities." He looked at Allenby. "Wrap him tightly in a tarpaulin and put him back in the yawl where the breeze can do us all a favor."

"Yes, sir," Allenby replied.

Chapter Thirteen

At Omaha the *Str. Barnard Clinton* churned toward the riverbank. There were two other steamers tied up already, but the waterfront could accommodate many more, so the *Clinton* positioned herself upstream, about a hundred and fifty feet from the next nearest boat. Many steamers on the river system of the United States were lost to fire. If the fire occurred while at a landing, the boat burned through its mooring lines and drifted down onto the next boat, which drifted down onto the next, and so on. Cautious pilots, and Charles Felden was certainly one of these, avoided anchoring, mooring, or docking downstream from other boats when possible.

Steamers usually approached a landing from downstream. If the steamer was traveling downstream, it would have to go below the landing and then turn in the river to come back. The *Clinton,* going upriver, had only to line up on the bank and reduce speed; she slowly came up to the riverbank, and the bow felt the bottom. As soon as this happened, men lowered one of the two stages, gangways, to the bank and ran ashore with heavy lines. They wrapped these lines around posts that had been driven into the riverbank and, in a matter of minutes, the *Clinton* was secure at Omaha. Danny Barton immediately went into the town proper to contact law enforcement about the body they had retrieved.

Barton had learned that Melinda LaFramboise had secured a cabin for the rest of the trip west. He related that information to Josephine, and she decided she didn't have to keep track of Melinda for the moment. She directed her attention to her job, selecting several horses to ride out and back for their benefit . . . and hers. If they stayed in port long enough, she would manage to let all the horses taste a little Nebraska air and feel Nebraska dirt on their hooves.

The captain stayed onboard to observe the offloading of freight. There were barrels of whiskey, barrels of flour and sugar, boxes of nails and railroad spikes, coffee, salt, gunpowder, lead, and even a well-used Abbott and Downing Concord stagecoach. Some of these items were for Omaha; some were destined for the railroad. He would also pick up some freight later from Council Bluffs, but not enough to replace the tonnage he would offload, and this was to his liking; the *Clinton* would be higher in the water for the Upper Missouri River.

Melinda waited in the main salon for the family whose cabin she would soon take over to gather their belongings and leave the boat. Delbert Gray had gone into Omaha alone. He offered to escort her into Omaha to see the town, but when she saw the muddy banks and the shabby river town in the distance, she reluctantly decided to stay onboard by herself. He had scarcely left her side since their meeting, and she was enjoying his company as much as he was enjoying hers.

When Melinda first met the businessman, her thoughts centered on curiosity about his wealth: how much money he had on his person, how much might be hidden in his luggage or perhaps in the captain's safe, and how much he might have in a bank somewhere. As they grew more comfortable in each other's presence, her thinking changed, and she began to think of him in a more affectionate, personal way. He was taller than she was, which was usually the case, since she was petite; he was good looking, well groomed, and well spoken. He seemed to have no flaws. Living with just one man for the rest of her life had never seemed like a realistic lifestyle for her, but she was wondering now what it would be like to be Mrs. Delbert Winston Gray.

"Miss LaFramboise?" It was the steward.

She looked up. "Yes?"

"Your stateroom is ready. May I show you the way?"

"No, thank you," she said, graciously. "But would you see that my luggage is taken up?"

"Yes, ma'am, right away." The steward handed her the key.

The *Clinton*'s purser stayed near the boarding stages at the bow whenever the boat was tied up. This made it convenient for him to book new passengers and arrange for freight deliveries. It was also his responsibility to prevent unauthorized boarding. The mate on watch likewise stayed near the bow to assist the purser and to supervise loading of freight.

It was difficult to make money with passengers, but transporting freight, especially freight bound for ports beyond Omaha, was lucrative. The Upper Missouri was dangerous. There were rapids, uncharted snags and sandbars, hostile Indians, extremes of weather, and no source of help for hundreds of miles. The high degree of risk was compensated for by high freight tariffs. But passengers nevertheless produced revenue that couldn't be refused, and the purser was now in the process of booking one Harold Robertson into the main cabin.

"Is there no way I can have a stateroom?" Robertson asked, thumbing the bills in his money clip in an obvious attempt to bribe the purser. The purser would have none of it.

"No, sir. I'm sorry to say, the last stateroom was just booked an hour ago. The curtained berths in the main cabin are quite comfortable."

"Very well, then, that will have to do," he said. "If a stateroom becomes available, please let me know."

"Yes, sir."

Robertson paid the purser for his passage and then carried his luggage up the stairs to the main cabin. He had given the purser the name Henry Rogers, and no one had seen him slip down to the waterfront to board. The *Clinton,* if on schedule, would leave before he was missed. He was through with Omaha, and it caused him no distress.

Passengers had gathered on the upper decks to watch the loading and unloading as a means of relieving the monotony of river travel. Also observing were the three men who had left the grounded *Missouri Princess* days before. They took note of the well-dressed man who had just paid for his passage, and they didn't miss the fat money clip that he had displayed in his vain attempt to bribe the purser.

Barton accompanied two roustabouts as they wheeled the cart carrying the wrapped body from the river up the street to the marshal's office. A few people on the street were curious, but most went about their business without paying notice. Using directions supplied by a man on the waterfront, Barton had no trouble finding the office, and he tapped on the door before opening it and walking in.

"What can I do for you, young man?" the marshal asked, looking up from his desk where he had been cleaning and oiling a revolver. Barton thought that in spite of the marshal referring to him as a young man, it didn't appear likely that the marshal had more than ten years on him.

"I'm from the *Barnard Clinton,* at the landing now," he said. "We recovered the body of a man about forty miles downstream." Barton thought this would be all he would have to say for the local law enforcement to begin an investigation. But he was wrong.

"Sounds like you need the undertaker. I'm the marshal," he said, and resumed working on his pistol.

"Well." Barton struggled for words, surprised at the man's indifference. "I reckon he might have come from Omaha. Maybe you could look and see if you recognize him."

"Hardly a week goes by that we don't see some poor fella floatin' down. River rats mostly. It ain't likely anyone in town would know him."

The captain's aide was becoming a little irritated. This marshal didn't seem very professional. "I'm not gonna take the body back to the boat," he said. "What do you want done with him?"

"Suit yourself, fella. It's nothin' for the marshal's office."

Barton walked out and motioned his men to wheel the cart up to the boardwalk in front of the marshal's office. "Let's put him right here in front of the door," he ordered.

They complied, lifting the wrapped corpse out of the cart and laying him on the boardwalk. They laid him across the walk so that anyone walking the boardwalk would have to step over him. The marshal, hearing the activity, came out onto the boardwalk.

"Whadda you think you're doing?" he asked angrily.

"You told me to suit myself," the aide replied, suppressing a smile, which is more than the two roustabouts did.

"I told you it wasn't for the marshal's office, now—"

Barton interrupted. "It's lost property that we discovered in the river. Every town I've ever been in, lost property is turned in to the law. So here y'are." He turned his back on the irate marshal and with hand gestures signaled the roustabouts to unwrap the tarpaulin that was around the body.

"Hey!" the marshal objected.

Barton answered with humor in his voice. "The tarp belongs to the *Clinton*. I can't leave it here." He nodded at the roustabouts to indicate they should continue unwrapping.

When the corpse was unwrapped, it presented a grisly sight as the men propped it up in a sitting position against the wall of the office on the main street of Omaha. The marshal was at his limit and was about to assert his authority, but he couldn't resist one look. He got a pained expression on his face.

"Oh, mother of God! It's John Swanson!" he exclaimed. His shoulders went slack, and after a long moment, he turned to Barton. "It's good your head's harder than mine. You were right; this man lived in Omaha."

Barton shrugged. "What can we do to help?"

"To start, wrap him up again. Then we'll take him to the doctor and see what he says." Barton nodded at the roustabouts, and they complied with the marshal's request.

Delbert Gray watched the gruesome scene from across the street. He had already decided that Omaha was no Seattle. He was relieved that he had not brought Melinda along on this sightseeing trip. He looked both ways along the street, and his eyes fell on a large sign that said LOANS. He thought this was the most likely place to find something to please the lovely young lady with whom he was just becoming familiar. Forty-five minutes later he was climbing the stairs to the main cabin aboard the *Clinton*. He walked past Harold Robertson, who was sitting in the main cabin playing solitaire, and found a steward, whom he addressed in a low voice. "Steward, I don't see Miss LaFramboise. Did she go ashore after all?"

"No, sir. She retired to her stateroom on the next deck."

"Oh. She managed to secure a stateroom, then?"

"Yes, sir," the steward answered, and then added, in anticipation of Gray's next question, "You'll find her in the Pennsylvania cabin."

"Thank you, my friend," Gray said, and pressed a coin into the man's hand.

At the door to the Pennsylvania cabin, Gray lightly tapped twice.

"Yes?" came a soft, Southern voice from within the room.

"It's Delbert Gray, Melinda," he answered, and in seconds the door was opened, and Melinda stood in front of him in one of her favorite dresses. It was so attractive, Gray was momentarily paralyzed.

"You may come in, Del," she said, in that same soft, Southern voice.

"Melinda, I . . ."

"It's all right, Del," she said. "This is the Missouri River, not St. Louis."

Del swallowed hard and finally got his unwilling legs to work, stepping into the room. In the room were two berths, a writing desk, and a chair. Melinda sat on the edge of one of the berths and motioned for him to sit in the chair.

"These staterooms do not compare to those on the larger Mississippi steamers," she said, "but they're ever so much better than the common cabin, don't you think?"

Del looked around and nodded in agreement. It certainly did more closely resemble military quarters than a private stateroom on a riverboat. But, like Melinda, he thought the privacy would more than offset the spartan furnishings. He put one hand in the pocket of his jacket and removed a small box.

"I must tell you, Melinda, that Omaha was a disappointment.

The only thing I found worthwhile was this little gift that I wanted to get for you." He handed her the box.

She opened the box and stifled a delighted cry. The box contained a small silver bracelet. It had been left as security for a loan by some traveler, and the loan had never been repaid. It wasn't bejeweled, but it was elegant in its simplicity. She handed it to him and then pulled back her sleeve, extending her arm so he could put the bracelet on her. This he did, and as he fixed the clasp, he clamped both hands around her wrist, as if to make sure the clasp had fastened, but actually just to feel her warm, pale skin. Her smile would have melted ice.

They dined together in the cabin, and when it came time to retire, Gray, ever the gentleman, excused himself and went back downstairs to the main cabin. After a long evening of intimate conversation with the beautiful Southern woman, he thought that it was more than possible she might consent to accompany him to Seattle. That presented a small problem.

It wouldn't do for them to travel alone together on the federal wagon road unless they were married, but a marriage after so short a courtship would hardly be proper. He reminded himself of her expression: "This isn't St. Louis; this is the Missouri River." The real problem, he decided, was whether or not she would accept a proposal. He went to his berth and climbed in, pulling the curtains closed, then undressed and put on his nightclothes. He would have many dreams this night, he was sure.

Melinda could not believe that Gray had not tried to make advances. There was a small mirror in her stateroom, and she looked herself over. She was her own harshest critic, and thus she could see the little imperfections that age was starting to endow her, but not many others would notice them. Objectively, she was as beautiful as ever. *Perhaps,* she thought, *he is not interested in me.* Maybe she should have listened more, talked less. No, maybe she should have talked more and tried to suppress her interest in him. Then she looked at the bracelet in the mirror. It was lovely and perfect. She smiled away her self-doubt for the time being and dressed for bed.

* * *

It was getting dark in Omaha as the marshal and the captain's aide laid the body of the telegrapher on a table in the doctor's office. The two roustabouts took the cart back to the *Clinton,* leaving the marshal, Barton, and the doctor with the corpse.

"How long was he in the water?" the doctor asked as he took off his coat.

"Don't know," Barton answered. "We pulled him off a snag Saturday morning about nine o'clock."

The doctor looked at Barton, wondering what the young man's interest in this death might be, but he rolled up his sleeves without comment and began examining the body.

"I've seen a dozen bodies pulled out of the Missouri, and I'm guessing that this one wasn't in the river long and that he didn't drown."

"How can you tell, Doctor?" Barton asked.

"I can't for sure, just a feeling. For one thing, John knew how to swim."

"Then it could be that he was injured before he entered the water."

The doctor had already reached that conclusion and was carefully going over the body, looking for such an injury, but he resented the young man's comment.

"Maybe you want to do this, and I can go have a drink," he said sourly. Barton pulled his chin in and stepped back from the table.

The doctor continued his examination, looking at every square inch of the man's body, which was now unclothed. He was methodical, going over the head first, then the neck, and now he was examining the chest.

"Here," he said, pulling at the skin below the man's sternum in two directions at once. A small incision opened up. The doctor probed the incision with a long, thin instrument. When he was done, he went to a basin and washed his hands. As he dried them on a towel, he faced the two men.

"I'm saying he was stabbed at that incision with a long, thin knife. Once the knife was deep in his chest, the killer worked it back and forth to injure the man's heart fatally. He didn't kill the man, he killed the man's heart." He said this last with a little bit of drama. "Then he threw the man in the water."

The marshal swore.

The doctor looked at Barton and asked, "Can you tell us anything else?"

"He had three keys, a pencil, a handkerchief, and seventy-five cents in his pockets. There was nothing else."

"No watch?" the marshal asked.

"No." Barton shook his head. He pulled the keys, pencil, and change from his pocket and handed them to the marshal.

"He carried that watch always. Somebody in town has a new gold watch," the marshal said. "I think I'll walk through the bars and see if I can spot it. Wanna come?" he asked Barton. The men were warming to each other.

"Sure," Barton said. "But I'll have to leave when I hear the *Clinton*'s whistle."

"Let's do it. Four eyes are better than two." The marshal turned to the doctor. "Thanks, Doc. I'll talk to you later."

Felden rang the ship's bell four times. Four bells. Ten P.M. His watch was half over. The first mate came into the pilothouse.

"We'll be done offloading by midnight, Mr. Felden," Steve Allenby said.

"How much freight are we taking on?" Felden asked.

"A couple of tons of personal belongings for people who have moved upriver. It'll take only half an hour."

"Provisions?" the captain asked.

"Liquor is good. We'll want to get eggs and pork every time we get a chance," Allenby answered.

"Cordwood?"

"Thirty cords. We'll get another twenty at Council Bluffs."

"Are all the passengers and crew onboard?"

"The off-watch officers are in town. And Mr. Barton hasn't returned from taking the body of the drowned man in."

The captain frowned. "When Mr. Barton returns, send him to me."

The pilot and first mate were silent. They knew that Barton was in trouble for not being present during offloading. The captain disliked spelling out a man's responsibilities in detail, preferring to let him find his own level of service, but in this case, he would undoubtedly let the young officer know he had fallen below the expected standard.

Felden wanted to get off the subject. "Are there any new passengers?"

"Yeah, eight. Three soldiers, a liquor salesman, two hunters, a Mr. Mike McDougall, and a Mr. Henry Rogers. Rogers looks to be well off. And we discharged Mr. and Mrs. Williams. The first person to ask for their cabin was the fancy lady, LaFramboise, so she's in that one." He rolled his eyes with unmistakable inference.

"I don't want . . . Tell the purser to keep an eye on her," the captain said.

"Yes, sir."

"When Mr. Singletary comes on watch, inform him that I desire to cross the river tonight. Sunday will be a day off so that everyone can attend church in Council Bluffs."

"Yes, sir." Felden and Allenby both answered. Each could see that the captain was irritated, and the source of the irritation was his security officer.

Barton and the Omaha lawman entered the third bar of the evening. They split up and took stations at opposite sides of the room. They watched every man in the room, waiting to see if anyone pulled a gold watch out of his pocket. It was a slow process, and Barton was anxious to get back to the *Clinton,* but he and the marshal had overcome their initial friction and were enjoying pursuing this investigation together.

The captain's aide was sure that the *Clinton* wouldn't leave until after midnight, but he felt like he should be there during the time the boat was in port. That was when it was most vulnerable, after all. Since he didn't carry a watch, and because he wanted to see as many watches as possible, he leaned over a card game and asked for the time. He looked on as several men pulled watches from their pockets to check the time for him. No gold.

"Thanks," he said, and moved to another spot in the room. This put him near the marshal.

A man approached the marshal, and Barton suspected his intentions were not good, so he put his hand inside his jacket on the butt of his revolver. The lawman carried his own revolver in a cavalry holster with a flap, butt forward. It was not the kind of rig that would let most men put their weapon into action quickly.

"Hey, marshal, remember me?" the man asked loudly.

The marshal wasn't intimidated. "Yeah, Jake, how could I forget the dumbest drunk I've ever seen?"

This was the wrong thing to say to the large drunken man, who produced a long knife from under his shirt. Barton started pulling his revolver from under his jacket, but before he could the marshal's gun appeared in his hand and he used the barrel to deflect the knife away. With his other hand he hit the man in the stomach. Barton was sure that the marshal's fist disappeared up to the wrist in the man's stomach, and the man's eyes bulged out. The lawman brought the barrel of his gun down hard on the man's hand and the knife clattered on the floor. The drunkard sagged to his knees as he tried to find air.

While this was going on, Barton scanned the watching crowd with his hand on his own revolver. Jake had some friends who had started to step forward, but they now froze in their tracks as they observed Barton backing up the marshal.

As Jake lay on the floor with his mouth open and his eyes bulging, the marshal picked up the knife and threw it at the wall, where it stuck with a twang. The big man sucked in a huge breath and laid over on his side.

"Dang, marshal, can't you take a joke?" he rasped.

"Jake, you never learn. Who gave you the knife?"

"I stole it."

"From where?"

"One a' them greenhorn outfits."

The marshal helped Jake to his feet. The big man was still breathing hard and all the fight was out of him.

"You go on over to the jail, Jake. Sit on the boardwalk and stay there until I get there, understand?"

"Yeah, all right, marshal."

"I'm going to have every bar in town cut you off. You can't drink."

"Yeah, but all my friends are here."

"Drink water, Jake. You'll live longer." The marshal pushed Jake toward the door. Jake stumbled once and then walked out of the saloon. The marshal and Barton followed him out.

"I was too slow to help you," Barton said as they walked down the darkened street.

"You did all right. I saw you pull your gun. If it had been anyone but Jake, I'd have needed help. Thanks."

They walked in silence and then Barton spoke. "Marshal, I've been thinking about the telegrapher."

"Yeah?"

"Do you think someone killed him just for his watch?" he asked.

"There are people in this town who'd kill you for a gold tooth," the marshal answered. "But no, probably not. Only because John didn't hang around that kind of person. I can't figure it out."

"I was thinking maybe he knew something that someone didn't want anyone else to know."

"I doubt we'll ever find out for sure," the marshal said.

"Maybe not, but do you still have the keys he was carrying?"

The lawman slapped his pocket. "Yeah."

"It might be worthwhile to look at his log in the telegraph office and see who received telegrams today."

The marshal slapped his new friend on the back. "That's a darn good idea, Danny. Wanna come?"

Barton wanted to come, but it was approaching midnight. "I'd better get back to the boat, marshal. Thanks for showing me the town."

"Thanks for the help. You'll be coming back this way?"

"Yeah, in a few weeks, if all goes well upriver."

"Stop by and see me, if I'm still alive," the marshal said with a smile. "Rake Angleton."

"Danny Barton." The men shook hands. "I'll do that." Barton started walking briskly toward the waterfront.

"Mr. Barton, I expect you to be on or near the boat when we are tied up," the captain said.

"Yes, sir." The security officer was standing stiffly in front of the cabin, just as he had done when in the Army.

"I know you had an official errand in town, but that doesn't excuse you from the rest of the day."

"Yes, sir."

"I'm withholding two weeks of your salary."

"Yes, sir."

"And if this kind of thing happens again, we'll terminate your services. The only excuse I'll take is that you dropped dead."

"Yes, sir."

"That will be all."

"Captain?" Barton wanted to tell the captain that the man they had found had not accidentally drowned, but had been murdered.

"That will be all, Mr. Barton."

"Yes, sir." Barton decided to walk around the boat until he could get his emotions in check. In any case, he needed to see what might have taken place during his absence.

He arrived at the pilothouse just as the watch changed at midnight. He remained silent as Felden brought Singletary up to date on what had taken place during his watch.

"When the cargo is all onboard, cast off," said the senior pilot. "Don't wake the captain until you're ready to nose in at the Bluffs."

Singletary looked at Felden's first mate. "How's the loading going?"

"We're waiting on some more livestock. Some horses for up-river, and some cattle for Council Bluffs."

"What's the delay?" Singletary asked.

"We just signed them on a few minutes ago. The shipper and two of our men went to fetch them."

"Where's our little hostler?"

"He . . ." Allenby looked around the pilothouse to see that there were only officers present and no one standing outside. "*She's* changing the corral around to accommodate the animals." All the officers had met Josephine as a woman by now, and they all felt protective toward her, honoring her request to keep her gender a secret.

"All right. I suppose the captain won't want the whistle to blow when we shove off?"

"He didn't mention it," said Felden.

"I'll keep it short," Singletary said.

That concluded the exchange of business, but Erickson couldn't miss the chance for a little sport. He nodded at Barton. "Glad to have you back onboard, Mr. Barton."

All the officers smiled—Felden looked at his feet as he did so—but the others looked at Barton's face to see his reaction. His face reddened as he met their gaze without blinking and said nothing. For the next few minutes there was an uncomfortable silence in the pilothouse and then, as the second hand came to twelve, Felden rang the ship's bell eight times.

Chapter Fourteen

The crossing to Council Bluffs was without incident. Even at night, it was a routine matter, and by two in the morning, the *Str. Barnard Clinton* was at the Bluffs. David Erickson, Greg Singletary's mate, awakened the captain as the nose of the steamer touched the bank. The captain's eyes opened instantly.

"Any problems?"

"No, sir. They're just lowering the stages now."

"It felt like we hit the bank with too much way on."

"Yes, sir, there's a large flatboat just north of us. The current is swirling around their stern and carried us in."

"How far north?"

"Fifty yards."

"Is this the landing spot that Singletary chose?" It was too close and the captain was unhappy about it. Plus, he didn't like flatboats under any circumstances.

"No, sir. The harbormaster waved us in here. He wanted us even closer to the flatboat, but Singletary ignored him."

"I'll have a talk with the harbormaster in the morning. If he wants us to stop here, he'll have to do better than that. Anything else?"

"No, sir."

"Very well. Unload our Bluffs cargo, but as soon as that is accomplished, everyone has until six this evening to do as they wish. I would hope that the officers will set an example for the rest of the crew and attend church in Council Bluffs. The pilot can be relieved by his mate for that purpose."

"Yes, sir. Thank you, sir."

"And Mr. Barton is to remain onboard until further notice."

"Yes, sir."

"Carry on, Mr. Erickson." The captain lay back down and Erickson let himself out of the room, stepping over the apparently sleeping Danny Barton.

Harold Robertson was restless. He heard the whistle signals and rightly guessed that the steamer was now at Council Bluffs. Even though he had covered his tracks well, he hoped they wouldn't be there long. Upriver was his best chance for safety and freedom. He pulled his curtain aside and swung his legs out to the floor. There was no one out in the main dining room except a dozen or so male passengers who were sleeping in various locations on the floor. Robertson pulled his boots on and donned his jacket. It was a good chance to look at Council Bluffs from the steamer without being seen. He let himself out and went to the rail to see what could be seen of the town.

Barton got up quietly as soon as Erickson left the captain's stateroom. Like Robertson, he also wanted to observe the town in the quiet of the early-morning hours. And he wanted to do better at his role as the security officer, watching to make sure there was no mischief being done to the steamer, vulnerable in the dark at a primitive waterfront. When he stepped out of the cabin quietly, he could hear footsteps on the deck below. He leaned over the railing and observed Robertson walking slowly toward the bow. Barton descended on the far side to the cabin deck and met Robertson on the bow.

"Good morning," said the officer, startling Robertson in the near darkness. Barton had his hand on the butt of his revolver. "I'm the captain's aide. Do you have a light?" he asked.

"Uh, yes, I think so."

Barton stepped back two paces. "How about lighting that lamp on the wall behind you?"

"What?"

"Turn around, light that lamp."

"It isn't necessary to treat me like this. I'm a paying passenger."

"Good. But I'm not asking you again. Light the lamp."

The tone of his voice let Robertson know he had used up the young man's patience. He lit the lamp and then turned around to face Barton, his face full of anger.

"What's your name?" Barton asked.

"Henry Rogers."

Barton looked at Robertson's face carefully. "Let me see your ticket."

Robertson removed his ticket from his pocket and handed it to him. Barton took his hand away from his revolver and stepped to the lamp to read the ticket, and then he handed it back.

"All right, Mr. Rogers," he said. "I apologize for the inconvenience. I hope you enjoy your trip." Robertson said nothing but went back into the main cabin and his berth.

On the deck above, the captain, who had followed his aide out of the stateroom a minute later and witnessed the confrontation, nodded silently and went back into the stateroom to get some more sleep.

Barton descended to the main deck and watched as Josephine separated the livestock and helped drive the Council Bluffs consignment out of the cargo bay and up the stage to a holding corral. When she walked back to the steamer, he was waiting on the bow.

"Do you ever sleep, Jo?"

"I get by. Where've you been?"

"I went into Omaha and helped the marshal investigate the body we found in the river."

"Are you going to hang around while we're in Council Bluffs?"

"Yeah. Why?"

Josephine shrugged. "Just wanted to know."

"Are you going to stay onboard?" he asked. "The entire crew gets the day off, you know."

"Yeah, I guess I'll stay," Josephine answered. "As long as I'm not the only one."

"I'll be here," he said.

"I'll see you later, then. I'm going to get some sleep" was her only reply.

After Josephine left, the officer went to the engine room.

* * *

"What's the matter, Barton, can't sleep?" the engineer asked.

"Just looking around, Lars. How're things in the power department?"

"Quiet. Hard to stay awake."

"Have you ever been to Council Bluffs before?"

"A couple of times. Not much there."

"You going in tomorrow?"

"Yes. I haven't been to church for a few weeks."

"When do you reckon we'll leave Council Bluffs?"

"Tomorrow morning. We're letting the fires go down to save fuel."

Barton turned to go. "I better get some sleep. I'll want to stay awake while everyone else is in town." And he was looking forward to spending some time with Josephine with few distractions.

At first light, the *Str. Inland Star* signaled her arrival at Council Bluffs. The harbormaster signaled her into the space between the flatboat and the *Clinton*, but she ignored him and slipped in just north of the flatboat. Felden, on watch in the pilothouse, thought to himself that if he had been piloting the *Clinton* he would have done the same thing. At least there was a hundred and fifty feet of separation between the *Clinton* and the flatboat, albeit for twenty-four hours. In the meantime he had instructed his engineer not to let the fires go out in case the *Clinton* needed to move without delay.

The captain entered the pilothouse at seven in the morning. "Mr. Felden, feel free to leave the pilothouse to partake in breakfast. The kitchen will be shutting down soon until this evening."

"Thanks, Captain. I'll fix myself something when I get off watch."

"Fine enough. Have you seen any activity on the flatboat?"

"Not much. I don't imagine they'll be casting off soon, or the harbormaster wouldn't have put us this close." The captain had no comment, so the pilot continued. "I told the engineer not to be too anxious to cool the boilers. I'd rather use a little extra fuel than be dead in the water below that flatboat."

"Very well, Mr. Felden. I agree. Pass that on to Mr. Singletary as my order."

"Yes, sir."

The captain left the pilothouse, climbed down to the main deck, and strode briskly into town. As soon as he was off the boat, Barton entered the pilothouse.

"Mornin', Charles," he greeted.

"Good morning, Danny. Sleep well?"

"I reckon," Barton said. "Anything going on?"

"No, just keeping my eye on the flatboat."

"When did that other steamer come in?"

"Hour and a half ago."

"That's a better berth than ours, right?"

"Yes."

"What did the captain think?"

"Same as you."

Barton had no reply to that comment. He watched two men walk down along the waterfront and board the flatboat. They were obviously suffering from too much whiskey but managed to walk a narrow plank onto the deck of the boat before they collapsed. They briefly tried to get on their feet, but it was too much effort, and they lay back down on the deck and were immediately asleep.

Felden broke the silence. "For what it's worth, the captain didn't want to dock your pay. He didn't say anything, but I could tell he was debating with himself."

"Well, he did," Barton said.

"He likes you a lot, son, but it would be better if you didn't put him in that position again."

"I don't intend to. And I can't argue too much with the punishment. It would go down a little easier if he had heard my side."

"Your side doesn't matter. The *Clinton* is the only thing that matters. She'll take care of us if we take care of her."

"I understand," Barton said.

"You can tell *me* your side."

The security officer raised his eyebrows and then started talking rapidly. "I know this is not an excuse, but I think it's important. The man we fished out of the river was murdered."

"Drowned on purpose?"

"No, stabbed."

"Oh," Felden said. "Oh, well, that *is* interesting. Who was he?"

"His name was John Swanson. He was the telegrapher in Omaha."

"How many people are in Omaha right now, Danny?"

"I don't know, maybe a couple of thousand."

"One of those people murdered a man."

"Yeah," Barton said, not sure what Felden was getting at.

"I would think he would want to leave town right away."

Barton made the connection instantly. "And he might be on this boat right now," he said.

"Have you met all the passengers who signed on in Omaha? Do you know how many?"

"No." He knew that Felden was making the point that he would have known about the passengers if he had been onboard when he should have been. "But I'm going to find out." He started to leave to talk to the purser, but Felden stopped him.

"The purser left an hour ago. There are eight new passengers."

Barton wished he had been here, but if he had been, then he wouldn't have known about the murder. He remembered that he had met one new passenger. Henry Rogers.

Delbert Gray tapped lightly on Melinda's stateroom. He was sure she was not an early riser, but he had decided to walk into Council Bluffs to attend church and wanted to let her know where he would be. And, more important, he wanted to give her the chance to accompany him. He heard a voice from behind the door ask, "Who is it?"

"It's Delbert Gray, Melinda."

"Just a moment, please."

Melinda opened the door. Although she had obviously been asleep, she was as lovely as ever, even in a bulky robe and without her makeup. She tilted her head slightly and looked up at him.

"Good morning, Melinda. I just stopped by to tell you I'm going to walk into Council Bluffs and attend church. I would be pleased if you would accompany me. It's a fine day for a walk."

Melinda raised a hand to shade her eyes and looked up at the sky. Then she looked at Gray, trying to make her brain process the situation. She had not attended church for many years and would certainly be uncomfortable there. She had an idea that this was something that was important to him, and it might even be a kind of test for her. But she felt she had to make at least a weak protest.

"Oh, Delbert, I slept late this morning, and I'm sure I couldn't get ready in time." She closely watched his face to gauge his reaction.

"In truth, Melinda, I have no idea what time the services start or even where the church or churches are located. I'm more than willing to wait until you can make yourself presentable, and then we can have a pleasant walk into town and see what we can find out."

Melinda's thoughts were on track now. "That's a wonderful idea, Delbert. If you'll just wait outside, I'll get ready as quickly as possible." She touched his arm briefly, as if to make sure he was real, and then closed her door. Gray stepped back to the rail to wait.

Melinda went to the bottom of her trunk to find a garment that was more modest than her usual dress. What she came up with was not much fancier than an ordinary housedress. It did have a fine lace collar and cuffs, which made it more proper for church. And it was the only dress she had that did not cling to her body. She didn't take the time to put on all the makeup she usually wore, and, in spite of what she thought, she didn't need much anyway. She found a simple hat and matching gloves and then opened the door to find Gray leaning on the rail, watching the river.

"I'm ready," she said. When he turned, what he saw pleased him more than he could express in words. The subdued costume and makeup made her more beautiful in his eyes than he had ever seen her. She smiled and took his arm.

Normally, Melinda looked forward to spending time with a man, but usually, before the time was over, she would invariably begin to look forward to the end. It was not that she liked being alone; it was that she needed only a short time to find out everything that interested her about whatever man she was with.

As she and Gray walked along together to town, they chatted about everything they saw, and she laughed often, as did he. She was in tune with everything around her, a most unusual experience for her. In contrast to her normal feelings, she hoped that they would be able to repeat this morning exactly, not just once more, but many times more.

They found a small church and were just in time for the service. Melinda watched Delbert carefully and did everything that he did. She didn't want to cause him any embarrassment; she wanted the morning to be as pleasing for him as it was for her. What she couldn't do was sing the hymns, so she mouthed the words silently but was treated to his resonant baritone singing voice. The morning was one perfect moment after another.

Delbert had had some misgivings about bringing Melinda to church. She had flirtatious eyes that she used on every man close enough to see them; she sometimes had a raucous laugh that was surprising and grating; she often made comments that were, to his mind, too racy. But this morning she was on her best behavior. The two of them made an extraordinarily handsome couple. He was enjoying the morning as much as she.

The sermon was on fidelity. It had minimal impact on Gray because he had never had anyone to be faithful to. For Melinda, however, it was fascinating. She had never embraced the concept of fidelity, of one partner for life. She looked around the room and realized that most, if not all, of these people were in lifelong relationships; something she had never known. What would that be like, she wondered?

At the conclusion of the service, the preacher announced that the regular potluck dinner would be served outside as soon as the chairs could be moved there and the food brought to the yard. He noted the several visitors from the *Str. Barnard Clinton,* urged the congregation to make a point of speaking with them, and insisted that they stay for the potluck, even though they had brought nothing, explaining that there was always too much food anyway.

Delbert Gray and Melinda LaFramboise stayed. He moved through the crowd easily, answering and asking questions. He was liked by everyone who met him. Melinda clung to his arm and answered questions as briefly as she could, deferring to Gray.

At midday Danny sat with Josephine on the bow of the *Clinton,* eating what food they could scrounge up from the cold kitchen. The day was warm, with clear blue skies and very little wind. It should have been a pleasure for him to pass time with the young woman, but he was restless. He had seen a dead man, investigated a murder, nearly been involved in a barroom fight, been disciplined by the man he respected most, and now was confined to the steamer.

"You're not eating much," Josephine said.

"I reckon I'm not as hungry as I thought," he said.

"You're not talking much either."

"Thinkin'."

"Think out loud. I don't get much conversation from the horses."

"Sorry, Jo," he said. "I just can't get my thoughts lined up for talking."

"Maybe you need to think of something else." Josephine leaned over and kissed him and then jumped away as if she had stolen the bait from a mousetrap and was waiting to see it spring shut. Danny's eyes opened wide and then he stood up. He looked at Josephine to try and see what meaning the quick kiss had.

Motion pulled his gaze from her face. Two men were running from the shack on the flatboat. He looked back at Josephine, but his eyes were drawn away again as the two men jumped to shore and continued running away from the waterfront toward town. When Danny looked back at the flatboat, smoke was issuing from the open shack. First a wisp of black and gray, and then the black smoke got thicker and rose faster.

"Hey!" he shouted over the fifty yards separating the vessels, but there appeared to be no one else on the scow. Quickly he climbed to the pilothouse, where he found Charles Felden and Steve Allenby examining a hand-drawn chart of the Missouri River. They were transcribing information onto the chart from Felden's notebook and were oblivious to the developing problem on the flatboat. Barton burst into the pilothouse, causing both of the men to look up in surprise.

"Flatboat's on fire!" Barton exclaimed.

Felden took one look and rang the engine room for steam. "I'm not sure there are enough deckhands onboard to stoke the boilers," he said worriedly.

Allenby went to round up what crew was available and prepare to cast off as soon as there was enough steam. Barton dashed to his stateroom, where he unlocked the gun cabinet and removed a lever-action rifle and a box of cartridges. Then he went to his old cabin where he found Abraham sitting with his wife, Elizabeth.

"Abraham, we're going to need help on the main deck. Hurry!" Barton dashed out, and Abraham followed.

Barton took the steps three at a time. On the main deck he found two roustabouts. They were following Allenby to the boilers. "Steve, Abraham is coming down to help, but I need one of these men." Allenby just waved assent as he walked briskly to the boiler.

Barton looked at the two. "Who's the best shot?"

Weedeater said, "Me." The other man nodded agreement. Barton handed Weedeater the rifle and the box of cartridges.

"Get up on the roof of the pilothouse and keep an eye on me," Barton said, adding a caution: "Don't be in a hurry to shoot."

Josephine didn't need to be told what to do. She started carrying cordwood from where it was stacked to the door of the firebox. Abraham and the remaining roustabout did the same. Allenby performed the fireman's duties, checking the try cocks on the starboard boilers, isolating the larboard boilers, and opening vents. He shouted to the engineer at the other end of the boat that they were firing the starboard boilers.

Barton ran up the stage to the bank and then toward the burning flatboat. He had anticipated what would happen as soon as the *Inland Star* saw the fire on the flatboat. The other steamer was separated from the flatboat by less than ten feet and any fire on the flatboat would more than likely spread to the *Star*. Officer Barton reached the mooring lines just as the mate from the *Star* did. His intentions were obvious; he was carrying an axe.

He stopped, put one foot on the mooring post, and pulled his revolver. "Don't try to cut those lines, mister."

"You ain't gonna shoot me." The mate was not going to back down. "Get out of the way!"

Barton pulled the hammer back and leveled the revolver at the man's head. "Go back to your boat," he ordered.

The man had no choice but to comply. There was no one on the railing of his boat to back him up.

Barton followed. "Do you have steam?"

"What do you care?"

"If you've got steam, start your doctor engine, get your pumps into gear, and we'll put this fire out."

The *Inland Star* was not as short-handed as the *Clinton*. And the *Clinton* was too far away for her pumps to be of use. The logic of Barton's order was hard to dispute. Although the first mate was enraged by the security officer's actions, he called for hoses and they appeared in minutes. The *Star*'s crew directed water toward the burning shack on the flatboat. The unrestricted hoses, however, had trouble throwing the water as far as was needed. The men choked the ends of the hoses with their hands and that helped, but not enough.

"We've got two nozzles on the *Clinton*. Send one of your crew over there." The *Star*'s mate complied, and Barton shouted back to the *Clinton* what was needed.

The mate took some initiative. He had his crew lay boarding planks between the *Star* and the flatboat so they could approach the fire, but they ran out of hose so Barton shouted back to the *Clinton* to send hose over with the nozzles.

They had to clamp pieces of pipe between the *Star*'s hose and the *Clinton*'s hose, but as soon as that was done, they were able to board the flatboat. Soon Barton had one crew with a hoseline, the mate had another crew with a hoseline, and they went into the shack to extinguish the last bit of fire. The cargo was mostly buffalo hides, and the *Star*'s crew moved these away from the shack. The shack was a total loss, but the boat and the cargo were saved. More important, neither the *Inland Star* nor the *Barnard Clinton* had ever been seriously threatened.

"You got a lotta guts, young man," the mate said. His face was blackened with smoke, as was Barton's. "But I gotta hand it to you. I seen a waterfront burn up, and it ain't an easy thing to stop." He extended his hand and the officer took it.

"We did it, mate," he said, and slapped the man on the back. Then he collected the *Clinton*'s hose and nozzles and returned to the steamer.

Captain Culpepper had seen the smoke from town upon exiting the church where he had attended services. He ran back to the waterfront and was greeted with the sight of his security officer dragging hose back to the *Clinton*. He boarded the *Clinton* and immediately climbed up to the pilothouse, where Felden was still on duty.

"You had a little excitement this afternoon, I see."

"Not as much as Barton did."

"I notice he has left the boat. What did he do?"

"He was the first to see the fire. He alerted us, found people to help stoke the fireboxes, and then went over to the flatboat and drove off one of the *Star*'s officers who was going to cut the flatboat loose."

"Drove him off?"

"Put a gun in his face while he stood over the mooring line."

"I see," the captain said.

"Then he and the same officer got some of the *Star*'s crew, and they put out the fire."

The captain nodded approval. "Everyone should be back onboard at four bells. I want you to stay in the pilothouse until then. We'll have an officer's meeting."

"Yes, sir."

At six P.M. all the officers excepting Singletary were in the pilothouse.

"Gentlemen," the captain opened. "Mr. Singletary has taken ill and is in the care of a doctor in Council Bluffs. I don't know the exact nature of his illness, but to be on the safe side, I am quarantining his stateroom. Mr. Felden will move in with me, and Mr. Barton will take a berth in the main salon. There are several available now.

"Mr. Felden will be on duty from first to last light. We'll be tying up every night from here on due to our unfamiliarity with the Upper Missouri. The first and second mate will rotate watches as usual, staying in or near the pilothouse during the time that Mr. Felden is off watch.

"Mr. Barton, nail the pilot's stateroom door shut. Find a lock and hasp and lock it. Let no one in."

"Yes, sir."

"For those of you not aware, Mr. Barton undoubtedly saved both the *Inland Star* and the *Clinton* and God knows what else from being destroyed by a fire this afternoon. I expect no less from any of the officers, but I am nonetheless moved to say, well done, Mr. Barton." Each officer, having already heard the story, leaned toward the young aide and either patted him on the back or shook his hand. The captain had one more thing to say.

"Our cargo should be loaded shortly after midnight. We'll cast off as soon as the eastern sky turns blue. From here on we'll be in a prairie wilderness. Keep your eyes open."

Chapter Fifteen

Melinda retired to her stateroom immediately when she and Delbert Gray returned to the *Clinton*. The walk into town, the delicious potluck dinner, and the fresh air had combined to make her drowsy, and she begged his leave to spend at least the early part of the evening alone. Delbert acquiesced and left her at her door and then descended to the main salon to impatiently kill the next few hours until he could again be with the lovely Kentucky woman.

The kitchen staff had fired up the kitchen and was producing meals for the first class and cabin deck passengers. Delbert had eaten his fill at the church potluck and sat down at an empty game table with a cup of coffee. He had purchased a newspaper in Council Bluffs and read news from a town about which he knew nothing.

Harold Robertson had not gone into town with the rest of the passengers and crew. He had also not helped fight the fire that threatened the *Clinton* or helped stoke the fireboxes whose steam might have been needed to save her. He had remained in the main salon, sitting in a chair in the darkest corner, wanting to be on his way upriver but powerless to make it happen. Now he decided to go to the main table, get his food, and then take it to the lounge area where he would be seen by fewer people. There was one table available as he was filling his plate at the main table, but by the time he turned around, there was a man sitting there, reading a newspaper. Robertson went to the table and addressed the man.

"Would you mind sharing your table?"

Gray looked up at the man who was about his size, his age, and dressed similarly. "Not at all. Please have a seat."

Robertson placed his plate and napkin on the table and sat down. Gray extended his hand across the table.

"I'm Delbert Winston Gray, from Seattle," he said.

"I'm Henry Rogers, from Philadelphia," Robertson said, using his assumed name and taking Gray's offered hand firmly.

"Pleased to meet you, Mr. Rogers," Gray said. "What brings you so far from Philadelphia?"

"I'm traveling on behalf of several eastern banks, evaluating investment opportunities," Robertson said. Virtually every answer over the next hour would be at least a partial lie.

"Well, I'm sure you'll find plenty of interesting opportunities out West. How far are you going?"

"It will depend on the capabilities of this steamer. Ultimately, however, I intend to spend some time in San Francisco and then book passage on a clipper ship back to New York."

"Mmm," Gray mused. "There are not many ways to get back to the overland stage route from the Upper Missouri."

Robertson had no idea of what the transportation picture was like in the West. Rather than bluff his way through this conversation, he confessed, "What would you suggest from Virginia City?"

"There may be a stage line that connects to Salt Lake City from there. I have heard proposals, so you might have success pursuing that course."

Robertson was anxious to end the conversation that was on a subject about which he knew nothing. "Well, I'll certainly keep that in mind."

"There is an alternative, however, if you don't mind a little adventure."

Robertson had hoped that his lukewarm response would stifle the conversation, but his table companion was persistent. He looked up from his meal, saying only, "Yes?"

"I myself am planning to take the federal wagon road system to Seattle. From there one could book passage on a coastal schooner to Sacramento or take a stagecoach, although the coach would be more involved."

"I have little knowledge of the federal wagon roads," Robertson said, the truest statement he had uttered.

"Ah," said Gray. "I have been over the roads in the recent past, and I have a wagon and team in the cargo hold. I had intended to travel alone, but two men would be much safer."

"Yes, I suppose so," Robertson said.

Robertson looked carefully at the stranger for the first time. What he saw was a middle-aged man, apparently well-off, seemingly enthusiastic about his endeavors, and this was the most interesting to Robertson, and possibly naive. There might be profit for him if he befriended him. But he had no intention of subjecting himself to a wilderness expedition with a stranger who had all the appearances of a man not at home away from civilization.

Gray looked at Robertson also. Some of what he saw he liked; Robertson had a hard, no-nonsense look, the kind of man who could take care of himself in difficult situations. But the cold blue eyes had no hint of humor or kindness, and these were traits that were also important to Gray. The sum of his impressions was that this man would be valuable as a traveling companion, but was not likely to be a close friend. This was acceptable.

"Would you be interested in joining me to Seattle?"

"I'd have to give it some thought," Robertson said.

"There is one more thing I would have to tell you, before you commit yourself," Gray admitted.

"Yes?"

"I have met a young lady and I intend to ask her to marry me and join me on this trip. That will certainly place an additional burden on me and anyone who joins me."

Robertson had a brilliant thought that made his decision easy. This man was his size, his age, and even bore a slight resemblance to him. He could take the man's identity if he killed him. Somewhere between the end of navigation on the Missouri and the western slope of the Rocky Mountains, he could kill Delbert Gray. By then he would know everything he needed to know to assume his name and business and continue on to Seattle. The woman would be at his mercy.

"I would like to inspect your wagon and team," Robertson said. He didn't want to appear too eager, and it seemed sensible to look at the equipment.

"Why, certainly. As soon as you finish eating, we'll go down to the cargo bay."

Fifteen minutes later, the two men descended the stairway to the main deck and walked through the cargo bay to a nicely finished wagon, stacked high with freight.

"This is it," Gray said.

"Is the freight yours also?"

"Most of it."

"Are there enough supplies for three people?"

"Yes. I procured more than I needed, thinking there was no use in driving an empty wagon when goods are so expensive in the Northwest."

"That seems logical," said the con man. "Let's have a drink, Mr. Gray."

The men returned to the main salon where Robertson manipulated the conversation to learn as much about his companion as he could. The only subject on which he found difficulty acquiring information was the woman whom Gray intended to propose to. All Gray would do was elicit a promise from Robertson not to mention anything about his intentions.

Melinda awoke and turned up the lamp in her stateroom. Outside it was pitch dark, and she had no idea what time it was. She was hungry, though, and was sure she would find Delbert in the main salon. She straightened her hair, freshened her perfume, smoothed out her dress, and walked out into the night.

Standing in the doorway to the main salon, Melinda gazed over the crowd. She could see Delbert across the room, sitting with a man who had his back to her. She smoothed her dress again and entered the room, walking to the table. When she arrived at the table, she smiled at Delbert and greeted him warmly, and then turned to face the man with whom he was sitting. Her breath stopped, and for just a moment the room went black. She swayed, but quickly she regained her composure as she looked at the spy, the gold thief, and her former sweetheart, Harold Robertson.

Robertson was as startled as Melinda at their meeting. He hadn't known if she were dead or alive, nor if she had escaped the

Federal patrol. But he also regained his composure quickly, standing up to receive her as if she were a complete stranger. It was a masterful performance for both of them.

Delbert spoke first. "Mr. Rogers, this is my very good friend, Melinda LaFramboise. Melinda, this is Henry Rogers. Henry is a businessman from Philadelphia."

"I'm pleased to meet you, Mr . . . Rogers."

"As I am to meet you, Miss LaFramboise," he replied, bowing from the waist. "Please, sit down."

After half an hour of small talk, Melinda, afraid her discomfort in Robertson's presence would betray her, excused herself, and Delbert accompanied her to her room. Naturally, she invited him in, and he accepted. She sat on the bed, and he sat in the chair, just as before. He had decided that in the matter of a marriage proposal, sooner was better than later. In his pocket was his grandmother's engagement ring. Before he could steer the conversation in that direction, however, she asked a question.

"How long have you known . . . uh . . . Mr. Rogers?"

"We met only this evening. Do you like him?"

Melinda could not say that it went far beyond liking. She and Harold had been in love. They had lived together, and they had killed together. But none of this would she mention.

"I'll have to wait to answer that question until I get a chance to know him better."

"Well, give it time." Del had to pause to think how to get back to the subject that he was most interested in. Melinda gave him the opening.

"What will happen to us after you leave the steamer, Delbert?" she asked in a smaller voice than normal for her.

Delbert took a deep breath and then looked into her eyes. He picked up both her hands in his.

"Melinda, I'm an adventurer. A risk taker. I have made several fortunes in my life and lost some as well. I have an idea and the resources for what I am sure will be a very successful business enterprise in Seattle. A week ago, this was the only thing in the world that was important to me, just as my past ventures were."

Melinda had received enough proposals that she had no

trouble anticipating what was on his mind. Two hours ago, her answer would have been easier. The appearance of her past love had left her mind and emotions in chaos. But she was able to hide her confusion from Delbert.

"For goodness' sake, Delbert, what are you trying to say?" It was the old coquettish Melinda, brought to the fore in self-defense.

"I can't help but feel that you're a risk taker, too, an adventurer. That we're kindred souls."

"Delbert! Please?" In spite of herself, she was anxious to hear the question that she knew was coming.

"I'm in love with you. I've never said that to a woman before."

"Delbert . . ."

"Will you marry me?"

Even though she knew well in advance what was coming, even though she had only an hour ago found a former sweetheart she had never forgotten, she felt a warmth come over her that was unlike anything she had ever experienced. All other considerations were forgotten.

"Yes!" she said.

He got up and sat beside Melinda on the bed. They embraced for so long he became fearful that he would succumb to temptation. He stood up abruptly and reached into his pocket for the ring. Then he lowered himself to one knee, took her left hand in his, and slipped the ring on her finger.

Melinda had not shed real tears since she was a child, but she fought them back now.

"Delbert," she said, then repeated softly, "Oh, Delbert." They embraced again at length. Delbert let her go and got to his feet again.

"It's become quite late, Melinda. We should retire, and in the morning we can talk about our future as we make our way on up the river."

Melinda stood up. She wanted more than anything for him to stay, but she knew what kind of man he was, and, reluctantly, she kissed him good night.

Chapter Sixteen

The sky had not a hint of lightness when Charles Felden awakened and dressed in the captain's stateroom. The captain stayed in his bunk until Felden was through dressing, and then he also arose, dressed, and followed Felden to the pilothouse.

Gary Singletary's mate, David Erickson, was holding the fort in the pilothouse. He had taken over just moments before from Steve Allenby. This was the captain's organization in the absence of two pilots. The rest of the officers would continue their normal watches, while Felden would be the pilot whenever the boat was not tied up.

"Good morning, Mr. Erickson," Felden said.

"Morning, Mr. Felden. Good morning, Captain Culpepper."

"Do we have steam in all boilers?" Felden asked.

"Yes, sir."

"How much wood?"

"Over forty cords."

"I see the stages are already up. That's good. Let go the lines as soon as the wheel starts turning."

"Yes, sir." The mate left the pilothouse to direct the deck crew. Felden rang the engine room for slow astern and let go a blast on the whistle. The deck crew was right on the job; just before the lines went taut, they slipped the loops and the *Str. Barnard Clinton* backed cleanly away from the landing at Council Bluffs.

By now the eastern sky had changed from black to a dark blue. Felden could see a few lights in Council Bluffs and, across the river, a dim light that was Omaha. He also had the stern lights of the *Str. Inland Star* to let him know when he was clear. Out in the channel, he rang for half ahead, and the big wheel slowed to a stop and then began churning forward.

Felden shared with no one that this was one of the moments he enjoyed most: the two-hundred-thirty-foot-long steamer using her momentum to go astern while the mighty paddlewheel churned the river in opposition, arresting her rearward motion and starting her toward her destination. To him it was poetry of the finest sort.

This was his first opportunity to talk to the captain about the incapacitated Singletary. "Any idea what's wrong with Singletary?"

"No."

"Not cholera, then?"

"The doctor wouldn't say no, but probably not. We'll have a telegram waiting for us in Sioux City if the nature of Singletary's illness is determined by then."

"If he recovers, will he wait for us to return?" Felden asked.

"Yes. He's still on salary."

Felden nodded his head in approval. He already knew that Captain Culpepper was a rare man. The fact that he himself was going to have to do the job of two pilots mattered less to him, knowing that the captain was as committed to his officers as he expected them to be to the *Clinton*.

The *Clinton* did not reach Sioux City that day. As it grew dark, Felden studied his chart and realized it would be after midnight if they continued on. Accordingly, he slowed the steamer and sidled toward the banks of the river, still just barely visible in the waning evening light. He called for a leadsman, and with his help, he soon had the *Clinton* snug against the bank. The roustabouts scrambled ashore with a timber the size of a railroad tie and used it as a "dead man" for one line. Then they tied another line to a large tree. It had been a long, long day for Felden, and he slapped his mate on the back as he left the pilothouse without formality.

Officer Barton recruited two men to stand guard. He didn't issue them rifles, but he gave them whistles to sound an alarm if needed. Then he crawled into his new berth in the main cabin.

Delbert Gray had likewise retired after walking Melinda

LaFramboise to her cabin and saying good night with a long kiss. Melinda had seemed a little distant to him tonight, but he thought he knew why. A woman accustomed to life in hotels and riverboats would be, should be, overwhelmed by the thought of crossing a mountain range on the seat of a wagon beside a man she had known for only weeks. But that was not the reason for her moodiness.

In short order Melinda was not alone in the stateroom. Harold Robertson had been waiting for his chance to see her alone, and when he saw Gray crawl into his berth, he waited for a few minutes and then exited his and quietly climbed the stairs to the upper deck. At her door, he tapped lightly, and Melinda, knowing it was only a matter of time until he sought her out, opened the door for him.

Harold immediately tried to take her in his arms, but she held him off.

"Melinda, it's been so long," he pleaded. "I've thought about you every single day." Another Robertson lie.

"Yes, and I've thought of you too, Harold, but things are different now."

"I can see that, but my feelings for you haven't changed." He waited for her to say something similar, but she didn't. After a long silence, he said, "Tell me, dear, do you need any money?" He wasn't actually going to offer her money; he wanted to find out if she had any of the gold left.

"I have a little," she said. "I'll be fine." She started to add that she would be married soon, but kept that fact to herself for the time being.

"Mr. Gray is taking care of you then?"

"No." She paused. "Yes."

"I'm happy for you, Melinda," he said, and then added: "He looks to have considerable resources."

Melinda shrugged. "He's a good man."

Harold didn't think for a minute that she was interested in Delbert Gray because he was a good man, but he didn't want to talk about Gray.

"What have you been doing for the last two years, Melinda?"

"I've been just trying to get by. It hasn't been so bad, I guess. How about yourself?"

For a few minutes they made small talk, each curious about the other's affairs during the two years they had been separated and each avoiding the frequent shabbiness of their existence to mention only the triumphs, however small. But as they talked, the closeness they once had slowly began returning. The air in the room was thick with suppressed emotions and nearly forgotten memories that had been suddenly revived.

"Harold," she said. "I think it would be better if you were to go." She unconsciously twisted the ring on her finger.

"Melinda, I can tell that you and Mr. Gray are serious about each other, and I don't want to ruin your chances, but I have missed you so much these last few years." He stood before her with his hands at his sides, palms open. "I don't know if I can give you up again."

This had the desired effect on Melinda, and she went to him and embraced him tightly. He returned the embrace, and then they kissed. It was sometime later that Robertson slipped out of the stateroom and returned to his berth in the main cabin. He was smiling and feeling very satisfied as he climbed into his berth. Melinda, alone in her stateroom, began crying and didn't stop until she fell asleep just before dawn.

The stop at Sioux City was mainly to replenish the wood supply, but it was possible that additional freight could be loaded or passengers booked. The captain was interested in finding out if there was a telegram waiting for him concerning his junior pilot, Greg Singletary. He also was taking a message from Barton to send to Rake Angleton, asking if the murder in Omaha had been solved. The security officer felt, and the captain agreed, that it was important to know if there was a possibility that the *Clinton* was being used as a refuge for a killer.

Immediately upon berthing at the riverside, Culpepper walked briskly into town, leaving the pilothouse and the steamer in the hands of Allenby. Felden also left the pilothouse to catch a nap during the few hours that the *Clinton* would be in Sioux City.

Josephine Wainwright and Abraham were taking care of the livestock in the cargo bay. Abraham sought Josephine out whenever he had nothing to do, wanting to help her, not only as payment for the help she had given him and Elizabeth but because she treated him as an ordinary man. He was good with animals, and he and Josephine learned from each other.

Josephine likewise enjoyed working with Abraham. He was smart and strong, and he could do the things that she wasn't big enough to do, like pushing stubborn horses in the direction they needed to go or actually carrying smaller animals like calves and pigs. She was eager to talk to him this morning, having a serious question on her mind.

"Abraham, how well do you remember the man who shot my brother?"

"I sees him now in my head, clear as then," he said.

"Have you seen him on this boat?"

"I doesn't go into the main cabin much, Miss Jo."

"We're done here. I'd like to take you up to the main cabin and have you look at a man to see if you recognize him."

"Sho', Miss Jo."

Josephine had not missed the fact that Melinda LaFramboise, who she watched every chance she got, was spending a lot of time with a man, Delbert Gray, who seemed to fit the description that Abraham had given her on the night her brother was killed. She put her hand into the jacket pocket that held the powerful little gun she had bought in Springfield.

"Don't you ever get too warm in that jacket, Miss Jo?" Abraham asked. "I don't reckon I've ever seen you not wearin' it."

"I just like to keep it on," she answered evasively. "Let's go look in the salon and see if he's there."

"Sho', Miss Jo."

They climbed the central stairs and entered the main salon at the aft end, near the ladies' cabin. Josephine guessed that the man she was suspicious of was more likely in the forward end of the main salon, near the bar, and she wanted to try to observe without being noticed by him.

Many passengers had decided to stay with the boat while

docked, and they were in the salon relaxing. At the far end of the room, which was one hundred and fifty feet long, there were two men sitting at a table, engaged in a lively conversation. It was Delbert Gray and Harold Robertson, aka Henry Rogers. Josephine waited for her eyes to adjust to the dimmer light of the salon. When she could see well, she whispered to Abraham and indicated the table with the two men. When he said he saw it, she asked him if that was the man. Abraham watched, and then walked closer to get a better view and to try and hear the voice, which he was also sure he would remember. Josephine followed a short distance behind. The two of them were starting to attract attention from the passengers. Abraham had seen enough and quickly ducked out the side door; Josephine retreated to the aft door and met him outside.

"He be the one, Miss Jo!" Abraham said excitedly.

"Thanks, Abraham. I'll talk to you later." Abraham left the cabin deck and returned to the cargo bay and his work.

Josephine was thinking hard. She had fought back the impulse to walk right up to the man and shoot him in the head, and it was a fortunate thing, because she had mistakenly assumed that Abraham had indicated Delbert Gray.

But Abraham had correctly recognized the other man at the table, Harold Robertson, as the traitorous spy who had double-crossed both sides, killed a man, and stolen forty thousand dollars of gold.

She really wanted to see her brother's killers tried and hung, but it would be difficult for her to accomplish this by herself. She needed Barton's help. He could arrest them, confine them, and turn them over to the authorities in Sioux City. She would leave the steamer at this point and wait for the trial so she could testify and see them convicted.

Barton was in the pilot house, conversing with Felden. The captain entered and handed Felden a telegram. Felden unfolded the telegram and read it, then smiled and handed it to Barton.

PATIENT RECOVERING STOP CAUSE STILL UNDETERMINED
STOP

"Well, that's certainly good news, Captain," Felden said.

"Yes. Tell the mate to have your stateroom cleaned as soon as Mr. Barton can reopen it. Put all your and Singletary's clothes and linens in the laundry as a last precaution."

"Very well, sir."

Steve Allenby and the purser came in at that moment to report that loading was complete and all passengers were onboard. The stop at Sioux City had been brief, taking on two more passengers, twenty cords of wood, and a hundred bags of seed grain for farmers upriver.

"Mr. Allenby, raise the stages and cast off," Felden said, and Allenby left to carry out the orders.

Josephine was just climbing the stairs to the pilothouse when the *Barnard Clinton*'s paddle wheel began to turn in reverse and the steamer backed away from the landing. She was too late to get her brother's killers incarcerated at Sioux City, but not too late to make sure they stayed on the boat. Danny saw her stop just outside the pilothouse and let himself out, realizing that she wanted to talk to him.

"Hi, Jo," he said.

"Danny, I need your help."

"What?"

"Abraham has identified the man who shot my brother two years ago. I want you to arrest him before he gets away."

"Who is it?"

"I think his name is Delbert Gray. He's been keeping company with Melinda LaFramboise. That made me suspicious, and when I showed him to Abraham, Abraham said he was the one. I can't let him get away." She was almost out of breath, not so much from climbing the stairs but from her anxiety to make sure the killer didn't escape.

"He can't go anywhere until we tie up tonight, and then he's not likely to. We'll not see a white man again until Fort Pierre."

"He mustn't escape," she insisted.

"Don't tell anyone what you told me," he said. "I think I'll have a talk with him."

"He mustn't escape."

"He won't, Jo. You have my word."

Josephine threw her arms around her surprised friend and he held her close, right out on the hurricane deck and in view of the men in the pilothouse. Then he leaned away and looked at her, seeing the dampness in her eyes.

"He won't get away," he said again. She held his hand to show her trust in his promise. "Let's go down to the main cabin and see if he's there," he said. "Anyway, I haven't had anything to eat yet today." She nodded and followed him downstairs.

When they entered the main salon, Gray wasn't there, but Barton's eyes fell on Harold Robertson. This was one of several men who the security officer thought might be involved in the murder of the telegrapher. It would have been opportune, he thought, if Robertson had been identified by Abraham as the murderer that Josephine had been seeking. Of course, the telegrapher's murderer was not necessarily on the steamer, but if one of the men who boarded at Omaha was the murderer, that would mean there were two killers onboard the *Clinton*. That didn't include Melinda La-Framboise, who was a participant in the killing of Josephine's brother. And both murders were cold and calculated. The safety of Josephine or any of the passengers and crew was at risk until both murderers were found and dealt with.

"Danny?" Barton put his thoughts aside and looked down at Josephine. "I thought you were in a trance or something," she said.

"I'm sorry," he said. "I was thinking about the murders."

"Murders?"

"Yes, your brother, and then last week the murder of the telegrapher in Omaha."

"But the telegrapher doesn't concern us," she said. She was totally focused on her brother.

"It might, if his killer boarded the steamer at Omaha."

"Oh, yes, in that case, I see what you mean." She grabbed his arm for comfort as they walked into the main salon and then immediately dropped it. Most people onboard still believed she was a young man.

There were leftovers on the food table from the afternoon meal. The *Clinton* fed four times a day: breakfast, lunch, dinner in the afternoon, and supper after the sun set. The dinner hour was just ending. Danny and Josephine filled their plates and found seats apart from the few people who were still eating.

"We haven't had a chance to talk since the fire," she said in a low voice.

"No," he answered, waiting to hear what she wanted to say.

"I kissed you," she said bluntly.

"Yes." He smiled a quick smile and then straightened his face.

"It didn't . . . it was just a kiss," she said.

"Oh."

Josephine thought she could see in his eyes and hear in his voice a measure of disappointment, but it was too late to say anything that might give a hint as to her deeper feelings. Maybe he would say something now that would give her an opening. If not, she thought, she would try again before they finished their meal. Why was it so hard for her to talk frankly with this man? She would plan what to say while they ate, and then afterward start over with her thoughts in order. The sound of a gunshot somewhere outside erased that possibility.

Danny jumped to his feet. "Stay here, Jo," he commanded and ran to the door nearest to the sound. He opened the door cautiously and peered around the door frame.

The *Clinton* had been fighting a narrowing of the Missouri River with full steam, but the main channel was too swift for her. Felden had worked the steamboat into calmer water near the shore with the help of a leadsman. By so doing, the *Clinton* was able to overcome the current and was making slow progress only a hundred feet from the shoreline. A band of about thirty Indians had witnessed her difficulty and had laid an ambush on the southern shore. Half of them had muskets, the others had bows, and they were making the deckhands dive for cover. Two men lay on the foredeck bleeding.

Barton took the stairs three at a time to the Texas deck as musket balls splintered into the wall beside him. He flew down the walkway to his original stateroom, where he unlocked the door and went directly to the gun cabinet. The captain was right behind him and took one of the rifles and a box of cartridges. Barton got one for himself and another for Weedeater, who appeared in the doorway. The three men went to the railing, where they could look from a superior height on the Indians crouching behind mounds of dirt and clumps of grass.

Weedeater was, as he claimed, an excellent shot, as were Barton and the captain. In minutes they had driven the Indians out of musket range. Felden continued working the *Clinton* upriver.

The Indians reloaded and tried to approach the river again, shooting as they came. The captain ignored the musket balls hitting the woodwork around him and went to the railing in front of the pilothouse.

"Somebody see to those men on the deck!" he commanded.

Three men scurried out from the cargo bay and dragged the wounded men into cover. The captain remained on the hurricane deck in front of the pilothouse, where he could see the river, see the foredeck, and watch the Indians, retreating again.

The *Clinton* was now making good progress up the river, and Felden eased back toward the swifter water to get the boat completely and permanently out of musket range.

Barton knew that Josephine was not afraid of blood, so he went to the main salon to fetch her. They gathered up some clean linens to use as bandages, and she descended to the main deck to tend to the wounded while he returned to the hurricane deck to watch for further attacks. The captain sent the purser to all the staterooms and berths to see if anyone else had been hurt in the attack.

Officer Barton slapped Weedeater on the back. "Weedeater, you have a new job. I'll square it with the captain."

"Do I get to keep this here rifle?"

"For now. You and I are going to stand guard on alternate watches; you take B watch, I'll take A watch."

"Whatta I have to do?"

"Stay awake, stay outside on the cabin deck or the hurricane deck. Watch for trouble."

"When does B watch start?"

"Soon. Four o'clock. Listen for eight bells. That's your time. When you hear eight bells again, I'll take over."

"Better 'n stackin' grain sacks, eh?"

"Maybe. Don't let that rifle out of your sight. Don't let it out of your hand!"

Barton descended to the main deck to see how bad the situation was. On the way down he met the purser, who told him everyone on the cabin deck had been spared injury, in spite of the fact that several musket balls had penetrated the flimsy cabin wall. On the main deck, in the cargo bay, he found Josephine taking care of the two wounded men. One had a wound on his head from a musket ball; the other had an arrow in one leg. They were both conscious and in good spirits, as was Josephine. Working on the men, it was not possible to disguise the fact that she was a woman, and she let them flirt with her to take their minds off their injuries. She swore them to secrecy, but she knew that it would be common knowledge on the boat in less than a day.

"How are you doing, Jo?" he asked.

"Well, these two men like to stand around so the Indians can have target practice. They think they're bulletproof, I guess." She smiled as she walked close to him and quickly took his hand, squeezed it, and released it.

"Every time we start to get somewhere, something happens," he said, grabbing her hand again and pulling her back. "These two fellas know all about you, I reckon." The men grinned in agreement. He wrapped his arms around Josephine and kissed her. "Now there's something for *you* to think about," he said after he released her.

During the attack, Delbert ran to Melinda's room to make sure she was safe. He cautioned her to stay inside while he went down to the main deck to see if he could be of any service. Half an hour later, when he returned, she let him in.

"Are you all right, Melinda?" he inquired.

"Yes. I'm fine now, but that fight was so horrible. Was anyone hurt?"

"Two men were wounded, but they'll survive their wounds. There'll be armed guards on duty from now on."

"Are you all right?" she asked. His customary well-groomed

appearance was in some disarray, and he was still breathing rapidly from the excitement and exertion.

"Oh yes, I missed all the action. But the captain and the officers performed valiantly. We're in good hands."

"It's good to hear that there will be armed guards. That means you don't have to take up arms and expose yourself to being wounded."

"No, in times like these, I prefer to be at your side to watch over you."

She sat down, relaxed at last. "You're very excited," she commented. "I've not seen you like this."

"I'm very happy today. I could think of nothing else but our marriage last night, and it caused me to sleep in a most pleasant state of mind."

Melinda couldn't look at him; she was afraid her eyes would betray her as she had betrayed him. He sensed something was wrong and lifted her chin to see her face.

"I promise you, I'll make you very happy and you'll have no regret," he said.

"Delbert . . ." Her voice trailed off. She already had regret, and she couldn't think of anything to say that would make her feel better or make her infidelity be less a barrier between them.

"What is it, my darling?" He still held her chin in his hand. She pulled away and went to the far side of the room.

"Everything is happening too fast."

"I see no reason to delay. I want to marry you, and the sooner, the better."

"You don't know anything about me."

"I know what I need to know," he countered.

"No, Delbert dear, I'm afraid you don't." Melinda motioned him to sit down. She intended to tell him all about her past life and misdeeds. It would be over between them, but she wouldn't go to Harold Robertson either. Maybe she would return to her home in Kentucky and reunite with her estranged family. Maybe . . . it didn't matter.

"I'm not the person you think I am," she said. "I'm not so nice."

Delbert was silent for a moment, considering how to say what he wanted to say. Melinda sat herself on her bed again, across from the chair where he was sitting. He leaned forward to better see her face.

"I, also, may be different from what you perceive. I am not the naive, inexperienced businessman that you may think me to be. I have met many people in every major city in America. I have always had the ability to assess a person's character after only a short meeting. I also have contacts who can supply me with information."

"But I . . ." She started to say something but Delbert held up his hand.

"If I am wrong in what I am about to say, I apologize in advance," he said. "The last thing I want to do is hurt you." She was silent. He took a deep breath. "You have pursued an unsavory lifestyle for several years. The police in Chicago and in New Orleans know you. You have . . . not been chaste. It's not that this doesn't matter to me; it's that I see underneath it all you are a good person and would lead a far more admirable life if given the opportunity. That is what I want to do."

"Oh, Delbert."

"I want to find a parson when we reach Fort Pierre and marry you. Then we can start making a new life for one another. And believe me, you will do as much for me as I will for you." She came to his side, sat on the floor, and rested her head and arm on his knee. She would never tell him about Harold Robertson.

Barton let the captain know that he wanted to have an around-the-clock armed guard on the boat, not just for the Indians but for the one or more murderers who were on the boat. The captain nodded in agreement. So, at eight, Danny took over from Weedeater and began patrolling the upper decks in the darkness. He noticed that Delbert Gray left Melinda LaFramboise's cabin at about ten P.M.

Robertson was always alert to what was happening in his environment. He had seen Weedeater standing guard and knew that it would be more difficult to return to Melinda's stateroom, but he was determined to do so. He observed Officer Barton relieving

Weedeater and walking the hurricane deck. He deduced that there would now be an around-the-clock guard on that deck.

The *Clinton* tied to the shore at about eight thirty. Barton lit every lamp on the starboard side, which was nearer the shore. This section of shore had been chosen because it was devoid of heavy brush. Robertson stood outside the main salon, under the hurricane deck, and listened in the silence of the evening to Barton walking around. He tried to detect a pattern to the security officer's movements, but it was unpredictable, making a half circuit sometimes, then retracing his steps or standing for minutes at a time in one spot while he searched the countryside, looking for movement.

At midnight Weedeater relieved Barton and Robertson returned to the outside walkway to listen for Weedeater's steps. Weedeater had a pattern, and he interrupted it occasionally to light a pipe and smoke it at a spot where he could observe the plains. After listening to this process repeat itself several times, Robertson quietly ascended the stairs to the deck and went to Melinda's stateroom door. It was so still, he could easily hear Weedeater on the other side of the row of staterooms as he lit his pipe and inhaled deeply.

Harold tapped on the door as quietly as he could, wanting to wake Melinda without alerting Weedeater. He always tapped on a door the same way, a certain rhythm and number of taps. Melinda would recognize his signal, he was sure. He tapped again and heard movement inside. Then the door opened, and he pushed inside just as Weedeater knocked his pipe out on the railing on the far side.

"Melinda," he whispered softly and reached for her in the dimly lit room. She pushed him away.

"Harold, it's over."

"No one saw me come up here," he said. To him that was the important aspect of the evening, not right or wrong, but the fact that there was little chance of being caught.

"Good. But it doesn't change anything. It's over," she reaffirmed.

"All right, Melinda," he said and backed away. "It's difficult for me to think that what we had may never be again." He tried to sound contrite.

"What we had was wrong, Harold. There was nothing good about it."

"If we hadn't run into that Union patrol, everything would be different now. We would be living in high style in Philadelphia or Boston. We would have wealthy friends and political connections."

"We were petty criminals."

"I wish we could try again," he said. Melinda shook her head.

"You and Delbert Gray?"

"I hope so."

"You are committed to this union?"

"Yes."

"You know, my dear, we have an excellent opportunity here."

"No, Harold."

"You haven't heard me out," he protested.

"I don't want to hear you out. I know what you want, and the answer is no."

"Melinda, even if you no longer have feelings for me, we make a good team. You owe me."

Melinda folded her arms in front of her. "I owe you nothing. I want you to get off this boat at Sioux City and never see me again."

Harold was not interested. "No," he said firmly. "You and I are going to travel with Delbert Gray to Seattle where I will be partners with him."

The image of Robertson shooting an innocent man in the dark of the Kentucky night two years ago came back to Melinda. She knew the same fate awaited Delbert Gray.

"No."

Harold's eyes narrowed. "If you don't cooperate, Melinda, I'm going to the authorities in Fort Pierre and have you arrested."

"They'll arrest you too," she countered.

"I don't think so. There is nobody to connect me with the gold theft. I was a nonperson. I didn't exist." He gave an evil smile. Melinda had no way of knowing his difficulties in Omaha and with the *Missouri Princess*.

"I can tell them plenty," Melinda said.

"Melinda, you make your living exploiting men. I'm a banker. What you say doesn't mean anything to anybody."

This was a bluff. The last thing Harold could afford was for Melinda to go to any authorities, to call attention to him in any way. She had a defiant posture.

"You go ahead with your marriage. Do whatever you want. I can do this without your help. Just stay out of my way."

"You're not going to do anything, Harold. I'll gladly go to jail to keep you from hurting Delbert."

Howard slowly slipped his hand into his inside pocket and his fingers closed around the letter opener that he had used on John Swanson. He removed it and held it at his side where Melinda couldn't see it.

"Melinda, I admire you. Maybe you will have a good life after all." He said this to make her relax her guard, and it had the desired effect. He stepped forward and plunged the knife into her chest just below her sternum at an angle to find her heart. "But I doubt it." He leered as he looked at her stunned face. She collapsed on the floor, took three more gasping breaths, and was still.

Robertson wiped the letter opener on her nightgown and returned it to his jacket pocket. Then he stood by the door and waited until Weedeater got into the part of his routine that would allow him to traverse the hurricane deck and descend to the cabin deck. When he heard Weedeater light his pipe, he opened the door, set the latch to lock on closing, and, unseen by anyone, returned to his berth.

Chapter Seventeen

Mr. Barton, I need you to come with me." It was the purser. Danny Barton was in the pilothouse watching Charles Felden navigate. He looked up at the purser.

"Right now?"

"Yes, it's an emergency, please," he said. Felden could only glance around before he had to return his attention to the river.

"Let's go," Barton said and followed the purser out of the pilothouse. They walked directly to the Pennsylvania stateroom.

The door to the stateroom was open and, looking in, the security officer saw Delbert Gray standing next to one of the beds where the motionless form of Melinda LaFramboise lay. The purser stopped at the door and turned to Barton.

"She's dead. Mr. Gray came to me this morning to unlock the door, as he was unable to get a response when he knocked. When we opened the door we found her on the floor."

Barton said nothing as he entered the room. He looked at the ghostly pale face of Melinda LaFramboise and then at Delbert Gray, who was almost as pale as Melinda.

"What happened here?" he asked.

"I don't know," Gray answered with a quavering voice. "She's dead," he said, and then repeated, "She's dead." He wiped his face slowly with one hand, as if covering his eyes momentarily would cause the scene to change.

Barton wanted to conclude that Gray had killed Melinda, but the man's emotional reaction caused him some doubt. He lifted one arm and felt the inside of the arm as compared to the outside. Both sides were cold, and the arm was stiff.

Gray did not want the officer touching Melinda. "Is that necessary?" he asked.

Barton countered with a question of his own. "Where were you last night?" As he waited for an answer he examined both of her hands, front and back.

"I would prefer that you not handle my fiancée," Gray protested.

Barton stood straight and faced Gray. Although he was extremely suspicious of Gray, the sight of Gray's grief-stricken face softened his approach.

"Mr. Gray, I want to know why this woman is dead. Since we are miles from any law-enforcement authority, I'm going to investigate as thoroughly as I possibly can. Now answer my question. Where were you last night?"

"In my berth!" he snapped. Gray's grief was being replaced by anger. It was only natural that he would direct it at the officer. But Barton was not intimidated.

"How long have you known this woman?" Barton asked.

"I met her on this boat, this trip."

Barton doubted that this was true, but he decided he would question Gray later. At the moment his best course of action was to concentrate on the dead woman.

"Is this how you found her?" he asked.

"No," Gray replied. "She was on the floor."

"On her back?"

"Yes."

Barton looked at the top and sides of her head. When he combed through her hair with his fingers, he heard Gray take a step toward him. He just glared over his shoulder at Gray and continued his examination.

"Then you picked her up and laid her on the bed?"

"Yes. The purser will tell you the same thing."

"What else did you do?"

Gray hesitated. "Her robe was open. I closed it."

"I'm going to open it," Barton warned.

Gray let out a long breath. "All right, if you must."

He opened the robe, revealing her in her nightgown from head to toe. There was a small bloodstain in the center of her night-gown just below her breasts. Barton turned to the purser.

"Find Weedeater and send him up here," he said.

"I need to get back to the kitchen," said the purser.

"Find Weedeater," Barton said again firmly. "Send the captain here too. Then you can go back to your job."

"Very well." The purser left.

"Mr. Gray, I'm going to open her nightgown now."

Gray hadn't noticed the small bloodstain when he had first found Melinda. Now he was more appreciative of what Officer Barton was doing.

"I understand," he said.

Barton unbuttoned Melinda's nightgown past the bloodstain. He carefully avoided exposing her breasts as he separated the sides of the nightgown. There was a slight amount of dried blood on her skin just below her sternum. He put his thumbs on her skin around the spot of blood and pulled in opposite directions, just as he had seen the doctor do in Omaha. It produced the same result, a small slit a half-inch long opened up in Melinda's pale skin. Barton stood straight again and faced Delbert Gray.

"Take your jacket off, Mr. Gray."

Gray may have thought that the officer was going to cover Me-linda with his jacket so he removed it without question or protest and handed it over. Barton pulled the jacket through one hand, feeling for a weapon, and then laid it on the table.

"Empty your pockets onto the table, please."

Now Gray understood that he was under suspicion. He accepted the fact and complied with Barton's order, grim-faced. Barton looked at the personal effects that Gray had placed on the table. There was no knife.

"Pull your pant legs up."

Gray did this, revealing nothing more than his legs and stock-ings, and dropped them. The captain walked into the room. He looked at the dead woman and then at Gray.

"Report, Mr. Barton."

"From what I know so far, this woman was killed last night by a stab wound to the lower chest. Mr. Gray and the purser discovered the body this morning. I find nothing implicating Mr. Gray, but he has been identified by another passenger as being involved in a murder in Tennessee two years ago."

"That's preposterous!" Gray exclaimed, hearing this accusation for the first time. "I was in Washington, D.C., throughout sixty-four, working for the Army."

Barton looked at Gray for a long moment, trying to decide if he was being truthful. If he did have an alibi for the murder of Josephine's brother, that would mean he was probably innocent in this murder also.

"That will be easy to verify when we reach Fort Pierre. Until then, I want to search your berth and your luggage."

"Fine. The sooner, the better."

"And I caution you, that if I see you with any kind of weapon in your hand, I'll shoot to kill."

Gray just snorted his disdain, saying, "Follow me, I'll take you to my berth." He paused to draw Melinda's robe closed.

Weedeater came to the door at that moment. He could tell something was wrong inside the stateroom, but he couldn't see the dead woman's body on the bed.

"Weedeater," Barton said. "Did you hear anything last night? Anything unusual?"

"No, sir. It was quiet all night until you came on at four, and right after that we pushed away from the shore."

"All right. I'm going to tell you something, but if you tell anyone else, you'll be swimming back to Sioux City."

Weedeater was taken aback, but stammered, "Ah . . . ah . . . All right."

"A woman was killed in this room last night. We don't know who did it. Everyone is under suspicion, and everyone is in danger. That makes your job as guard the most important job on the boat."

Weedeater whistled a breathy, quiet whistle.

The captain entered the discussion. "Mr. Barton, find another roustabout as reliable as this man and give him your rifle. You'll have enough to do for a while without taking four-hour watches throughout the day and night."

"Yes, sir," the captain's aide agreed. "There's one other thing, Captain. The wound in this lady's chest is identical to the wound that killed the telegrapher in Omaha."

The captain accepted this news stoically, but his admiration for the young security officer was growing.

Barton examined the lock on the door to Melinda's room and then locked it as he left. He and Delbert Gray went to Gray's berth where he searched it, finding nothing incriminating.

"Let's go have a cup of coffee, Mr. Gray. I have a lot more questions."

"I think I'll have a drink, if you don't mind," Gray said.

"One thing for sure," Barton told Gray when they were seated at a table in the salon, "you didn't kill the telegrapher. I don't believe that you had anything to do with your fiancée's death either, but I'm going to continue my investigation without taking shortcuts."

"I understand," Gray said.

"And I want you to know that my sympathies are with you for your loss. Were you close?"

"Yes, very."

"Do you have a key to Miss LaFramboise's room?" Barton asked.

"No. I told you I had to find the purser to open the door."

"Yes. And you're positive that it was locked this morning when you went there?"

"Yes."

"Did Miss LaFramboise have any other friends onboard?"

"No."

"She let someone in whom she trusted."

"She didn't know anyone else," Gray insisted.

"You boarded at St. Louis?"

"I did, and she was, as you probably know, one of the passengers that we took from the grounded *Missouri Princess*. It was several days on the river before I made her acquaintance."

"Did you ever see her in the company of a man?"

"She was popular at the poker games, but she didn't favor any one man during the time I observed her."

"What do you know about her past?"

"That's not germane to your investigation," Gray snapped.

"Let me ask the question another way," he said. "If you can think of anything in what she's told you of her past that might help me, please tell me."

"I will. I want this killer caught more than you do, believe me."

"For what it's worth, I'm starting to."

"We had planned to get married at Fort Pierre." Gray's voice was tremulous again. Barton's lingering doubts vanished as he looked at the man's sorrowful face.

Danny found Josephine in the cargo bay feeding the horses. He glanced around to make sure no one was within earshot.

"Josephine, Melinda LaFramboise has been killed."

Jo considered that statement for a moment before asking, "Where's Delbert Gray?"

"I just finished an interview with him. I don't think he's the man who murdered your brother."

"Abraham had no doubt when he identified him."

"He claims he was in Washington, D.C., throughout 1864, and we'll be able to verify that at Fort Pierre. He also claims he had never seen Melinda before he boarded the *Clinton* in St. Louis."

"And you don't think he killed her?"

"No, I won't bet my life on it, but he seems truly grief-stricken."

"Over Melinda?" In Josephine's mind, Melinda LaFramboise was human trash who had no redeeming qualities.

"They were going to be married."

"He's better off without her," Josephine said sullenly.

Josephine stared at the ceiling of the cargo bay as she turned these facts over in her mind. She wasn't sorry to know that Melinda was dead, but she wished she could have seen the woman tried in a court of law. Worse than that, with Melinda dead and Delbert Gray likely innocent, she had no trail to the murderer of her brother. And then it hit her: the killer of Melinda was possibly her brother's killer also.

"Who do you think killed her?"

"Melinda was killed just like the telegrapher in Omaha. A

single knife wound in the chest. No struggle, not much bleeding. The killer is most likely one of the eight men who boarded at Omaha."

"What are you going to do?" she asked.

"I'm sending a telegram to Marshal Angleton in Omaha asking if they found the telegrapher's killer and requesting information on the passengers who boarded there. About the only other thing I can do is keep my eye on them."

"I'll help."

"No, Jo. You have to be careful. The killer might decide that you're a threat and try to do something about you."

"I'm ready," Josephine said grimly.

"Don't try to do anything on your own, Josephine," he said. She made no reply, even when he reached for her hands and held them.

Barton left Josephine to her work and went to the pilothouse to confer with the captain.

"Captain Culpepper, I want to talk to each of the passengers who boarded at Omaha. It's very likely that one of them was the killer."

"Why do you think that?" Culpepper asked.

"Melinda was killed exactly like the telegrapher in Omaha. A single stab wound in the center of the chest. In John Swanson's case, the wound went up into his heart. It was probably the same with Melinda."

The captain didn't reply for a moment. Then he said, "Mr. Barton, I remember a command officer's briefing where we were told of a training program for Southern saboteurs that included a technique of assassinations similar to what you described."

"That agrees with what Josephine told me about her brother's murder. She said the killer was a double spy who betrayed both sides when he stole forty thousand dollars of gold with Melinda LaFramboise."

The captain nodded his head. "Very well, Mr. Barton. Arrange to bring them to my cabin one at a time. I'll be present during the interviews."

The officer decided the best strategy was to interview the least likely killer first. He could improve his tactics with each interview. And the real killer would grow nervous with the passage of time and possibly make a mistake. Accordingly, he started with the three soldiers. It took him no time at all to conclude that there was little likelihood any of the three was guilty. The same was true of the buffalo hunters. The liquor salesman, out of habit, was very wily about admitting to anything, and Barton couldn't eliminate him from suspicion. His interview lasted for over an hour, and, at the end, Barton decided he needed a break.

"I'm not sure about him," he told the captain, "but I can't believe the soldiers or the hunters were involved."

The captain nodded.

"I'll start with Henry Rogers tomorrow."

Chapter Eighteen

Harold Robertson relaxed in the main salon. The death of Melinda LaFramboise was not common knowledge, so he could not seem aware of that fact. When Delbert Gray came into the main salon, he would approach him as if there were nothing amiss. He wanted to maintain the relationship they had developed, and he would take care to console Gray without betraying himself. Unless Gray, in his sorrow, abandoned his business plans, it was yet possible to travel with him, dispose of him, and assume his identity. He had learned that Gray had liquidated his assets in the East, so it was more than possible that he was carrying a large amount of cash also. Melinda was out of the way, Omaha was many miles downriver, and he had the beginning of a trusting relationship with a wealthy man. He made a silent toast to his good fortune.

The main table was being set for supper, and Robertson sat down with the other cabin passengers. This included the three soldiers who sat next to Robertson and began conversing about their interview experience. Robertson had not heard that the security officer was interviewing passengers. Danny Barton had been clever enough not to reveal any details or even why he was interviewing. His questions had been mostly limited to establishing alibis for the night Melinda was murdered, whereabouts during 1864, and getting permission to search personal effects. But Robertson knew that the soldiers and the hunters had boarded in Omaha, just as he did. He didn't know why Omaha was the focus of Officer Barton's questions, but he deduced that he would probably be questioned also. He began going over his story in his mind.

Gray was standing on the aft hurricane deck, watching features

149

on the river recede in the distance. A sandbar with a coyote on it, a snag jutting up high with ravens sitting in the branches, a small cabin that looked to be abandoned. Gray looked at these things without recognizing them, so deep in his thoughts was he. Although he had told Melinda that he knew a lot about her, he didn't know enough to have any idea who might have killed her. Was she just an unfortunate single woman traveling alone and crossing paths with a person who was bent on doing harm for an unknown reason? Did someone kill her for revenge? Or was it someone from her past; someone who knew she had a secret that could cause him harm and had enough of her trust to kill her in the manner she died? The last scenario seemed more likely.

He had examined her room at Officer Barton's request and was sure that nothing of value was missing. Why did she have to die? How did someone gain entry without breaking the door or the latch? The answers to all these questions evaded him, and he hung his head low, resting his elbows on the railing. Josephine Wainwright walked up behind him at that moment.

"Mr. Gray?"

He turned to see her. "Yes?" he said.

Josephine didn't know what she wanted to say. She had sought him out to satisfy herself that he was not the killer she had believed him to be on the basis of Abraham's pointing him out. But she had not given much thought to how to question him.

"I . . . I heard about Melinda LaFramboise's murder. It is horrible. I'm sorry for you."

"Thank you, young man," he answered. He had seen the little hostler several times before, and he couldn't understand why he would be expressing sympathy. "Were you acquainted with Miss LaFramboise?"

Josephine had one hand on her gun in her jacket pocket as she purposely removed her hat with the other. "Yes, we both grew up in southern Kentucky." She watched his eyes for any sign that she looked familiar as she tightened her grip on her pistol.

Delbert looked closely at the hostler he knew as Joe. Joe looked very feminine to him, but his gentlemanly manners would not allow him a comment or question. "Were you good friends?"

"No. Less than friends." Although Josephine had liked the LaFramboise family, she had not taken a liking to Melinda.

"But you were acquainted with her family?"

"Yes, their farm was thirty miles from ours," Josephine said. She replaced her hat on her head, kept her hand on her gun, and went on. "Have you ever been to Kentucky?"

"Yes, before the war."

"Not since then?" she asked.

"No, and may I ask, what is your interest?"

Josephine decided to lay all her cards out. "My brother was killed by a traitor in 1864 near Russellville, Kentucky, and a friend of mine who was present pointed you out as the killer. He was very sure."

"This friend is a passenger, isn't that right?"

"Yes."

"I am aware of this accusation," Delbert said matter-of-factly. "I don't need to know who he is, but have him take another look at me. He was mistaken."

Josephine was now beginning to have doubts in her own mind about Gray's guilt. And what he said next erased most of those.

"Perhaps you could do me a favor, young . . . man."

"Perhaps," Josephine said.

"I don't know how to get in touch with Miss LaFramboise's family. I would like very much to write to them and explain what I know about what happened to her."

Josephine thought she had never seen a person look so sad as Delbert Gray did at this moment. Whatever animosity she had toward him, and for that matter Melinda LaFramboise, evaporated. She took her hand out of the pocket that held the gun.

"Give me a piece of paper and a pencil, and I'll write the address of her family's farm for you." This he did, and she wrote the address and handed it back to him.

Gray looked at the address, folded the paper into his pocket, and lifted his eyes to the fading evening horizon. A hundred miles back, Melinda had been alive, vital, charming, sensual, and ready to devote herself to him. What had cost her her life? Why did she have to die? What was the secret that she had not shared?

"I believe it's suppertime," he said. "Are you hungry?"

"I'll have to wait and eat with the deck passengers," Josephine said.

"Very well. Thank you for your sympathy . . . and for the address." He turned abruptly to descend the stairway to the main salon. Josephine watched him walk away, feeling an immense sorrow.

Delbert wasn't hungry, but he was determined to carry on with his normal life. He entered the main salon and found a seat next to his new friend, Henry Rogers, at the main table.

"Mr. Gray, nice to see you this evening. Where is your companion?"

"She won't be joining me," Gray answered.

"I see. Perhaps later?"

"I don't think so."

"She is very charming. I'm sure you miss her, ah . . . when she is not with you." Robertson tried to speak of Melinda as if ignorant of her death.

Gray wanted a change of subject. "The *Clinton* has been making good time, I believe."

"Yes," Robertson said. "I think we'll be in Fort Pierre in the next day or so." He dished food onto his plate. "Forgive me for saying so, Delbert, but you seem not yourself today."

"I suppose not," Gray said. He wished he had a close friend to talk to. Although he found Henry Rogers a pleasant dinner companion, their friendship had not developed. If he continued to his objective, however, and if Rogers accepted his invitation to join him across country to Seattle, they would eventually and inevitably become close. "I'd like to confide in you, if you don't mind, Henry," Gray said.

"Please do," Robertson said.

Gray took a deep breath and let it out. "Miss LaFramboise has passed on."

Robertson had to feign surprise, and he did it convincingly. "Oh, my word. What happened?"

Gray didn't think he should reveal more. He said, simply, "She was found dead in her stateroom this morning."

Even a good liar gets ahead of himself sometimes, and this is what happened to Harold Robertson. He anticipated that Gray would tell him that Melinda had been murdered, and he started to give himself away. "Who di— . . . uh . . . how did she die?"

Gray seemed not to notice the slip. "I'd rather not say just now. I want to respect her and protect her memory."

"Yes, of course," Robertson said. "Please let me know if there's anything I can do for you."

"Thank you, Henry. I will."

Robertson put some effort into making small talk while the two men finished their meal. Then Gray excused himself and went outside to be alone while he walked the deck under the stars. The *Clinton* was tied to the shore again as it had been every night since leaving Omaha. The fires were low and the engines were still.

Robertson went to the bar, purchased a drink, and sat at a card table to plan his next move. He must ensure that Delbert Gray remained on track; that he would still begin his journey over the Federal wagon roads; that he would still want the man he knew as Henry Rogers to accompany him.

The following morning, Danny confronted Harold Robertson in the main salon.

"Mr. Rogers, I'd like to talk to you in private as soon as possible."

"It might as well be right now, young man. I have nothing else to do." Robertson remembered his confrontation with the officer in the wee hours one morning. He didn't like him.

"Very well. Follow me, please." Barton climbed the stairs to the Texas deck. He leaned into the pilothouse to signal the captain that he was going to begin another interview, and then he opened the door into the captain's stateroom and waved Robertson in.

"Make yourself comfortable, Mr. Rogers," Danny said, pointing at the bunk. Harold sat down, but he was unable to make himself comfortable, as the bed was higher than a chair, and worse, he couldn't lean back because the wall was too far away. Barton had arranged the room with this in mind. He sat comfortably in the only chair, with a small table in front of him. The captain came in and stood, as he almost always did in the presence of others.

The security officer began the questions. "Mr. Rogers, what did you do during the war?"

"I was an auditor. For the Union. I traveled around the areas of deployment, reviewing payroll and procurement records. I held the rank of major at the conclusion of hostilities."

This was partly true. But he left out the fact that he was also a scout for the Army of Northern Virginia, the Confederacy.

"What did you do in Omaha?"

"I'm now a bank auditor. I was working in the bank. The Missouri River Bank."

"And what is your destination now?"

"I'm on vacation. I thought I would take the steamboat upriver to the end of navigation and then return to St. Louis. I'm also looking for investment opportunities."

"Are you carrying any weapons?"

"Yes, a pocket pistol in my kit. Purely for my own protection. Why are you asking these questions?"

"We've had an incident onboard, and I'm gathering information for the authorities."

"What kind of incident? Surely I am not under suspicion."

Barton didn't answer. "What's the name of your company?"

The last auditor with which Robertson had dealings was Carruthers and Sons. He used that name.

"How can I get in touch with Carruthers and Sons?"

"I would prefer that you not contact them. They're very conservative and old-fashioned."

Barton made a point of writing the name in large script across the piece of paper in front of him. Then he added a question mark. Robertson scowled.

"I consented to a conversation," Robertson said angrily, "but I find that I'm being questioned as if I were a criminal."

Barton remained calm. "This *is* a criminal investigation. I'm gathering information from a number of passengers. I'm sure you want to cooperate."

Robertson glared at the security officer and then looked at the captain to see if he could gain some support from him. One look told him that the captain was not on his side.

"Ask your fool questions, but I warn you, I'll tolerate neither innuendo nor insinuation."

"These are basically the same questions I've asked other passengers. You can answer them or not," Barton said, "and I'll relay that information to the authorities in Fort Pierre. Then they can pursue the investigation as they see fit."

Robertson couldn't think of a retort. He folded his arms across his chest, saying nothing.

"What time did you retire night before last?"

Before Robertson could answer, Steve Allenby and a crewman came into the stateroom. They placed on the table in front of Barton a Colt pocket police revolver, loading paraphernalia for the revolver, a pen knife with a two-inch blade, a massive skinning knife with a wide, thick blade, a letter opener, and a leather wallet containing a photograph of Robertson in a Union Army uniform on one side but no photograph on the other. Robertson exploded.

"This is outrageous! You have had my personal effects searched." He started to stand up, but Allenby pushed him back down where he had been sitting on the edge of the bed. He sat there in a silent rage.

The officer examined each article. The revolver was loaded and capped. He carefully laid it to one side and then picked up the pen knife and opened the blade. He looked into the slot for any trace of blood, but found none. The skinning knife held no interest for him, but the letter opener did. It was only half an inch wide at the widest place and about one-sixteenth of an inch thick. The edges were not particularly sharp, but the point was. Robertson was ignorant of the fact that the doctor in Omaha had examined John Swanson's body and had described the murder weapon as a long thin blade. Robertson didn't believe an ordinary letter opener would attract attention, but Barton thought it was a very significant find. He kept his thoughts to himself.

The officer looked up at Allenby, who was standing by to restrain Robertson again if required.

"Thanks, Steve. This was all you found of interest?"

"Yes."

"Very well, you can go." Allenby and the roustabout left. Barton addressed Robertson. "Again, Mr. Rogers, what time did you retire night before last?"

"Around eleven, as near as I remember."

"You sometimes arise in the middle of the night and walk around. Did you do so on that night?"

"No."

"How long have you known Delbert Gray?"

"I met him on this boat only days ago."

"Did you know he has been identified by a passenger as being involved in a murder and theft of gold some years ago?" Barton asked this question for the shock value, hoping to get a revealing reaction. A muscle on Robertson's face twitched.

"That's ridiculous. He's a fine gentleman." This answer was credible. But Robertson suddenly had the fear that Delbert Gray might be detained and thus ruin his scheme to travel with him. He felt it was important to add, "I'm a good judge of character, and I'll personally vouch for Mr. Gray."

Barton had one more trick to pull, and while Robertson's mind was preoccupied with defending Delbert Gray, he tried it.

"Why did you and Melinda separate after the war?"

Robertson didn't answer immediately. Instead, he looked at Officer Barton with cold eyes, while he rapidly assessed the question. If the officer actually knew anything, he, Robertson, would be in handcuffs at this point. But, he thought, he must have enough information to make him suspicious, to try a line of questioning designed to offend and confound. And if it were actually the case that there was someone onboard who witnessed the murder in Tennessee, that person might realize that the identification of Gray was a mistake and, after reconsideration, identify him, Harold Robertson.

"Young man, I had never met Melinda LaFramboise until I boarded this boat, which I am beginning to regret."

Danny Barton acted surprised and said, "Oh. Hmm." He looked at his notes and then said, "Very well, Mr. Rogers, you may go. I'm going to keep these articles for a while, but you'll get them back as soon as we can clear you." Then he added, "If that turns out to be the case."

Robertson stalked out, slamming the door.

"That man is lying," the captain said as soon as he had gone.

Barton nodded in agreement. "I'm going to question the last two men anyway."

The captain nodded approval.

Robertson had much to think about after he left the stateroom. He wished he had a private stateroom of his own so that he could think in peace. He went instead to the bar, bought a drink, and sat by himself, swirling his drink in the glass.

He and Delbert Gray were nearly the same height and build. It seemed obvious that whoever identified Gray had mistaken him for Robertson. Contributing to the error in identification may have been the fact that Gray was keeping company with Melinda. If someone had been present two years ago when he shot and killed Jonathan Wainwright, who might it have been? There had been a passing noise before the cart came along the trail; perhaps it was a scout or a guide. The con man thought back to all he could remember about that day.

The gold had been loaded into a cart at Jonathan Wainwright's farm in Tennessee. Melinda had told him about the trail that wound through the forest into Kentucky to another farm. He remembered that she had described the Wainwright family to him, but he had not met any of them, other than Jonathan, and wouldn't recognize them. Then it struck him. There were black people in the cart; that was the original reason for the trip, and the gold was an afterthought. He remembered the people slipping away in the near darkness of early morning as he rode up to Jonathan Wainwright and killed him. One of them must have gotten a look at him before they all ran away. Over the two intervening years, the image of Harold Robertson had blurred until now the witness confused him with Gray.

Robertson settled on two possibilities. Wainwright had had an accomplice nearby when he was murdered, or one of the escapees had seen him.

There were several black men working as roustabouts. If one

was a former slave who escaped through Tennessee into Kentucky, he was likely the one who witnessed the killing. The other thing for Robertson to do was to get a look at the passenger and crew roster to see if there was a Wainwright name on it. That might be a family member of the slain Jonathan.

Robertson finished his drink and walked out of the main salon and toward the bow where he could watch the outside work. Delbert Gray saw him walking the outside deck and joined him.

"Did you ever own a slave?" Robertson asked.

"No. My father did when I was young."

"Do you suppose those blacks down there are former slaves?" There were three black men working on the bow, cutting wood for the boilers.

"Two of them are. My guess is that the smaller one was born free or freed when he was young."

"How do you know that?"

"The little roustabout has none of the body posture or demeanor of a slave. In contrast, the big man on the left has still not adopted the behavior of a free man. If he's as old as he looks, he was a slave for fifty years or more," Gray said. "Watch the expression on his face every time a white man walks up to him."

Robertson watched for a few minutes, but was not perceptive enough to see what Gray had explained. "How about the other big one?" he asked.

"I had a conversation with him," Gray said. "His name is Abraham. He told me that he and his wife escaped from a brutal master two years ago. They're headed for Montana." Gray turned to Robertson. "Did you ever own a slave?"

Robertson's heart was pounding. This man named Abraham was, without doubt, the man who had witnessed the killing of Jonathan Wainwright. He must be dealt with at the earliest opportunity. He suddenly remembered Gray's question and answered blankly, "No." But his mind was already planning another murder.

Chapter Nineteen

Did you finish the interviews?" Josephine asked.

"Yes," Danny replied.

"What did you find out?"

"Not much," he said. He didn't want to reveal to Josephine that he thought he knew who the murderer was, for fear that she would try to take action on her own. But he couldn't bring himself to lie to her either. "There is one person who stands out. Because of the way I questioned him, I'm thinking he'll try to find a way to get away from the *Clinton* as soon as he can."

"There's nothing but wilderness. Where could he go?"

"We have reports that there are three steamers upriver. He might try to get on one of those or on a flatboat. When we get to Fort Pierre, we'll watch him closely."

"What if he gets off? How can you stop him?"

"He won't get away from me."

"Have you eaten supper?" she asked.

"No, I missed it."

"Come on," she invited. "You can eat with me and the other deck passengers. We'll be right on time."

They walked into the main salon, filled their plates, and sat down.

"When this is over, what will you do, Jo?" he asked.

"I could go back home to Kentucky, I suppose," she replied, watching his face. "What about you?"

"I haven't had time to give it much thought. This is as far west as I've ever been. I want to see the Rocky Mountains. The captain told me we might get close enough to see them in the distance."

"Do you think you'll stay out here?"

"This is lonely country. I wouldn't want to try to make it on my own," he said.

"Nor would I," she said.

"That sounds to me like you've given some thought to exploring the West."

"Yes, I have. California appeals to me."

"Gold?"

"No," she said. "Farming. I've heard fantastic stories of how things grow in California."

Barton reached across the table and took one of her hands in his. "Promise me that no matter what happens with this murderer, you won't leave suddenly without talking over your future plans with me."

"We could talk right now," she said.

"Josephine, I"—he wasn't prepared to say what he wanted to say and what he hoped she wanted to hear—"I have so much on my mind, I can't think clearly. Just promise me you won't leave suddenly."

"I promise," she said, hiding her disappointment.

When they had finished their meal, Danny went up to the pilothouse and Josephine went to the corral to tend to the livestock. It was now dark, and the *Clinton* was feeling her way along the banks of the river for a place to spend the night.

Charles Felden had a leadsman on the bow and all the side lanterns lit as he made his way slowly upriver. There was enough depth near the eastern shore, but the bank was mostly mud. Then the leadsman called out depth less than four feet, and Felden rang for stop. The channel had apparently swung away from the bank. The *Clinton* coasted to a stop just as her bow touched the bottom. Then the current pulled her back, and Felden rang for slow ahead and put the wheel hard over to larboard. Before the *Clinton* could respond to the rudders, Felden rang for more speed and then slowly brought the rudders amidships as the *Clinton* made her ponderous maneuver in the black of night on a river wilderness.

The bank disappeared and the side lanterns lit only the black swirling water of the river. The leadsman found nine feet of water. Felden called the mate to the pilothouse and in minutes David Erickson was by his side.

"This could go on all night, Mr. Erickson," Felden said. "I'm going to work my way back over to the bank, and as soon as we get clear of the channel, I'll stop the engines. Drop two anchors for me. We'll lay at anchor out of the channel until light."

Erickson turned to his task without discussion. On the bow he formed two anchor crews, and they began laying out the chain and shackling the anchors. "As soon as they dig in, set a tattletale on a half-inch line and flag the cleat so each watch can check it." The crew knew what to do. "Jimbo," Erickson said. "When the anchors are set, get four men and take the yawl to the shore so we'll know where we are on the river. The rest of you men fill all the lamps and keep them lit until dawn."

Abraham had been helping Josephine again when the second mate organized the anchoring crews. Josephine was not needed, but as soon as she finished her tasks, she went to observe the anchoring crew at work. Barton also watched the action, but from the hurricane deck in front of the pilothouse.

The anchors were considered to be too heavy for one man to lift, but Abraham was able to carry one by himself to the bow. Then he held it while another roustabout shackled the chain to it, and when that was done, he stepped up onto the gunwale. When the leadsman called five feet, Felden rang the engine to stop, and the *Clinton* suspended her battle with the current. On signal, Abraham heaved the anchor over. Four men on the starboard bow accomplished the same thing, and the chains rattled over the gunwale until the ends were stopped. The bow of the *Clinton* dipped slightly as its motion in the current was arrested, and a bow wave developed. Two men brought a small anchor forward and dropped it over the bow with a lot of slack. The current carried the anchor and the line under the bow. They cleated the line off and tied a colored rag to the cleat. Without reference to the shore, the *Clinton* had the appearance of being towed by the two chains, her bow cutting the water at the speed of the current.

Barton returned to the pilothouse. Felden had already left to get as much sleep as possible, and Erickson, the second mate, was on duty.

"What's a tattletale?" the security officer asked the second mate.

"An anchor on a slack line. If the anchor rode goes taut, we'll know we're moving over the bottom."

"Then what?"

"Set another anchor or two, wake the pilot, make sure there's adequate steam to hold station."

Jimbo came into the pilothouse at that time. "The eastern shore is fifty yards off and the western shore is at least two hundred. You're in five and a half feet, and that holds steady downstream for a hundred yards. We didn't go any farther. The channel is a hundred feet west."

"All right, Jimbo. Make sure the tattletale is checked every ten minutes all night." Erickson made notes in the log, and Jimbo left.

"Mr. Erickson, I'm going to stay up until the main salon beds down, and then I've got an armed guard outside all night."

"All right, Danny. It should be a quiet night."

Barton left the pilothouse. He circled the staterooms and then descended to the cabin deck. He opened the door into the main salon. There were several card games in progress. A woman was playing the piano while several women stood by appreciatively, and the bartender was polishing the bar while conversing with several gentlemen. Barton noted that Henry Rogers and Delbert Gray were seated together. He didn't know how two men who looked alike could be so different. He watched for a minute and then left to walk the main deck and the cargo bay. He wanted to give Abraham another opportunity to identify Jonathan Wainwright's killer.

"What are your plans now, Delbert?" Robertson asked his new friend.

"I want to see Melinda given a proper funeral."

"Of course. And please count on me to assist you in any way I can."

"I appreciate that, Henry," Gray said.

"And then what?" Robertson asked.

"I've considered going back to Kentucky to meet her family. I've even written them a letter describing our relationship and the circumstances of her death, but I hesitate to impose myself on them until I receive a reply, so since my mailing address is in Seattle, it's best if I continue with my original plans."

"She let you know of her family and their whereabouts?" Robertson was a little surprised at this. Melinda had always wanted to distance herself from her origins when Robertson knew her.

"Actually, no. I met someone onboard who had known Melinda and gave me her family's address."

"What an unusual coincidence. Who might that have been?"

"The hostler, Joe."

It was like an icicle in Robertson's chest. Another person from his past. But it was also another piece of the puzzle in place. The hostler may have been driving the cart and ran with the slaves when he approached to shoot Jonathan Wainwright. Robertson changed the subject. "Are you still desiring to travel with someone when you leave the river?" he asked.

"Yes, of course. Are you still willing to accompany me?"

"Yes, it fits nicely with my plans." This was an understatement. His escape to the Northwest depended on Delbert Gray. Everything was falling into place except that Officer Barton might let the black man or the hostler have another shot at identifying him. Robertson's habits of avoiding places where people on the boat congregate, of sitting in the shadows of a corner, of wearing his hat even when indoors, were all designed to make his countenance less memorable. His strategy to minimize his visibility as a constant rule had so far paid off, and he wanted it to continue. And if he couldn't avoid the black man and the hostler, he could render them ineffective. He now had *two* murders to plan, but his pistol was still in the possession of the young security officer.

"I'm somewhat uneasy, Delbert," Robertson told his new friend.

"It's been an unsettling and unhappy few days," Gray granted.

"Yes. I'm given to understand it is likely that there is a murderer aboard."

"Yes. There is no doubt."

"Although I am proficient with most weapons, I rarely travel with one. The war is over, and I prefer to tell myself that violence is behind us, even when that is not the case."

"You have no sidearm?"

"No, and I feel very foolish. It seems I worry less about my own safety than the safety of others who may look to me for assistance. When the Indians attacked us several days ago, I was powerless to help defend the boat."

"I can offer you my Colt Navy revolver, if that would ease your mind."

"Will that deprive you of a weapon?"

"Hardly. I'm well armed for wilderness travel."

"In that case, I would be very grateful."

"I'm ready to retire for the night, Henry. Come with me to my berth, and I'll give you the pistol and the paraphernalia."

A short time later, Delbert Gray was sound asleep in his berth, and Harold Robertson was prowling the *Clinton* with a loaded revolver and murder on his mind. He had learned that Abraham was staying in a stateroom, although he worked on the main deck as part of the ordinary crew. The walkway on the main deck was only two feet wide and there was no railing, just a few handholds along the wall. This walkway was only for the crew to use when docking, loading through the side doors, working across sandbars, or doing maintenance on the buckets. The stairway up to the cabin deck was set into a recess in the wall of the main deck to avoid blocking the narrow walkway. This feature left it in the shadows, even when the side lamps were lit. A good place for an ambush.

"Abraham, I need you to take another look at the man you said killed Jonathan Wainwright."

"Sho', Mr. Barton. But I don't have no doubts about it."

"I believe you, Abraham, but the man you pointed out was somewhere else at the time, and he says he can prove it," Danny said.

"I ain't no liar."

The officer was at an impasse. He didn't know what to do now, but he didn't want to insult Abraham.

Abraham was also at an impasse. He started to feel a sense of betrayal that he had not felt since becoming free. His thoughts went back ten years.

"Abraham, this horse is lame. I have told you not to ride him, he is for plowing only. Did you ride him in spite of my wishes?"

"No, sir. I plowed the south field like you asked and he done good. I didn't ride him."

Abraham looked at Cordell Junior for help. Cordell had done the riding, and Abraham had objected, but Cordell had ignored him, riding fast across the field and jumping ditches; he brought the horse back lame.

"Abraham, Cordell has told me that it was you who rode the horse."

"Ah ain't no liar, Mister Billings." He could see the smirk on Cordell Junior's face.

Josephine stepped in. She took one of Abraham's hands in her own and held it for a minute before she spoke. "We both believe you, Abraham. And if you don't want to do this, that's it. This is important, but keeping you as a friend is even more important." She didn't release his hand, but looked up into his eyes.

"I'm a free man, Miss Jo. I'm goin' to be with Elizabeth and my baby now. If you still want, I'll look at that man again tomorrow for you." He met Danny's gaze without blinking. Josephine let go of his hand, and he left them in the cargo bay to climb to the Texas deck.

Josephine and Danny went to the bow to watch the river flow against the bow and split into two streams around the *Clinton*. The water was lazy this close to the shore and the air was still and heavy under a cloudy sky, and so the evening was quiet except for an occasional owl. Josephine had had many conversations with slaves and former slaves and could understand things about which Danny had no concept.

"Neither of us can have any idea of the things he has had to endure to get to this point," she said. "He'll help us in the morning."

"Sure. I just wanted him to trust me."

"He will. . . . What was that?" They both heard a splash from the river side of the steamer. Danny turned and ran down the side of the main deck, trying to see what could have made the sound.

In the dim light of the side lamps he could see a man's arm waving from the river, fifty feet behind the stern wheel. He dropped his jacket and dove into the river to find the arm that he was sure belonged to Abraham. Harold Robertson quietly ascended the stairway to the cabin deck as Josephine ran by, oblivious to him.

Abraham had been walking the narrow walkway, brooding over the conversation with the young officer and was completely surprised by Robertson's big boot that kicked him over the side into the dark water of the Missouri River. Now, just as two weeks ago, he was again in water shallow enough to let him keep his mouth above water but not shallow enough to let him stand his ground against the current. His fear was overwhelming. He kept trying to dig his bare feet into the bottom, but when he would plant them, the current would sweep him back, his head would go under, and he would struggle to get his feet underneath himself again so that he could open his mouth for a breath. Half the time he could get a quick breath, and half the time he swallowed some of the river. He was losing strength, unable to get enough air to sustain the exertion.

When Danny entered the water, Josephine turned and ran up the stairs, almost bowling Robertson over. He recovered quickly.

"What is it, son? What's the matter?" He feigned ignorance.

"Man overboard. Get out of my way."

Robertson missed his chance to eliminate the boy. He could have thrown the hostler into the water also, but the boy was desperate to get to the pilothouse and wriggled past him. As Joe ran up the stairs to the Texas deck, he could have shot him with his newly acquired pistol, but the mate appeared at the head of the stairway just as he put his hand on the butt of the Navy Colt. He put his hand back at his side, and to continue his charade, followed the boy up the stairs, as if to help.

Josephine shouted to Steve Allenby as she ascended the stairs. "Abraham fell over and Danny jumped in after him!"

Allenby ran back to the pilothouse and blew the whistle until the second mate appeared in the doorway of his stateroom. "Man overboard, Erickson! Take over the watch, I'm getting a crew into the yawl!"

David Erickson went to the pilothouse, pushing his nightshirt into his pants as he walked. When he got there he began blowing a short blast every fifteen seconds. Roustabouts came running up the stairs to the Texas deck where the yawl was stored under the davits, and in minutes the yawl was in the water with lanterns, four oarsmen, a coxswain in the stern, and Allenby as a lookout in the bow.

Josephine went to the aft hurricane deck where she could try to see what was happening downstream. There was nothing to see until the yawl went by with its lanterns alight, but soon it was also out of sight. Because of the incessant steam whistle at fifteen-second intervals, there were twenty or more passengers on the hurricane deck also. They all pointed at the yawl as it made its way downriver and chatted excitedly, but after a few minutes, they grew bored and began conversing among themselves. When it started to rain, they turned, one by one, and went back down to the main cabin. Soon, Josephine was alone on the hurricane deck. That is, she thought she was alone. Robertson was in the bathhouse, the last room in the row of staterooms. He quietly opened the door and looked all around the hurricane deck. It was deserted except for Weedeater on the far side of the staterooms, doing his patrol duty.

Harold started timing the whistle. He recited a verse to himself in time, and when he could predict the exact moment of the short blast, he raised the pistol, aimed at the hostler's back, and as the whistle blew, he pulled the trigger. Josephine let out a short cry that was lost in the echo of the whistle and pitched over the end of the hurricane deck.

The *Barnard Clinton* was in turmoil. Through the middle of the night the whistle sounded every fifteen seconds, making it impossible for anyone to sleep. Somewhere on the Missouri River two men were either drowned or fighting for their lives. There was also a yawl with six men aboard, groping through the darkness and the strengthening rain, trying to find the lost two.

Felden had just laid down when the excitement began. Now he was in the pilothouse with Captain Culpepper and second mate David Erickson. In the main salon, everyone was awake and trying to ignore the fifteen-second blasts on the whistle. Some men stuffed cotton in their ears.

In the excitement, no one noticed that the tattletale anchor was now ahead of the *Clinton*. It wasn't until Erickson went down to check on the wood supply that it was realized that the *Clinton* was dragging its anchors. It was not known if the Clinton had immediately dragged the anchors or if it had slowly backed down on the tattletale, since no landmarks on the shore were visible. He ordered the tattletale anchor retrieved and reset so that he could judge the speed that the steamer was losing ground. He knew from experience that an anchor often took a few hundred yards to hook up solidly, and he hoped that was the case with the two big anchors that were ahead of the *Clinton*. There were no more anchors this heavy aboard the *Clinton,* so to reset the anchors would entail starting the engines and pulling ahead until the anchors could be winched off the bottom and then set again. The decision not to start the engines would turn out to be critical to the life of a young woman.

It was after one in the morning when the yawl found its way back to the *Clinton* in a heavy rain. The men were exhausted from their battle with the current. It took them only half an hour to get five miles down the river, but it had taken them two and a half hours to make their way back. They couldn't see the banks of the river, so they meandered from bank to bank, sometimes not able to determine whether they were going upstream or downstream. Only the sound of the *Clinton*'s whistle had saved them from being lost also, and this was frequently confusing as they negotiated the twists in the river.

Allenby wearily climbed up to the pilothouse to make his sad report.

"Captain, I fear those men are lost."

"Very well, Mr. Allenby. We'll keep the whistle blowing, reduce it to once every two minutes."

"Do we know who the other man was?" Allenby asked.

"Yes. It was the big black man Abraham, whose wife just had the baby. I've let her know that her husband fell off the boat and that a crew in the yawl was looking for him."

"Poor Danny," Allenby said, shaking his head sadly. "I'm going to miss that kid."

"Get some rest, Mr. Allenby," the captain said. "We'll send the yawl out again at first light."

Chapter Twenty

Danny Barton was not an excellent swimmer and was encumbered by his boots, but he was determined to find Abraham. He was half swimming and half running on the river bottom, heading downstream with his head swiveling in all directions. The dim lights of the *Clinton* were rapidly fading into the distance behind him.

Abraham coughed violently and then swallowed yet more water. Danny heard the cough and worked his way in that direction. Because of his swimming efforts, he had overtaken Abraham but was fifty feet to the west, toward the deeper channel. Abraham had managed to work his way to the east, where the water was less than five feet deep, but in his weakened state, he was in as much trouble as he had been in the deeper water.

Danny stopped for a moment, realizing that swimming downstream would take him past Abraham. Floating with the current in the darkness, he had no sense of direction unless he put his feet on the bottom, which he could do only some of the time. The clouds blacked out the stars, Danny was weightless, there was no sound or smell, and all he could feel was the cool water around him. He wanted to turn three hundred and sixty degrees and tried, but he was completely without any means to orient himself. He only estimated that he was turning. He realized that saving himself was going to be as difficult as saving Abraham. Then he heard Abraham take a rasping gasp just a few feet away.

"Abraham, I'm here. Say something!"

Abraham could make only unintelligible sounds, but that was enough. Barton found him.

Abraham had exhausted his adrenaline and his strength. He couldn't even hang on to Danny's arm; the young officer had to hold him while he worked his way to what he hoped was the shore. The relentless current continued taking them downstream, but eventually they were in less than three feet of water and could resist the water's flow. Barton estimated that they were more than two miles downstream from the *Clinton,* whose lights were no longer visible.

The men were too tired to stand, but the water was too deep for them to crawl. They were both on their knees, heads just above the water's surface, trying to regain strength. Abraham was the first to his feet, and he helped Danny stand. Then they had to try to determine the way to the nearest shore. Abraham thought he knew, and he found words for the first time since being pushed off the boat.

"This way, Mr. Barton."

He followed without questioning. They slogged through the water, and it became shallower as they struggled across the current. They got to a dry sandbar and collapsed from their exertion. When they were very still, the distant sound of the steam whistle came to them, but they were far too tired to make their way upstream. Oblivious to the rain, they both went unconscious from exhaustion and relief, and minutes later the yawl, with lanterns aglow, passed them in the rain.

Their sleep was ended when the rising river began washing over the sandbar where they were lying. They got on their hands and knees and found each other.

"We'll have to find higher ground, Abraham," Danny said, voicing the obvious. It was still pitch black in all directions.

"Yes, sir," Abraham said. "Follow me."

They got to their feet and began walking, but their first twenty steps put them into deeper water. Danny was following Abraham with his hand on the black man's back and he stopped.

"Are you sure this is the right direction?" he asked.

Abraham replied, "I done a lot of runnin' in the dark." He grabbed Danny's hand and continued in the direction he had been walking.

Five minutes later they ran into brush that was in six inches of water. They fought their way through the brush until they encountered a steep slope of grass. Here they lay down again to gather their strength for a few minutes, and then they started walking upstream along the side of the grassy hill. Frequently they would encounter brushy areas, and they would climb the hill to get around these. The hillside was slick with rain, and they fell and slid down often, but they always managed to find each other again and continue.

When they had been walking for about an hour, the rain let up some. Below them, five hundred yards out in the river, they saw the lights of the yawl, fighting its way upstream. They shouted as loudly as they could, but the yawl continued its slow progress up-river. The oarsmen in the yawl were working so hard, they couldn't hear the shouts of Abraham and Danny, over a quarter mile away.

Barton thought about plunging down the banks and into the water, but he realized he would be far too late to swim out to the yawl. They were better off to stay on the hill and continue walking toward the sound of the *Clinton*'s whistle. Abraham reached the same conclusion, and they resumed their trek, Danny's hand on Abraham's back.

Elizabeth was told by the captain that the yawl had returned without finding the missing men, but it would start again at first light. She thanked the captain and closed the door of the stateroom. She feared that she would never see her husband again. Her baby boy sensed her distress and refused to nurse, crying and fussing. She arose, wrapped the infant in a blanket, and went out onto the hurricane deck. She walked to the aft end of the deck where his cries would be less likely to disturb other stateroom passengers. She sang a song to comfort herself and the restless child.

Don't cry little baby,
You're in momma's arms.
Don't cry little baby,
Daddy's coming home.

Don't cry little baby,
Trouble's on the run.
Don't cry little baby,
Morning light will come.

And when the morning light came, the infant boy was asleep in her arms as she stood on the aft hurricane deck to watch the yawl again head downstream with a crew of eight this time.

Delbert Gray climbed to the hurricane deck to watch the sunrise. He had slept poorly since Melinda's death. He reached the top of the stairs and walked slowly toward the aft end of the deck, realizing as he walked that there was someone already there. It wasn't so much that he was afraid of disturbing someone else's reverie as that he wanted to be by himself, but before he could retreat, the person turned at the sound of his footsteps. It was a black woman holding a baby. He had seen her infrequently onboard the *Clinton*, but he had not met or spoken to her.

"I didn't mean to disturb you," he apologized.

Elizabeth looked the man over, but she said nothing and turned back to watch the yawl disappear in the dim light of early morning.

Gray stood for a long time, also watching the yawl and strangely comfortable in the black woman's presence. He had no way of knowing that the two of them had something in common—grieving for a lost loved one.

"Do you know where they are going?" he asked.

Elizabeth answered without turning. "They goin' to look for my husbin' and Mr. Barton."

"What happened?"

Elizabeth turned now to see Gray. "Abraham fell overboard, and Mr. Barton jumped in to fetch him."

"That was last night." Gray, like others, had been disturbed by the whistle all night. It was still blowing.

"They look for three hours last night. They tryin' again this mornin'."

"I'm sure they'll have success once the sun comes up." His brow furrowed because he noticed as he said this that there were little patches of fog forming along the river. That certainly wouldn't help, he thought.

"Abraham, he still alive. He somewhere on the river."

"Is your baby a boy?" Gray asked, trying to change the subject.

"Yes." She lifted a corner of the blanket that covered his face. It was then that Gray looked down into the wheel to see the motionless form of Josephine Wainwright, partly folded across one of the buckets of the stern wheel. Elizabeth saw also and let out a little cry.

"Stay here!" he said and ran toward the pilothouse.

"Mr. Felden, we're dragging again," Erickson said.

"We've got enough light now to stay out of trouble. Get a crew on the anchors and we'll get under way."

"All right," Erickson said.

"Once the anchors are up, I'll turn the *Clinton* around and follow the yawl downriver. We can see more from the hurricane deck, and if those men are above water, we'll find them."

Erickson left the pilothouse and nearly ran into Delbert Gray at the door.

"Captain! There's a body in the paddles!"

Felden shouted to Erickson, "Wait!"

Erickson returned to the pilothouse door. "Did I hear correctly?"

"Yes. Get to the engine room and tell the engineer to keep the brake locked. Then get a crew and pin the wheel."

The engineer had put the brakes on the wheel to keep it from spinning all night in the current, putting unnecessary wear on the pitman arms, bearings, and pistons. This and the reluctance of Erickson to pull the anchors in the darkness had kept Josephine's body in position at the top of the wheel.

Gray and the captain ran to the aft end of the hurricane deck to see for themselves, but once there they could only look helplessly at the motionless form of Josephine. Gray started to climb down to where Josephine lay.

"No!" the captain ordered. "We'll have to wait until the wheel is pinned."

They dared not put any weight on the wheel for fear that that weight, combined with Josephine's, would overcome the brake and let the wheel turn, shredding her body against the stern of the *Clinton*. They could walk to one side, though, and watch as the crew inserted a pin through the hub of the wheel to lock it in place. They looked up and signaled the captain that the task was done.

Gray jumped down to the wheel and lifted Josephine in his arms. Two men climbed up over the pitman arm, and he handed her body to them. They passed her down to two more men on the walkway.

"Up here!" the captain shouted to them. "Up here! Bring her up here!"

They ascended the stairway to the cabin deck and then the stairway to the Texas deck. Elizabeth knew what the captain wanted to do and opened her door to her stateroom. She laid her baby in his makeshift crib and threw back the covers on her bed. To a man, the crew believed that Josephine was dead, but Elizabeth knew she was still alive.

"She be alive, Cap'n," she said.

"I hoped that was the case. Can you tend to her, Elizabeth?"

"Ain't nobody else can. I gon' need a man to fetch fo' me."

"He'll be right here. Report to me as soon as you know anything."

"Yes, sir," she replied. The captain left to tend to his vessel. Elizabeth began removing Josephine's clothes. She was curious about a heavy lump in the pocket of Josephine's coat and set the coat aside as she began her examination.

The sun was just about to come over the eastern horizon and patchy fog was forming along the river. In the pilothouse Felden was again preparing to move the *Clinton*. Erickson had directed the crew to remove the pin on the wheel and was now attaching rope to the anchor chains so that the crew could use the capstans, powered by the doctor engine, to lift them off the bottom.

Felden rang for slow ahead, and the wheel that would have snuffed out whatever remained of Josephine's life began churning the brown water. He discontinued blowing the steam whistle. Five minutes later the anchors were on the foredeck, and the *Clinton* began a slow turn into the main channel to follow the yawl. Almost every available man was on the hurricane deck to watch both sides of the river for any sign of Abraham and Danny.

Captain Culpepper had his binoculars to his eyes and examined the eastern shore, in spite of the sun that washed out the image. He worked the glasses back and forth, taking advantage of the changing angles to ensure that he would see every inch. He looked in the water, along the shore, into the wetlands, and atop the bluffs. The patches of fog were consolidating over the river in advance of the rising sun.

Shortly they found the yawl, still heading downstream, without success. The yawl, realizing that the big boat was able to see more, pulled alongside and tied off. They hoped they would be needed for rescue, so they left the yawl in the water for the time being.

Danny was devastated. The *Clinton* had come around a bend while he and Abraham were fighting their way through head-high brush and gone past while they struggled to get out into the open. The two men watched disconsolately as the boat sped downstream.

"They'll be going much slower on the way back upstream, Abraham. Then they'll see us," said the young officer. "And if they don't, we're only a day or two from Fort Pierre on foot. We're not going to die out here."

Abraham had seen many men separated from their wives in the fields, only to find out later that the wife had been sold and would never be seen again. Mothers were separated from children, brothers from sisters, and wives from husbands. It was the prospect of this that had motivated Abraham and Elizabeth to risk their lives to escape. "I don't want Fort Pierre," he said firmly. "I want Elizabeth, and she be there on that boat."

Danny faced Abraham squarely. "You stick with me, Abraham, and I'll make sure Elizabeth gets you back. I promise."

"Mr. Barton, I b'lieve you." Then he grinned. "You stick with me and I'll make sure Miss Jo gets you back."

"I haven't asked you, Abraham. How did you come to fall off the *Clinton*?"

"I was kicked, Mr. Barton."

Danny swore. "Did you see who did it?"

"No, sir," Abraham said. "I jes' felt a big boot."

They turned to the task of finding a spot where the lookouts on the *Clinton* could not miss them. Danny found a point above the river that had no brush on it, only foot-high grass. "How about right here, Abraham?"

"No, sir," Abraham answered. "Time that boat gets here, the sun be behind us."

"You're right," he said, turning to squint at the sun.

"Let's us go 'round this bend and get on that hill yonder."

"We'll have to get across the hollow before they come back or we'll be missed again."

"Let's get on our hosses then," Abraham said. They both began to trot down a long slope to a swampy hollow, filled with fog, that led to the desired hillside position.

"Mr. Felden, I see no point in going any farther downriver. Let's turn and try to fetch up Fort Pierre this afternoon."

"Very well," Felden said. He could sense how disappointed the captain was, and he was equally upset. Danny and Abraham were surely drowned, and there was nothing more to be done.

Felden picked a wide part of the river to make a slow turn. The swollen river was less of a problem to navigate than it had been, but the fog was persistent.

"I'll go slowly for a few miles, and we'll have one more chance to find them," he told the captain. Captain Culpepper started to tell him it would be better to make faster time before the fog made progress dangerous, but he didn't have the heart. It would do little harm to hold the speed down for three or four miles, and in the meantime, the fog might burn off.

Felden completed the turn and began working along the western bank. He had the *Clinton* at two-thirds, which, with the current in opposition, held them to about two miles per hour. In an hour and a half they were almost back upriver as far as their night's anchorage, but on the far side. Felden sent Allenby down to haul the yawl onboard as he rang for full speed. The captain put his binoculars to his eyes, recognized the spot where they had spent the night, and knew that the men would not be found farther upriver.

The captain reluctantly set his binoculars down and looked downriver one last time. This was the final resting place of two good men, he thought to himself. Felden began a maneuver to avoid a snag that appeared as a patch of fog lifted. He rang for slow ahead and let the current take him down a hundred yards and then rang for full speed again with the wheel hard over.

The high spot that Abraham had selected overlooked the previous night's anchorage. Each man took off his shirt and fastened it to a long stick. They could hear the *Clinton*'s engines and see the stacks, but the fog cloaked its approach. They stood ready to swing the sticks and shout as the sound of the engines grew nearer. Then the Clinton came out of the fog, but it was on the far side. They didn't bother shouting over the distance, but they waved furiously until the Clinton disappeared into the fog again. They got one more glimpse of her rounding a bend far upriver, and then they were alone.

Elizabeth examined the supine Josephine from head toe. Occasionally she would mumble "Mmm-hmm" to herself. A man opened the door and looked in.

"Get yoself in here and help me turn this girl over," Elizabeth commanded the roustabout who had been sent to help her.

He protested. "She's nekkid!"

"She ain' gonna care, fool. Get in here!"

Josephine's back was crusted with dried blood and there was a hole high on her right shoulder. Elizabeth carefully washed the blood off and looked at the hole. Then she looked at the big, awkward roustabout.

"You can step back now. I'll do the lookin' and you do the waitin'!" she said sternly. The roustabout complied.

A .36 caliber ball with a normal powder charge barely penetrates a half-inch board. Josephine's shoulder was broken, but the ball had gone no farther. Elizabeth was able to remove the ball using one finger and the blade of a knife. Then she carefully picked out the shards of fabric that the ball had picked up going through Josephine's clothes. The wound began bleeding, and she wrapped a dressing tightly against it. She decided that was as much as she could do. She left Josephine lying on her stomach and pulled the bed covers over her.

"Now take all this water away and bring me some more," she ordered the roustabout. When she had done as much as possible for Josephine, she picked up Josephine's jacket and felt in the inside pocket. What she found was the pistol that Josephine had been carrying for weeks.

Elizabeth was smart. In her care was a young woman who had been shot, but not killed. To her, that meant that she was not only responsible for medical care but for the woman's defense (and hers). She had never held a gun in her hand, but she had seen men shoot a variety of guns, and it was easy for her to learn how the gun worked. When she was satisfied that she could shoot it, she slipped it into the pocket of her dress.

When the roustabout had replenished the water, Elizabeth told him, "I'm goin' to talk to the cap'n. You fetch me if she does anything."

"Yeah, all right."

"You can say 'Yes, ma'am,' can't you?" she asked.

"Yes, ma'am," he answered.

Elizabeth picked up her baby and walked out to find the captain.

In the pilothouse there was no conversation. Felden and the captain were each silently mourning the loss of the two men. They both liked Danny Barton, and all the officers had become familiar with Abraham and Elizabeth because of their presence on the Texas deck and considered Abraham a friend also.

"Cap'n?" Elizabeth said, as she peeked into the pilothouse through the open door.

"Come in, Mrs. Jackson," the captain said.

Elizabeth walked in, looking around at the interior of the pilothouse, a place she had never been before.

"Mrs. Jackson, I regret to tell you that we have abandoned our efforts to find your husband and Mr. Barton. I am very sorry."

"Abraham still be alive, Cap'n," she said.

"What makes you say that?" the captain asked.

"I jes' know. He's alive."

The captain doubted it, but he wouldn't say so. "If he is, he'll be found, Elizabeth. We'll all pray that you are right."

"Thank you, Cap'n."

"How is the girl?"

"She still alive. She been shot in the back. An' I s'pose when she fell on the paddles she done broke some ribs. She lost blood, an' she hit her head, so she ain't woke up. But she breathin'."

The captain had suspected that Josephine had been shot, but shot in the back seemed worse.

"Thank you, Mrs. Jackson. Your only duties for now will be taking care of Miss Wainwright," the captain told her.

"She be needin' me, for sure."

"Let me know when Miss Wainwright can speak and answer questions."

"Yes, Cap'n. I'm goin' back to take her care now."

"Very well."

Harold Robertson had climbed into his berth in the early morning as soon as the whistle stopped blowing. He was one of the few men who had not been on the hurricane deck watching for the missing men. He wanted to get some sleep, and he definitely wasn't going to help find the two men who had become such a problem for him. He was unaware of the finding of Josephine. He had assumed she had fallen into the river.

He wakened and pulled the curtain aside on the little window in his berth. The sun was getting high, the fog had burned off, and the *Clinton* was pulling steadily upriver. He dressed without opening the curtain and stepped out into the main salon.

The main salon was empty except for a few men sleeping on the floor. It had been a long night on the *Clinton,* and everyone was catching up on their sleep. Robertson went to the main table where he found some food that was left over from breakfast. He stretched and helped himself to a biscuit and ham. Things were looking good for him, he decided.

Chapter Twenty-one

As the *Clinton* disappeared upriver, Danny and Abraham sat down on the hillside and hung their heads, but only for a minute. They stood up and looked all around. There was no sign of a human as far as they could see from the top of this bluff overlooking the Missouri River.

"I reckon we'll be walking to Fort Pierre, Abraham." He looked at Abraham and then noticed for the first time that he was barefoot. "You don't have any boots." He was concerned that Abraham would not be able to walk any great distance.

"No, sir. Miss Josephine done give me some boots two years ago when she take me north. I still got 'em, but I don't like to wear 'em without no good reason."

"Fort Pierre is about twenty-five miles from here."

"We be there tomorrow, Mistah Bahton." Abraham started walking in long strides.

"We'll have to get across the river, Abraham."

"Mebbe so, but for now, let's us stay over here. This high ground is better than the swamp on that side yonder."

"All right." Danny matched Abraham stride for stride.

He took inventory. Abraham had a shirt, a pair of pants, and a belt knife. He himself had a pair of pants, a shirt, a vest, a pair of boots, and his revolver. The cartridges and caps had been in his coat that he left on the *Clinton* when he jumped into the river. The cartridges in his revolver were wet, making the weapon useless. Additionally, although it was presently without value, and he had not thought of it, he had a month's salary in a pocket of his pants.

The young officer checked his shadow frequently, and, when it began to get longer, he knew it was after midday. He had studied the maps of the river, but not with an eye to walking it. He tried to remember the major features, such as islands and inflows. As near as he could calculate, they had covered thirteen miles. That left approximately twelve, but he knew they were both traveling slower now than they had in the early morning. If they could maintain the pace, and if they could find a way across the river, they might get to Fort Pierre before total darkness.

Several times they crossed little creeks that flowed into the Missouri River. They drank their fill at these cool creeks, and that helped fill their empty stomachs, but it didn't provide nourishment that they were beginning to need. They would start walking again after the briefest of rests. Danny was anxious to get back to Josephine, to resume his job of finding a killer and protecting her and his other friends. He didn't want to get back just in time to see the *Clinton* disappear around a bend upriver from Fort Pierre. Abraham wanted to get back to his wife and baby boy, fearing that any separation was likely to become permanent, however illogical that fear may have been.

Danny knew that the *Clinton* needed wood. If there were a woodhawk between where he and Abraham were and Fort Pierre, he felt sure the captain would stop. That would delay them for perhaps an hour. He also remembered that the captain was waiting for an answer to his telegram concerning the murder of John Swanson and wanted to inquire about the military record of Henry Rogers. He would be in Fort Pierre long enough to secure that information. That would give them a few more hours.

There were other glimmers of hope. Another steamer might come their way and stop for them, if they could get the steamer's attention. Or they might come to a farm or ranch and borrow horses that would let them cover ground faster. But Danny knew these thoughts were more likely just vain wishes. The reality was that the *Clinton* was most likely already at the banks in Fort Pierre and would soon be under way again. They walked on.

It was the middle of the afternoon when the two men topped a hill and saw below a small cabin and a cultivated field. The cabin was situated near a creek that was timbered. Near the river were stacks of cut wood. The *Clinton* might have stopped here for wood, but it was out of sight now. He and Abraham walked down the hill.

As they continued down the long hill, they spotted a man and several children cutting wood near the creek. The man looked up to see them approach and then went back to cutting wood. His children, dressed in rags and thin as rails, stopped and clustered anxiously around him, forcing him to stop work. He waited for Danny to speak.

"Hello."

"Hello," the man replied.

"We're from the steamer *Barnard Clinton*. Did she stop here for wood?"

"No."

"Did you see her go past?"

"Yeh."

"How long ago?"

The man squinted at the sun. "Near three hour."

"How far are we from Fort Pierre?"

"'Bout seven mile."

"We need to catch up to her. Is there a faster way to get there than walking?"

"No."

"Would you be willing to loan us two horses? We could pay a little now, and more when we catch the *Clinton*."

The man casually placed one hand on the bed of the wagon, and Danny saw that he had a rifle there. "No," the man said.

Danny didn't acknowledge that he saw the rifle. "Well," he said, "could we just get a little food from you, and then we'll be on our way?"

"I got to get my wagon loaded. Then you can follow me to the house."

"We'll load the wagon for you." Danny didn't want to waste any time, and he wanted to do something for the man in exchange for the food.

It took the three of them only five minutes to load the wagon. The children were of some help, but most of the wood was carried and loaded by Abraham. When it was done, the man climbed onto the seat of the wagon.

"I'll get some food for you at the house," he said. "Follow me."

The farmer started his horses toward his cabin and his four children followed, along with Danny and Abraham.

When they all arrived at the cabin, the farmer quickly jumped down from the wagon with his rifle and went to the door. Danny could see that there was a woman inside, but the farmer pushed her back inside and then followed her, closing the door after him.

A moment later, the farmer came back out with some dried fish and biscuits. Danny noticed that the door latched behind him.

"This is about all I got," he said, and gave each man some of what he had. He divided the rest among his children.

"Where do you want your wood stacked?" Danny asked. "We'd be happy to stack it for you." Although he hated to lose the time it would take to stack the wood, he rationalized that the food would give them additional strength to make up whatever time they lost.

"I'll take care of it," the man said. Danny knew the farmer was worried about losing his horses to two strangers and didn't want them to be around the wagon now that they had food. The officer reached into the pocket of his pants and pulled out a dollar.

"Here, then, take this for the food." He handed it to the surprised man, and he and Abraham turned to go.

"Hold up," the man said. Danny and Abraham stopped and turned back to the man. "I've got a skiff down in the reeds to take you across the river. There's a road on the other side."

"We'd pay you for that." Barton was elated that they were finding a way across the river, a problem that had bothered him all day, knowing that Abraham couldn't swim.

"No," the man said. "You can do me a favor."

"All right," he said.

"My oldest boy, Noah, will go with you. Buy me a dollar's worth of coffee and salt and give it to him to bring back. They cheated him last time."

"Let's go."

Minutes later the four of them were on the west side of the Missouri. The farmer took Noah by the shoulders and talked to him in low tones that Danny couldn't quite make out. Then the boy took off running down the road toward Fort Pierre.

The farmer gave the dollar back. "My boy can run like a deer. He'll go ahead and tell your boat you're coming. He'll be waiting for you at the trading post. Coffee and salt." Danny shook hands with the farmer, and then the farmer went to Abraham and shook his hand before stepping back into his skiff and starting across the river to his home.

Chapter Twenty-two

Barton had been correct in his guess that the *Clinton* tied up at the banks of Fort Pierre about noon. And the steamer would have cast off within an hour of her arrival but for two situations: The captain wanted to secure medical help for Josephine Wainwright, and the mate was having difficulty procuring cordwood.

When the *Clinton* pulled into the banks at Fort Pierre, there were two other steamers tied up there. The *Str. Great Plains,* a smaller vessel, had filled her decks with cordwood and was making ready to cast off. The *Blackfeet Princess* had come from upriver and was loading cordwood onto the foredeck. There was not enough wood available for all three vessels. The *Blackfeet Princess* had contracted for all the wood that was left at the waterfront. Felden had passed up the farmer's wood station seven miles back on the east side because he knew the *Clinton* would be in Fort Pierre more than long enough to procure wood, and he had wanted to make up the time they had lost. It was turning out to be a mistake. The price in Fort Pierre was higher due to the fact that so much timber had been cut around the village for construction; wood for burning and timber for construction had to be hauled by wagon from several miles away.

Felden left the problem in the hands of the first mate, Steve Allenby, and went to his stateroom, intent on getting an hour's sleep while the *Clinton* was tied up.

Allenby was telling the first mate from the *Blackfeet Princess,* which was headed downriver, that there was a woodhawk just seven miles away. But the first mate was not willing to give up wood that was ready to be loaded on the strength of a report of wood from another steamboat.

While Allenby negotiated, the captain and the purser walked into the village. They tracked down a person who professed to be a doctor. In a little frame house the man was seated behind a worn desk that was covered with stacks of old newspapers, books, and ledgers. There were bookshelves on all the walls, tilted forward precariously from the weight of the books on them.

The man who was the town's only doctor was dressed in sturdy work clothes that were as worn looking as he was. His hair was long and he had a full beard, but his eyes were the eyes of a younger man, bright and alert. He beckoned them in through the open door of the little shack without words and now waited for them to speak.

"I'm Captain Culpepper of the steamer *Barnard Clinton*. I'm looking for the doctor."

"I'm the doctor. Phil Underwood. What can I do for you?"

The captain extended his hand, and the man shook it.

"We have an injured woman onboard the *Barnard Clinton*," Culpepper told him. "I'd like you to take a look at her."

"Sure, Cap'n," Underwood said. "What happened to her?"

"She's been shot, and she fell about ten feet."

"Uh-oh," Underwood said. "We're currently without a town marshal."

"What I need is medical help, not law. In any case, it didn't happen in this jurisdiction."

Underwood shrugged, put his bag on his desk, opened it, and started putting supplies into it. "Where was she shot?" he asked.

"In the back, right shoulder," the captain answered.

"And you don't need the law?" Underwood finished filling the bag and closed it.

"I'm the law on the *Barnard Clinton*."

"Lead the way, Admiral," he said.

"My purser will take you. I'm looking for the telegraph office."

In most frontier towns it was not too difficult to find the telegraph office; one just had to follow the telegraph lines into town.

The captain had not noticed any lines along the river or through the town, but he had hoped, in spite of this, that there was a telegraph office somewhere.

The doctor looked at him with a wry grin. "There isn't any telegraph here, Captain. We get our news from Sioux City by steamer. You're in the West now. The river is our telegraph."

The captain received this information stoically and led the doctor and purser back to the *Clinton*. He would not be able to verify Delbert Gray's claim that he was in Washington, D.C., throughout 1864, and he wouldn't get any news from Omaha about the murder of John Swanson.

Dr. Underwood observed Captain Culpepper as they walked to the waterfront. His uniform was clean and sharp, his hair and beard were neatly trimmed, and his stride was strong, erect, and confident. He had seen many riverboats come through Fort Pierre, and based on his observations of the captain, he formed a mental picture of how the *Barnard Clinton* would appear. He wasn't disappointed. She lay between the *Blackfeet Princess* and the *Great Plains* like a polished stone between two lumps of coal.

The captain took the doctor to the stateroom where Josephine was being tended by Elizabeth. The doctor acknowledged the black woman and infant son, but he said nothing. He went directly to the bed where Josephine lay, still on her stomach. Her face was pale, her hair was matted, and she was unresponsive. He pulled the bed covers back to see the bandage on her back, soaked with blood. Gently, he removed the bandage.

"Who cleaned the wound?" he asked.

"I did," Elizabeth answered. Her baby fussed at the sound of the doctor's voice, and she lifted him out of his crib to comfort him.

"Is the bullet still in there?"

"No. I plucked it."

"Mmm." The wound was oozing blood. The doctor took clean dressings from his bag and covered Josephine's shoulder. He looked at the gash on the side of her head. It had not bled much, and Elizabeth had cleaned it but left it unbandaged. He felt Josephine's head around the gash. Next, he looked at the bruises on Josephine's side. "What position was she in when you found her?"

"She was folded over one of the paddles on her stomach. Her head was on the nextest paddle," Elizabeth answered.

"Does she have bruises on the front of her chest too?"

"She sho' does."

"Any other wounds in front?"

"No."

The doctor put his stethoscope on Josephine's back in several places, nodding as he did so. He felt Josephine's lower ribs. "I see no reason to turn her over." He examined her arms and legs and then pulled the covers over her again and stood up.

"What's your name?" he asked Elizabeth.

"Elizabeth."

"And your baby's name?"

"We still decidin' that."

"Can I see him?"

Elizabeth handed her boy to the doctor. The doctor looked him over briefly.

"That's a fine young boy." He handed the baby back to Elizabeth.

"Yes."

"I wouldn't have done anything different with this girl than what you did. If she wakes up, try to get her to drink something. No whiskey."

"No."

"And keep her warm."

"I do that."

"How long will you be in Fort Pierre?"

"I doesn't know."

"Very well. I'm going to talk to the captain. Good day."

The doctor walked out of the stateroom and easily found the adjacent pilothouse. The captain beckoned him in.

"Thoughts, Doctor?"

"She's obviously lost some blood, so she needs to get fluids and nourishment at every opportunity. And it's very important that she be kept warm. She would be better off in a hospital, but what we have in Fort Pierre doesn't really qualify. If I put her in my office, she'll be left alone too often. The black woman is doing a good job of taking care of her. How far up the river are you going?"

The captain answered, "We'll go to Fort Benton if the river permits."

The doctor was troubled by this answer. "That means you'll be in wilderness for many days."

"Weeks," the captain contradicted.

"Is the black woman going to stay with her?"

"Yes. She has nowhere else to go at present."

"She's done a good job. The young woman is probably being taken care of as good as we could expect on this side of the Mississippi."

"That's good to hear, Doctor."

"Don't misunderstand me. She's in danger, but there's nothing I can do about it out here. She needs a really good hospital, but there's no one here who could care for her better than the black woman."

"Very well. I'll see that she's well tended aboard until she gets better or . . . dies."

"That's probably the best, Captain. Could you tell me how she got shot?"

"I'm not sure. She wasn't found for several hours."

"Do you know why?"

"She witnessed a murder two years ago. The murderer wasn't caught. That's all we know."

"Have you discharged any passengers since she was shot?"

"No."

"It strikes me that the river is not the biggest danger you face."

"I can't help but agree, Doctor," the captain said with a trace of weariness.

"How long will you be in Fort Pierre?"

"Only another hour, I think."

"I've heard steamboat food equals that found in fine hotels."

The captain was embarrassed. "Yes, of course. Follow me, Doctor, and we'll see what we can find in the main salon."

* * *

Harold Robertson and Delbert Gray were sitting together in the main salon, having finished lunch. The deck passengers had taken over the main table, and the full-paying passengers had left for other pursuits.

For a reason that he couldn't understand, Gray did not share with Robertson the episode of finding Josephine in the wheel. He was beginning to become uneasy about Robertson. It might have been the fact that he had told Robertson that Little Joe had been a witness to a murder, and then the little hostler was shot. And he remembered that he had pointed out Abraham to Robertson in a seemingly harmless conversation, and Abraham had also met with tragedy. But more than anything else, his sixth sense was telling him that Robertson might not be the man he purported to be.

Gray was by no means ready to accuse Robertson of anything, but neither was he willing to entrust him with anything or any information of value. Gray resolved to engage Robertson in more conversations in order to evaluate whether or not he wanted the man to share his journey to Seattle.

"Fort Pierre, for being a village of many years, is certainly wanting of the marks of civilization," Gray commented, breaking an awkward silence.

"I understand that we will not be here very long," Robertson said.

"No, I guessed the same thing," Gray said. "Only a few officers went to the village, and the entire crew stayed aboard," he added.

"I suppose the captain wants to make up the time we lost this morning," Robertson offered, referring to the search for Danny Barton and Abraham.

"What a tragedy. This has become a very sad journey." Gray stared into space, not concerned about his suspicions for the moment, but suddenly reminded of the woman he had won and lost.

"The frontier takes its toll, Delbert."

"Yes. Well, I've seen too many people die in the last five years." But the one that had affected him the most was the beautiful Melinda LaFramboise. Although Gray was a strong-minded person, he was still troubled greatly by her death.

Robertson realized he had been insensitive and tried to make amends. "Like you, I had hoped that I had seen the end of killing, but it seems that is not the case."

This comment did not console Gray. He decided he would rather be alone than spend any more time delving into Robertson's personality. He finished his drink and stood up. "Please excuse me, Henry. I've taken to spending some time by myself every afternoon, as a sort of memorial to Miss LaFramboise."

"By all means. Join me for dinner later, won't you?"

"Certainly. Good afternoon to you."

Gray left the main salon and climbed to the hurricane deck. From there he could see most of the shabby little village that had grown up around the Army outpost. Across the river was a large island and above that was a high, muddy bluff topped with grasslands. It seemed to him that everything was plainer, drabber, lacking contrast and detail, since Melinda had been killed. He found a bench next to the bathhouse, sat there, and was lost in his thoughts for a long while.

Captain Culpepper watched as Delbert Gray walked past his table and out the door. As Gray was walking out, Allenby came in, looking for Culpepper. He walked to the table where Culpepper was sitting with Dr. Underwood. The captain stood to meet him.

"Captain. I managed to talk the *Blackfeet Princess* out of ten cords of wood," Allenby said. "It's being loaded now. The woodhawk says he'll have two more wagonloads here in two hours."

"How much in each wagon?"

"Three cords each."

"Singletary's chart shows a woodhawk sixty-five miles ahead. We'll be there at midday tomorrow. I think we'll go ahead as soon as the other six cords come and are loaded. We'll try to get wood ourselves this evening when we stop for the night."

"We could go back to the woodhawk we passed an hour ago," Allenby said.

"That would be going backward," the captain said. "Let me know as soon as the six cords are loaded." The captain was affording Felden a little extra sleep.

"Yes, sir." Allenby left.

"How common is it for a steamboat this size to go to Fort Benton?" Dr. Underwood asked.

"Although the *Clinton* is long, she's actually lighter than many boats that are smaller. She's drawing under four feet right now. But the answer to your question is that the *Clinton* will likely be the largest boat to ever reach Fort Benton."

The captain took Dr. Underwood to the main deck. He showed him the boilers, the engines, the doctor engine, the driving linkage, and the stern wheel. The doctor was fascinated by everything. They ended up on the foredeck in time to see the first of two wagonloads of cordwood drive up. Allenby directed the wagon to drive down the stages onto the foredeck to speed loading. It was now midafternoon, and he knew that the captain wanted to get well upriver before dark.

As the captain and the doctor stood on the foredeck watching the work, a teenaged boy came running up to the riverbank. He seemed momentarily confused as he looked first at the *Clinton* and then at the *Blackfeet Princess*. He shouted to the captain.

"Is this the *Barnard Clinton*?"

The captain looked at the boy who was breathing hard. He decided the boy was probably unable to read, as the vessel's name was in giant letters on the side of the cargo deck walls. He was dressed in ragged overalls and wearing a flour sack for a shirt. His shoes were homemade.

"It is," the captain replied.

"Are you the captain?"

"Yes. I'm Captain Culpepper. And what is your name, young man?"

"Mr. Barton and a colored man are trying to catch up to you, Captain Culpepper," the boy said breathlessly, taking care of his prime responsibility first. Then he added, "My name is Noah."

This was amazing good news. They had survived after all. The captain walked briskly down the stage and took the boy by the shoulders. "Where are they, Noah?"

"'Bout four mile downriver."

"This side?" the captain asked.

"Yes, sir."

"Are they hurt?"

"No, sir. Tired I 'spect."

The first wagon was empty, and the driver expertly backed the team up the stage to the riverbank. Then the other wagon drove down the stage to unload. The captain went to the first wagon driver.

"Is the road south passable for your wagon?"

"Yep, why?"

"There are two men walking this way, a young man named Danny Barton and a black man named Abraham. I'll give you fifty cents to drive down and give them a ride back."

"How far?"

"About four miles."

"Make it a dollar."

"No."

"Make it six bits."

The captain started to walk away, but the wagon driver stopped him.

"All right, old man, fifty cents then."

"Take this boy with you."

"All right, anything else?" he asked sarcastically, but he didn't want an answer and didn't wait for it. Noah jumped up onto the seat beside the driver as he turned the wagon toward the road.

"Dr. Underwood, I have just received such good news I am having trouble believing it," Culpepper said. The doctor raised his eyebrows with the obvious question in his eyes. "Last night, a black man fell overboard, and my aide jumped in to save him. They were never seen again. We searched downriver for hours through the night and again this morning and found no trace of either man. It seems impossible, but somehow they have survived a night in the river and are walking up the road in an attempt to catch us before we cast off."

Chapter Twenty-three

The three men in the corner of the main salon talked in low tones. Since leaving the *Missouri Princess,* they had kept to themselves, and other than occasionally allowing another male passenger to join one of their card games, they had spoken to no one.

"The slick one is wearing a money belt. I can tell by the way his coat hangs." He was referring to Harold Robertson, known as Henry Rogers on the *Clinton.*

"Well, he'll be easy to take down," the second one said. He was known as Bacon and he was speaking to his little brother, Junior. The oldest of the three brothers was Thomas Franklin, commonly called Tank.

The Franklin brothers had made a name for themselves in Philadelphia, so much so that they had found it prudent to leave the state of Pennsylvania.

"How 'bout that other easterner?" Tank asked. "What do we know about him?"

"Every time I see him, I get a bad feeling," Bacon said. "I think I've seen him before."

"Prison?" Tank asked.

"Nah," Bacon replied. He was quiet as he thought. "You guys remember that fight in front of the courthouse?"

Junior smiled. "We busted some heads that day, didn't we?"

"Yeah, yeah," Bacon agreed. "But that guy who took your Colt. Remember him?"

"Yeah," Junior said. "He almost had me in handcuffs. You think that's him?"

"Could be."

194

"Well, let's take him out first, just to be safe. If he's the same guy, he's tougher than cobblestones and broken glass."

"Suits me," Tank said. "Just do it quick. We got a lot to do."

"Are we gonna get the boat's gold?" Junior asked.

"No gold, Junior. Cash to buy gold."

"Better," Bacon offered.

"Bacon, you take the two city guys down. Use a knife if you can, but do it quick. Junior and I will get the cash in the safe."

"You know where it is?"

"No. We'll persuade the captain to show us." Tank smirked.

"How about that young guy with the pistol under his coat? He looks like trouble," Bacon said.

Tank knew what his brothers had yet to learn. "He was the one who fell off the boat. They never found him."

"Was he some kind of boat sheriff?" Bacon asked.

"Maybe. But he's just catfish food now," Tank answered.

"When?" Bacon asked.

"I'm thinking as soon as the boat gets around the first bend," Tank said. "After we get whatever we can get, we'll make the pilot run into the bank. We'll blow all the steam and water the fires. Maybe punch some holes. This stinkin' boat'll be helpless. We'll take all the horses, ride back to Fort Pierre, and take the *Blackfeet Princess* back to Omaha."

"Why not just take the money now?" Junior asked impatiently.

"And then what?" Tank asked sarcastically. "The *Barnard Clinton* is big enough to run down any of these other steamers. We'd have to leave the river and ride through Indian country. Stick with my plan, Junior, and this time next week we'll be in Omaha with a woman on each knee, pourin' whiskey."

"Yeah, all right, Tank. I'm with ya."

"Me too," Bacon said.

"Good. Let's just hunker down here until the boat pulls out."

Abraham saw the wagon coming before Danny did and pointed. "Mr. Barton, yonder comes our boy in a wagon."

Danny and Abraham had been walking fast without resting, and they were both exhausted. They separately hoped that the wagon had been sent for them. They weren't disappointed. The driver found a wide place in the road and wheeled the wagon around as they walked up to it.

"I been sent to pick you fellers up," the driver said.

"Not a minute too soon," Barton said as he and Abraham climbed into the wagon.

"The captain said you'd give me a dollar if I found you," the driver said slyly, hoping for a little extra profit.

"Liar," the boy said.

The driver started to strike the boy who was still sitting beside him on the seat, but the officer grabbed his arm.

"The captain already give him four bits," the boy said, leaning away from the driver in self-defense.

"All right, son," Danny said. "Just get us to our boat, mister. We won't cheat you."

The driver clenched his jaw and slapped the reins on his team to start them back to Fort Pierre. Danny and Abraham sat in the back, and Noah remained on the front seat with the driver, feeling very important, indeed.

Josephine was still lying on her stomach when her eyes opened. She could see a washstand.

I'm in a room somewhere. Where's Danny? Oh. Danny's in the river. With Abraham. But I'm here. I've got to get to the river. Danny needs me. Don't die, Danny. Don't die. This is a stateroom. I've got to get out of here and get to the river.

Josephine tensed up. It was not in an effort to get up. It was a move to locate her limbs, to verify that she still had them. They seemed to be where they should be. She could feel her arms, her hands, her legs, her feet. Her back.

Oh, Lord, that hurts so much. I can't move if it hurts that much. I've got to get to the river. Somebody help me get up. Danny, help. Help, Danny.

"Danny!" she said hoarsely.

"Girl! It's about time you woke up. You must be near-starved."

"Elizabeth?"

"Yes, I'm here. Let me help you turn over, girl, and we'll stuff some food down you."

"Water!" Josephine demanded.

"Sho', Miss Jo, water. Now let me help you turn over and sit up." She pulled Josephine's covers back and then helped her roll over onto her back. Josephine cried out in pain, but kept her eyes open and strained to help Elizabeth roll her over in spite of the pain it caused.

"You doin' good, girl. Now come on."

Elizabeth pulled Josephine up and propped blankets and pillows behind her back. Then she covered her up again.

"There you are," she said. "Now jes' sit still while I bring you some water." She went to the nightstand and poured water from a pitcher into a cup.

"Here, Miss Jo. Drink it slow like."

Josephine sipped at first and then drank. She hadn't realized how thirsty she was. She started to gag, and Elizabeth took the water from her.

"Slow down, girl. And don't let yourself cough, hear?"

Josephine gasped and swallowed. "More," she said.

"That'll do for now. You rest a spell."

Josephine let her head lay back on the pillows. "Where's Danny?"

Elizabeth looked deep into Josephine's eyes. "Danny and Abraham be in the river somewhere. But they gonna come back. I believe that strong." She took Josephine's hands in hers. At length she said, "I'm gonna fetch you some soup. You set still and don't try to move. You got a hole in your shoulder that ain't closed."

"It feels like I'm lying on a hot cannonball."

"I 'spect so. Jes' lie still. I'll be back directly."

Elizabeth looked at her sleeping baby boy, let herself out, and locked the door behind her.

Harold Robertson and Delbert Gray were again sitting together in the main salon, waiting for the dinner announcement. Gray had decided that unless he learned something really suspicious about Rogers, he would proceed with his plans to travel to Seattle with Rogers' assistance. He could think of nothing that Rogers had said that was positively incriminating or proof of any wrongdoing.

"I'm surprised that we have not cast off from Fort Pierre," Robertson said.

"I believe the captain is addressing two problems," Gray replied. "He's allowing the pilot some additional rest and is awaiting delivery of wood."

"Do they know the destination of the *Great Plains* and the *Blackfeet Princess*?"

"The *Princess* is headed downriver, and they graciously shared wood with us the knowledge that there is a well-stocked woodhawk only a few miles downriver. I have been told that the *Great Plains* is going up the Missouri as far as Fort Buford, and then up the Yellowstone."

"Where will that lead?" Robertson asked.

"From the end of navigation there is usually a stagecoach to Virginia City, the gold fields, and beyond."

"That sounds complicated."

"It's not as comfortable or safe as steamboat travel."

"Has the hostler been found?" Robertson asked.

Gray's heart sped up. Something was wrong with that question. He realized that Rogers had misspoken. So far as Gray knew, the assault on Josephine had not been reported or shared with anyone on the *Clinton,* outside of the men who rescued her. Only he, a few of the officers, two roustabouts, and Elizabeth knew. Had news of the assault on Josephine been shared around the boat, or did Rogers know more than he should know? He had to consider his response to this question carefully. He wanted to encourage Rogers to talk more without tripping any alarms.

"No," he said. This answer would serve to protect Josephine if Rogers was the person who had attempted to kill her. "Another mystery to ponder, without doubt."

"I would assume that he fell overboard." Robertson said. "I've often seen him working on the narrow walkway."

"Perhaps," Gray answered. This statement confirmed that

Rogers was aware that Josephine had met trouble, but was unaware that she was still alive. *Every person who knew that she had been assaulted also knew that she was alive in Elizabeth's cabin, except the would-be killer.*

"Perhaps?" Robertson wanted clarification.

"There could be other explanations," Gray said.

"Surely you don't mean to imply that foul play was involved. In any case, it seems doubtful that a person of that station would have enemies."

At this statement Gray was afraid his eyes would betray him. It was obvious to him that Rogers was leading him away from a conclusion that someone had killed or, in this case, tried to kill the hostler because of a perceived threat. Gray looked away for a moment.

"I just mean to say," Gray stated, "that we should not reach a conclusion until all the facts are known."

As he said this, Gray saw the black woman Elizabeth slip through the salon and go into the kitchen. If that meant that Josephine had regained consciousness, there might be more facts to be had. He hoped that the captain was still pursuing the investigation, just as the young security officer would have. He was ever more sure he was sitting in front of a killer, but he didn't know how to proceed.

Robertson had also seen Elizabeth slip into the kitchen, and this would not have meant anything except for the fact that she was not carrying her baby. He had not seen her without her child since the child's birth. Something unusual was going on. Gray seemed more than a little distant, and this heightened his suspicion. Did Gray know something that he was not sharing?

There had been three people who could spoil Robertson's scheme. Danny Barton had been openly suspicious; Little Joe claimed to be a witness to the murder that he himself had committed; and Abraham was also possibly a witness. But all three of these people were dead. Was Elizabeth the unnamed witness? Or had one of the three previously said something to Gray that had aroused his suspicions?

Robertson knew he had to play his cards very carefully from

now on. Although he could see no connection anyone could make between him and what he believed to be his successful killing of the hostler and the black man, he certainly didn't want anyone fishing for information in Omaha. He thought the best outcome would be for Gray to forget his suspicions and renew his invitation to accompany him to Seattle. But if that were not going to be the case, and if Gray had damaging information, he would have to dispose of him.

Chapter Twenty-four

Danny Barton saw the smoke from the *Clinton*'s stacks from a mile away. He wanted to jump out of the wagon and run, but he was in no condition for that.

"Whip those horses up, mister," he shouted to the driver.

"They ain't racers. They're goin' their own speed."

Danny fished a dollar out of his pocket and handed it to the man. He was afraid the *Clinton* was about to cast off.

"Make 'em go *my* speed for the last mile."

Without making a reply, the man slapped the reins on the back of his horses and they broke into a trot. Noah grinned as he hung on. This, the boy thought, was more like it. In spite of the lurching of the wagon on the rough road, Danny and Abraham both stood up to look ahead.

In ten minutes the wagon pulled up at the boarding stage to the *Clinton*. Danny and Abraham jumped down before it stopped rolling. Noah did likewise.

"You got to take me to the trading post for coffee and salt, mister," Noah said.

"You come with me, Noah. I'll get all the coffee and salt you can carry, and you can keep the dollar." Danny walked swiftly up the boarding stage, and Abraham and Noah followed.

The captain had been waiting on the foredeck with the doctor since sending the wagon for his aide and Abraham. He strode forward to meet Barton and extended his hand.

"Welcome back, Mr. Barton," he said as the young officer shook his hand. "We had given you up for dead." Then the captain took

Abraham's hand and shook it also. "Welcome back, Abraham. Your wife told me you would return. She'll want to see you."

"Yes, sir," Abraham answered and ran up the central staircase, taking three steps at a time.

The captain detained Danny. "Mr. Barton, I have some bad news for you. Miss Wainwright has been shot. She is alive, but in serious condition."

"Where is she?"

"She's in my old stateroom with Elizabeth, but before you go there, let me say a few words."

Barton anxiously waited to hear what the captain had to say.

"It is an inescapable conclusion that there is a killer onboard this boat. Find him and incarcerate him or kill him. Soon. Do you understand?" The expression on the captain's face was something Barton had not seen since the battle in which he was captured during the Civil War.

"Yes, sir," Barton said. He was practically dancing in his anxiety to see Josephine.

"Go talk to the girl," the captain said, putting his hand on Noah's shoulder to keep him from leaving. Barton left like he had been shot from a gun.

The captain looked at Noah, who had not moved. "What can I do for you, young man?" he asked.

"Mr. Barton was supposed to take me to the trading post and see that I got a dollar's worth of coffee and salt for my father."

Culpepper smiled a rare smile. "Mr. Barton has other things on his mind at the moment. Come with me."

Culpepper and the doctor took Noah to the kitchen where the captain filled a sack with coffee, salt, sugar, crackers, and gumdrops.

"It'll be dark in three hours, Noah. Will you be home by then?"

Noah squinted at the sun and replied, "Yes, sir," and was off at a run to proudly show his father his treasures.

Captain Culpepper shook Dr. Underwood's hand. "Doctor, we'll be casting off in a few minutes. It's been a pleasure talking with you. We'll stop on our way downstream in a few weeks, and I'm sure I'll have some interesting stories to tell."

"I look forward to that, Captain. Have a safe journey." The doctor walked up the boarding stage to the riverbank and turned to watch the preparations for departure.

Robertson was considering what might be his best course of action. There seemed to be some evidence against him, although incomplete. The information he had gained from Gray presented another possibility to him. He could leave the *Barnard Clinton* and book passage up the Yellowstone on the *Great Plains*. It might be prudent to kill Gray, especially if there were a good opportunity to do so. On the other hand, leaving him alive would not pose much risk. Robertson thought he might be able to get away from the *Clinton* without being seen and board the *Great Plains,* which had still not cast off.

The outside doors into the main salon were open to let light and air in during the warm afternoon. As Robertson pondered his plan and absently stared out an open doorway, Abraham rushed by outside. It took a minute to register in Robertson's mind. The big black man! Where did he come from? He started to get up and then stopped.

Gray noticed Robertson's distress. "Are you all right, Henry?" he asked.

"Uh. . . . yes. Yes, I just thought of something I wanted to do before dinner, but it can wait," Robertson said, fabricating an excuse.

"It's still almost an hour before dinner will be announced."

"Um, yes. I'll . . ."

At that moment, Barton rushed by the open door. What was going on? Had they been hiding somewhere on the boat for some obscure reason? Robertson could see no way possible they could have rescued themselves and caught up to the *Clinton.* He had an almost irresistible urge to run from the boat and get lost in the wilderness west of Fort Pierre. He had to find out what had happened, so he would know how best to escape. And who he might need to kill. Killing had always been his solution to the problem of staying out of trouble, and he was good at it, but time was running out.

Gray had also seen Barton and he arose and excused himself.

Robertson got up and went to his own berth where he hurriedly packed his valise.

As soon as the doctor left, the captain climbed to the pilot-house where Felden was ready to take the *Clinton* into the river. "Mr. Felden, in case you didn't see, Abraham and Mr. Barton have been found and are onboard," the captain said.

"That's very good news, sir. When we get into the channel, I'll hear the story," Felden said. He signaled the mate to raise the stages. The mate set the crew to the task and went to the engine room to make sure the engineer was ready.

As one crewman on the foredeck wrapped the stage halyard around the capstan and the stage began lifting, Harold Robertson came down the central stairs to the foredeck. He was too late to get off the *Clinton* without attracting attention. He pushed his valise into a corner behind some boxes in the cargo bay and watched the shore retreat as the *Clinton* backed into the river. He was cornered.

Danny burst into Josephine's stateroom without knocking and just as quickly Elizabeth turned him around and put him back outside.

"This girl ain't ready to have company. You jes' wait out here." It was only a minute until she came out and motioned him in with a nod of her head. She was carrying her baby and followed by Abraham. They walked down the hurricane deck and Danny went in to find Josephine sitting up against a stack of pillows and bedding and dressed in a nightshirt.

"Danny," Josephine said softly.

"I'm sorry, Jo," Danny said. "I'm sorry," he repeated.

"For what?"

"I never should have left you. I never . . ."

"Did you save Abraham?" she asked.

"I reckon we saved each other," he said.

"Sit down and tell me," she said.

"Well," he hesitated. "I've got to find out who did this. I can't stay."

"Oh," she said and looked down at her folded hands.

"I reckon I've got a minute or two," he said, and he went to the side of her bed and knelt down. He put his elbows on the bed and picked up her hands in his. Neither of them spoke. He pressed the back of her hand to his face and then stood up.

"I'm going to get a deckhand to stand guard at your door," he promised.

"Elizabeth can handle it," she said.

He nodded, but told himself to get a man to guard anyway.

"Be careful, Danny," she told him as he left the room.

Chapter Twenty-five

Delbert Gray found the captain on the hurricane deck, watching as the *Clinton* made sternway into the lazy current of the Missouri.

"Mr. Gray," the captain said. "I have a feeling you want to talk to me."

"Yes, Captain," Gray said. "I wanted to know how many people are aware that Josephine was shot."

"I've told no one, so it's myself, yourself, Felden, Erickson, and the four roustabouts. Oh, and Elizabeth," the captain said. "I asked the roustabouts to keep the information to themselves, but it would be unreasonable to think they told no one."

"Henry Rogers knows about it," Gray said. "I doubt that he spends much time chatting with ordinary laborers."

"Let's talk in the pilothouse, Mr. Gray," the captain said. The two men went into the pilothouse where Charles Felden was at the wheel.

The captain addressed Delbert Gray. "What significance do you attach to his knowledge of the assault on Miss Wainwright?"

Gray chose his words carefully. "I have become uneasy about his intentions, and in a conversation only moments ago, I learned that he was aware that the hostler had met with misfortune, but apparently he does not know that she was found alive. This seems to be a contradiction."

The captain held up his hand to silence Gray as Felden rang for slow ahead. He and Felden watched carefully as the wheel changed directions and the sternway she had been making slowed.

The *Clinton* became motionless in the stream and then began moving ahead.

"You're mine now," Felden said in a low voice. He prided himself on making as few changes as possible with the engine room telegraph.

The captain turned again to Gray. "Go on, Mr. Gray."

"The knowledge that Miss Wainwright met misfortune must logically be accompanied by the knowledge that she is still onboard, unless someone witnessed her being shot but did not witness her rescue from the wheel."

Danny Barton came in to the pilothouse at that moment.

"Mr. Barton, find Henry Rogers and disarm him. Then bring him to me," the captain ordered.

"Yes, sir," Barton replied. "I have to get a fresh gun from my kit."

"See to it," Culpepper said, "but find him before someone else is killed."

Gray spoke. "I'll go with you, if you don't mind, Mr. Barton."

"Do you have a gun?" Barton asked.

"Yes," he patted his side.

"Let's go," Barton said.

While Harold Robertson had hurriedly packed his valise, Bacon had watched from the corner table, and as Robertson walked along the cabin deck walkway, he followed from a distance. He observed the stage being lifted and saw Robertson's frustration that he had not been able to disembark. Then Robertson disappeared from his view into the cargo bay. This was good, Bacon thought. The crew was out on the bow and the lower walkways as the *Clinton* got under way, all busy with their various tasks. So much the better to find and dispose of the city slicker without being noticed. And then he would be near the engine room and could handle the engineer as well. Bacon slowly descended the main stairway.

Tank had a double-barreled shotgun and a pistol; Junior had a repeating rifle. They bided their time until the *Clinton* shifted into forward and began picking up speed against the current of the Missouri.

"Junior, you go up the far stairs all the way to the hurricane deck. I'll be on the other side. The mates are on the bow. The captain and the pilot will be alone in the pilothouse."

"Right," Junior said.

"We'll go in from opposite sides. I'll hold my scattergun on them. You cut the captain's throat."

"Yeah." Junior tried to sound enthusiastic.

"By then we'll be out of sight of Fort Pierre. I'll make the pilot run the boat into the western bank. Then you cut his throat too."

"Yeah."

"Then we've got to get to the engine room before the engineer has time to do anything, although there won't be much he can do."

Junior remained seated.

"Come on, little brother," Tank ordered. "Let's get it done."

The two men got up and exited the main salon on opposite sides.

Robertson walked aft in the cargo bay, past the firemen at the fireboxes and into the jumble of cargo between the boilers and the engine room. He knew events were closing in on him. He wanted to stay out of sight until he could develop a plan. He found a place where he could observe without being seen. The cargo bay was deserted; all hands were on the main deck.

Bacon entered the cargo bay and waited for his eyes to adjust to the dim interior. He, as well as his brothers, was proficient in close quarters with a knife. He told himself he would need just two quick moves: one to take the life of the city slicker, and one more to cut his money belt loose. His fingers curled around the handle of his knife, and he walked farther into the cargo bay.

Robertson, the former double spy, had been hunted before. He saw Bacon enter the cargo bay and his pulse quickened. He immediately identified Bacon as a threat to his safety, even though he had scarcely taken notice of him previously. A shot in the open area of the cargo bay might be heard by the firemen and strikers.

His technique of stabbing his letter opener into his enemy's heart would not work unless he faced his attacker, and, since Bacon was stalking him, he would have to approach from behind. But he had more than one deadly trick. He pulled a silk cord from his jacket pocket and waited in the shadows.

Tank was walking along the Texas deck on the larboard side, and Junior was advancing along the starboard side. Junior, nervous and unable to assess his older brother's progress, was almost to the pilothouse, well ahead of Tank on the other side. Delbert Gray stepped out of the pilothouse on the side where Tank was walking and began descending the half staircase to the Texas deck. The stairs faced forward, and he didn't notice Tank coming from behind. Tank quickly brought his shotgun up to kill the unaware businessman when he felt the barrel of a rifle against his neck. Weedeater had watched the men climb the stairs with their long guns in hand and decided this was exactly what he was being paid to prevent.

"Lay that double on the deck, yahoo, or die right now!" Weedeater commanded.

Tank made to lower the gun but instead of putting it on the deck, he shoved it back into Weedeater's face. Weedeater's rifle fired, taking a chunk of skin out of the side of Tank's neck. Weedeater fell back, his face bleeding from the jab of the gun barrel.

Tank ignored his wound and fired the shotgun at Gray who, alerted by the commotion, had pulled his own revolver and fired at Tank from behind the post supporting the stair railing. Buckshot pierced Gray's legs and chest. He cocked his gun and fired again and then fell behind the half staircase for cover as Tank let go with the other barrel.

Weedeater had dropped his rifle after the heavy blow and was at Tank's mercy now as Tank pulled his revolver and kept Gray pinned behind the stairs. He turned to finish Weedeater.

At this moment Barton came out of the pilothouse and saw Gray lying on the stairs at his feet and Tank in front of the Iowa cabin, taking aim at Weedeater. He pulled his Colt and took aim. Tank smashed into the door of the Texas cabin to get out of the officer's line of fire. Barton's hammer fell on the cap, but the wet powder did nothing. Tank was already in the cabin and didn't realize that Barton's gun was waterlogged.

Junior entered the pilothouse from the other side and found only Felden and Captain Culpepper, both unarmed. He was momentarily confused because he had expected to find Tank in the pilothouse. He had never been on a steamboat before and wasn't even sure which man was the captain and which was the pilot. He needed Tank to give him direction.

"You fellers don't move or I'll kill you where you stand!" he threatened. But now he was out of ideas. Where was Tank?

Weedeater had found his rifle, and now he and Barton faced each other on the walkway while Tank stood just inside the cabin door. He could step out and shoot at either Barton or Weedeater and then duck back in, and neither of them could afford to shoot back for fear of hitting the other. Barton started to take cover in the pilothouse and realized that there was an armed man in there. It was a complete impasse for all of them for the moment.

Tank took a minute to look around the cabin to see if there was another way out. There was a black man and woman against the far wall, watching him with eyes wide.

"You! Woman!" he pointed to Elizabeth. "Come here!"

Elizabeth's hands dropped to her sides and seemed to gather the folds of her dress.

"Right now!" Tank shouted.

Elizabeth walked across the small room and, just before she came within his reach, she raised her right arm, which was holding Josephine's gun, and she shot the surprised Tank between the eyes. He fell backward out onto the walkway, killed instantly by the wife of a former slave who had never held a gun in her hand until a few days ago.

Barton, trying to stay out of sight of the stranger in the pilothouse, began helping Delbert Gray. Weedeater walked up to Tank's lifeless body to check it and find out who had shot him. He was amazed to see Elizabeth holding a smoking pistol and watching Tank's body.

"I never shot no man before," she said in shock.

Weedeater took the gun from her hand as Abraham came forward to take her in his arms. Elizabeth turned to Abraham.

"Is my baby all right?"

"He just fine, 'Lizbeth," Abraham told her tenderly. "You be all right?"

"I s'pose," she replied. "I ain't never shot no man before."

"Elizabeth, you done real good," Weedeater said. "Where'd you get this?" he asked, indicating the little pistol.

"That belong to Miss Jo."

Weedeater looked from Elizabeth to Abraham and shook his head.

Junior was in the pilothouse, holding his rifle on Felden and Captain Culpepper while waiting for his brother to arrive and tell him what to do next. It was a difficult job; the captain stood at the back wall of the pilothouse and Felden was at the wheel forward. Junior would point his gun first at the captain and then at Felden. After a few turns of this, the captain lost patience. He stepped forward and grabbed Junior by the throat, lifting him off the floor with both hands. Junior had never levered a shell into the firing chamber, and it was too late now.

Junior wasn't the only one having trouble breathing. His big brother, Bacon, was turning blue as Harold Robertson tightened the silk cord around his neck. In minutes Bacon was dead on the floor of the cargo bay.

Robertson was unaware of what was taking place on the Texas deck and in the pilothouse. He did not know if Bacon was just another riverboat thief or had been sent by the captain to detain him. It made no difference. He had to get away from the *Clinton*. He took Bacon's revolver, shoved it into his belt, and then made his way to the engine room. Entering the engine room, he aimed the revolver at the engineer.

"Stop the engines!" he ordered.

"Who are you?" the engineer demanded to know.

"I won't tell you again," Robertson said and cocked the pistol. "Stop the engines right now!"

"Go to blazes!"

Robertson didn't have to worry about a gunshot inside the engine room being heard. He had a vague idea about how the engines worked and felt sure he could stop them. He shot the engineer in the chest.

The striker had been working on the opposite engine and now came from behind it, shouting. Robertson turned and shot twice, but the striker dove behind the engine on which he had been working.

"Get out here and stop the engines!" Robertson shouted to him.

There was no answer. The hatch cover adjacent to the engine had been open and the striker slipped into the hold and away from Robertson.

To the uninitiated, the engine room was a tangle of pipes leading in all directions. Robertson looked overhead and located the main steam line coming from the boilers. There was a valve with an extension so that it could be turned without the necessity of a ladder, but he found it impossible to turn. Looking around, he saw a valve wrench and it took him only seconds to deduce its purpose. He shut off the main steam line. The pitman arms slowed and stopped, and outside the wheel ceased turning.

"Captain, we've lost power!" Felden exclaimed. It had happened so suddenly that Felden was caught off guard. The *Clinton* yawed in the current and began drifting broadside downstream. The captain dropped Junior in an unconscious heap on the pilothouse floor and walked out and down the half stairs to the forward Texas deck, overlooking the bow.

"Get an anchor down!" he shouted. First mate Steve Allenby had already become aware of the loss of power and was getting an anchoring crew organized.

"Right away, sir!" Allenby answered.

Allenby's crew knew what to do and knew what danger they were in. The first anchor was a smaller one, but quicker to get overboard. They tied a heavy line to it and threw it into the Missouri. The other end they snubbed around a cleat with a hundred feet of slack. The current was strong here, but the anchor was heavy enough to slow the *Clinton* and turn her bow into the current. While they accomplished this, Abraham, not taking time to descend the stairs, had jumped from the Texas deck to the cabin deck and then to the main deck. He pulled fifty feet of chain from the locker while three men wrestled the *Clinton*'s big anchor to the bow. They had it rigged in seconds and Abraham lifted it overboard. The line paid out much more slowly than the first because the little anchor had slowed the *Clinton*. Disaster had been averted for now.

Robertson found two lanterns in the engine room. He lit them both and then tossed them out into the cargo bay. They might not start a catastrophic fire, but they would divert attention from him. The aft door of the engine room exited onto the walkway just ahead of the stern wheel. There was a ladder up to the hurricane deck from here, and Robertson quickly ascended it. He wanted to somehow get the ship's yawl over the side and drift back down to Fort Pierre.

On the Texas deck, Elizabeth was tending to Delbert Gray's wounds while Weedeater stood guard over Junior. Culpepper and Barton, who had borrowed Gray's revolver, were descending the main stairway to the bow to find out why the engines had stopped. Neither man had any illusion that it was an accident. At that moment someone shouted, "Fire!" A roustabout ran to the fire bell and began ringing it. Smoke had filled the cargo bay. Allenby began organizing a firefighting crew.

With no way to use steam, pressure built up in the boilers and the safety valves began to lift, making a loud screeching whistle. The smoke was too thick by now to read the gauges, so the firemen had no choice but to water the fires and try to reduce the pressure before it overpowered the safety valves and caused one or more boilers to explode.

Men were running in all directions; some passengers on the cabin deck were preparing to jump into the water rather than be blown to pieces in a boiler explosion. The horses were panicked by the smoke and noise and broke down part of the corral that Josephine had built.

Until now, David Erickson had been assisting the anchoring crew. Now he headed for the engine room to see if he could remedy the trouble with the engines. He had to feel his way through the smoke and dodge the loose horses. In spite of there not being much real fire, the smoke was thick and plentiful. Erickson found the door to the engine room and entered. There was only light smoke in the engine room.

"Lars!" Erickson coughed out. No answer. Engineer Lars Hansen was dead on the floor. William Brown, the other engineer, was now groping his way through the cargo bay to find out why the engines had stopped. Erickson found Lars and glanced quickly around for the striker who had escaped through the hold. At that moment Brown entered. He closed the door behind him to prevent more smoke from coming in.

"What happened?" he asked Erickson, who was kneeling over Hansen's body.

"Don't know."

"Is Lars dead?" Brown asked.

"Yes. Can you figure out why the engines stopped?"

"The boilers have overpressured. Both banks. The line is blocked in somewhere." He grabbed the main valve. Robertson had thrown the valve wrench overboard, and Brown didn't waste time looking for it. "Give me a hand here," he asked Erickson. Even with their combined strength, the men were not able to turn the huge main valve without the valve wrench.

"We're dragging both anchors, William," Erickson said. "We need to get steam to these engines, or we're going to drift into trouble."

"We can bypass this valve!" Brown shouted to Erickson. "Follow me!"

The engineer and the mate ran forward to the boilers where the fireman and stokers were getting ready to inject water into the fireboxes. The air had cleared enough for the engineer to read the gauges.

"Don't water the fires yet!" Brown ordered the fireman. "Keep your eye on the gauges and if they get above one-forty, put the water in. Got it?"

"All right, Mr. Brown," the fireman answered. "D'you want me to keep stoking?"

"Not now. I'll let you know," Brown answered. He motioned to Erickson to follow him as he scrambled over piles of freight in the cargo bay.

Standing on some crates, he pointed out a valve to Erickson. "Open that one," he said and he jumped down and ran across the aisle to more boxes. He climbed up on them and began opening another valve.

By the time Barton arrived to help with the fire, the crew had made headway against it, and he decided to keep going. He entered the engine room and took the scene in with a glance. A mate and an engineer were taking care of the mechanical problems, and another engineer was beyond help. He walked quickly through the engine room and exited the door next to the stern wheel. Whoever killed Lars Hansen must have gone this way. Barton shoved Delbert Gray's revolver into his belt and climbed the ladder to the hurricane deck.

Harold Robertson had managed to lift the yawl off the blocks but didn't know how to swing the davits out. He decided to push the yawl sideways with his feet and cut the lines, letting the yawl fall thirty feet to the water. Then he would jump in and swim to the yawl, pull himself aboard, and drift away. The problem was that his knives had been confiscated. He struggled with a knot. At that moment the young officer climbed onto the hurricane deck.

Robertson pulled out Bacon's revolver and fired once at Barton without taking aim. The shot went wild. Barton instinctively drew his own gun from its holster, instead of the one he had borrowed from Gray, cocked, pulled the trigger, and heard only a dull pop as the cap detonated against a soggy powder charge.

The two men were separated by only thirty feet. Robertson fired again without taking aim and missed again. He used the yawl for as much cover as it would provide.

Barton pulled Gray's gun from his belt. The grip felt strange in his hand, and the sights were not familiar. He shot at Robertson and the bullet threw splinters from the yawl. He cocked and fired again, and missed again.

Robertson stepped from behind the yawl to get a clear shot at the officer, and the hammer fell on an empty nipple. The gun was empty. Robertson ducked behind the yawl as Barton fired the third time and Robertson felt the bullet whistle past his ear. He realized that Robertson's gun was empty and slowly walked forward, keeping his own gun level and watching Robertson to make sure he had no other weapon.

Robertson was out of options, but not ready to give up. When Barton was close enough he charged, counting on the young man to miss again if he fired and relying on his own prowess at hand-to-hand combat. Barton pulled the trigger and found that his borrowed revolver was also empty. Robertson hit him like a bull and the two men fell backward onto the hurricane deck, each trying to gain an advantage.

Robertson had been a boxer at one time in his life and knew how to land punches that would incapacitate his opponent. Barton had grown up on a Missouri farm with two brothers, and he knew how to take care of himself. They traded punches, and then the officer went into a clinch, and they went down again.

Robertson was very tough, although he was ten years older than Barton. Danny had had several exhausting days and was not in his best shape. He was beginning to get the worst of it and held on to his clinch until Robertson's fists on his ribs forced him to let go. Robertson got to his feet, grabbed an oar from the yawl, and swung it at Barton's head. It missed and struck the deck hard. He grabbed the end of the oar to prevent Robertson from swinging it again and as they struggled with the oar, Robertson stepped off the end of the hurricane deck and fell on the stern wheel. It was at this time that Erickson and Brown managed to bypass the main valve to the engines and the stern wheel started forward. Barton watched in horror as it crushed Harold Robertson, aka Henry Rogers, against the stern and then submerged his lifeless body in the Missouri River.

Chapter Twenty-six

A week later, life was almost back to normal on the *Barnard Clinton*. The steamer had passed the mouth of the Yellowstone and was working her way up the upper Missouri River, where few steamers had previously gone.

Weedeater was promoted to striker, and the striker who had escaped Robertson's gun was promoted to engineer. Lars Hansen was given a Christian burial on the banks of the Missouri. The captain spoke over his grave. Bacon and Tank were also buried nearby, but no one spoke over their graves. Robertson's body was never found.

Delbert Gray had eight pellet holes in his body, but none serious. There was a lot of paint missing from the stair railing from the two blasts of Bacon's shotgun, however.

The fire in the cargo bay had done little damage. Only two horses were injured during their panicked escape from Little Joe's corral.

Delbert Gray offered Danny Barton a job anywhere in his various enterprises in Seattle.

"I appreciate the offer, Mr. Gray. I have committed to two voyages with Captain Culpepper this year. If the offer is still open next year, I'll be interested."

"Very well, Danny. The offer is open until I go out of business!"

Gray also offered Abraham a job and told Elizabeth that a small cottage and garden in Seattle went with the offer. They eagerly accepted.

"You understand, Abraham, that we will have a challenging journey over the Federal wagon roads to the Pacific Coast."

"Miss Josephine told me what they are. As long as 'Lizabeth be with me, we'll make it."

"My baby gon' have a home," Elizabeth said happily.

Josephine was making a good recovery, although she was too weak to negotiate the stairs. When Danny told her of the offer from Delbert Gray, she was as interested as Danny had been.

"If you take a job with Mr. Gray next year, will you be going alone?" she asked. She thought she knew the answer, but Danny erased all doubt.